It had been a go...

And at least for the mo... ... to keep his hands off Sam... ...er.

He hadn't counted on Sunny all of a sudden turning to him and throwing her arms around his neck.

"Thank you," she whispered.

"Really?" he croaked, brilliantly. Which was about when it occurred to him where his own arms were and what they were doing.

"Really," she murmured. She was touching his face… Her hand lay softly along his jaw.

He looked back at her and knew he would kiss her now. And knew it was right and inevitable, and that it didn't matter if he'd only known her a couple of days—didn't know her at all, in fact—and she was Sam Malone's granddaughter and heir. Kissing her seemed like the most natural thing in the world to do…like taking his next breath.

* * *

Dear Reader,

Welcome once again to June Canyon Ranch in the beautiful southern Sierra Nevada Mountains of California, where eccentric and reclusive billionaire "Sierra" Sam Malone continues to try to form the elusive bonds of family that have eluded him for most of his nearly one hundred years. This is the second book in the series The Scandals of Sierra Malone. It should have been Sunny's story, but as you will see, it isn't really hers after all.

When I first began writing this book, I thought it was about choices, those that, whether easy or difficult, for better or for worse, shape the pathways of our lives. But as time went by, I began to realize it was about family, and roots, and what it means to a child to grow up surrounded by love and acceptance...or without it. Of course, families come in all shapes and sizes, and if you are lucky enough to have one, no matter how ungainly or embarrassing or eccentric it may be, I hope you will say a little prayer of thanksgiving...and perhaps also ask for the patience to put up with them, the strength to forgive them, and the wisdom to appreciate all they've given you.

Kathleen Creighton

KATHLEEN CREIGHTON

The Pretender

ROMANTIC
SUSPENSE

Recycling programs
for this product may
not exist in your area.

ISBN-13: 978-0-373-27763-6

THE PRETENDER

Copyright © 2012 by Kathleen Creighton-Fuchs

This edition published by arrangement with Harlequin Books S.A.

For questions and comments about the quality of this book
please contact us at Customer_eCare@Harlequin.ca.

www.Harlequin.com

Printed in U.S.A.

Books by Kathleen Creighton

Harlequin Romantic Suspense
‡*Sheriff's Runaway Witness* #1656
‡*The Pretender* #1693

Silhouette Romantic Suspense
**The Awakening of Dr. Brown* #1057
**The Seduction of Goody Two Shoes* #1089
Virgin Seduction #1148
**The Black Sheep's Baby* #1161
Shooting Star #1232
***The Top Gun's Return* #1262
***An Order of Protection* #1292
***Undercover Mistress* #1340
**Secret Agent Sam #1363
The Sheriff of Heartbreak County #1400
The Rebel King #1432
Lazlo's Last Stand #1492
†*Danger Signals* #1507
†*Daredevil's Run* #1523
†*Lady Killer* #1559
†*Kincaid's Dangerous Game* #1563
†*Memory of Murder* #1607

*Into the Heartland
**Starrs of the West
†The Taken
‡Scandals of Sierra Malone

Other titles by this author available in ebook format

KATHLEEN CREIGHTON

has roots deep in the California soil but has relocated to South Carolina. As a child, she enjoyed listening to old-timers' tales, and her fascination with the past only deepened as she grew older. Today, she is interested in everything—art, music, gardening, zoology, anthropology and history—but people are at the top of her list. She also has a lifelong passion for writing, and now combines all her loves in romance novels.

For My Family,
(which has turned out to be
even more far-flung and eclectic
than I could have imagined),
but especially for those members of it
who would never dream of living anywhere else
but in the Kern River Valley.

Prologue

From the memoirs of Sierra Sam Malone:

I never thought I would live so long. For the fact that I have done so I must give credit to the Man Upstairs, I suppose, but also to three beautiful women, all of whom loved me a damn sight more than I deserved. Lord knows I never did right by any of them, but maybe there is still time before I die to make up for some of the wrong I did. I sure do mean to try.

Telling the story—the whole truth—well, I reckon that's as good a place to start as any.

That day outside of Barstow when the railroad bulls beat me senseless and threw me off the train and left me to die in the desert wasn't the first time Death came for me and went away empty-handed. Not the first time, but I thought sure it was the last, and my last day on earth before I'd reached the ripe age of eighteen.

For some reason—instinct, I reckon, or Divine Guidance, or maybe it was just because, being a mountain boy born and bred from the green hills of West Virginia, I had no wish to die in the desert—and so I didn't try to follow the tracks back to Barstow but instead kept stumbling my dogged way toward the mountains I could see off in the distance. Could just as well have been a mirage, but it wasn't. It was mountains, real ones, and something in me told me there might be water there, somewhere.

Well...there was water, and I don't know what led me to find it, hidden deep in the gold mine that belonged to a sweet bit of a girl named Elizabeth. (I'd say it was the Hand of God that guided me, but I can't for the life of me think why the Good Lord would bother to save the miserable life of the likes of me, Sam Malone. That is a mystery I've not been able to figure out to this day.) But find it I did, and with it the great-est treasure any man could wish for.

Ah, Elizabeth. I was too young and stupid to know it then, but you were the real thing...the treasure I had in my hands, that I threw away to go chasing after Fool's Gold.

In my defense, I will say that she was beautiful, more beau-tiful than anything I'd ever seen. As beautiful, I thought then, as an angel.

But, I see that I am getting ahead of my story, so if you will bear with me, I will proceed with it.

Part Two—Barbara

Elizabeth found me in that mine, and for some reason decided against shooting me for a trespasser. Instead, she took care of me and brought me back to good health, and I married her for her trouble. We worked the gold mine her daddy had left her, worked it together, and she could swing a pickax as well as any man. There wasn't a lot of gold left in that mine, but it was enough to keep us comfortable, and after she bore me a son, a bright and beautiful boy we named Sean—for her daddy, not mine—we had everything anyone could possibly need in order to be happy.

Except, me being the kind of man I am, I wanted more. Maybe I always had that restlessness, that something or other that kept me with one ear cocked to the distant call of adventure. So when the movie people came to our corner of desert and I heard they were looking for horses and men who could ride them, the excitement drew me like a moth to flame.

Well, sir, it wasn't long before those people discovered I could not only ride, but was more than a little foolhardy. In no time at all I was doing stunts for the likes of Duke Wayne, and Coop and Alan Ladd. Westerns were big back then—somebody was always filming something out there in Red Rock, or up at Lone Pine, or over on the Kern River—Roy Rogers and Gene Autry, Bill Boyd—you'd maybe know him better as Hopalong Cassidy—all the great ones. I got to know 'em all, and I had as much work as I could handle. Elizabeth, she got tired of it after a while and went back to our home and the raising of our son, Sean. But I'd got hooked on the glamour of it...the excitement. And, I confess, on all the temptations that went with that.

Then came the War. I went to join up when I heard what had been done at Pearl Harbor, but those railroad bulls—or maybe all the spills I'd taken doing the movie stunts—had inflicted more damage on me than I'd thought, enough that the army wouldn't take me. Which was a disappointment at the time, me being like any other man too young and dumb to value his own life, but it turned out to be one more piece of Good Fortune I didn't deserve. Because 'round about that time something was discovered in that played-out gold mine of ours, something I'd never heard of before, that was worth far more than gold or the bodies of brave young men. Something called Uranium.

By the time the war ended I was a rich man. I still loved the movie business, but I'd quit falling off horses and was making my own movies now. I moved Elizabeth and Sean into town, set them up in a big house up there in the Hollywood Hills, even though I knew she'd never be happy there. And I confess

I didn't spend much time with my wife and child during those days, being too busy hobnobbing with the glamorous and beautiful people that surrounded me day and night. I know the stories must have found their way back to her, though, about the booze and drugs and beautiful women. Oh, my Lord, the women...

Then one day I walked onto the set—we were shooting interiors for Sierra Gold, *I believe it was—and there she was. No, not the most beautiful woman in the world, God knows, because I'd seen more than my share of those already. But there was something about her... She had hair like flame and dark, tragic eyes, which was something of a contradiction, something of a mystery, and that beguiled me from the first. She had skin like rose petals and a smile like an angel's, so sweet it made your heart ache...and then when she spoke or sang, her voice was cigarettes and whiskey and dark dive bars full of pure sin.*

There'd been women before—I think I've made that plain enough. But she was different. For her, I gave up everything.

Elizabeth, it's true you were the earth, the world, practical and real and as vital as food and drink to me. But, they say a man can't live on bread alone, and she...well, she was the food of my spirit. My soul. Her name was Barbara Chase, and I flew to her, and for a time, God help me, I did believe I'd found heaven.

Chapter 1

Abigail Lindgren buried Sunny Wells on a cold rainy day in April. Or rather, she watched while cemetery workers placed the small box containing her roommate and best friend's ashes in a hole in the muddy ground.

Abby took some comfort in the fact that she wasn't the only person who'd bothered to show up at the cemetery to say goodbye in spite of the gloom and the steady drizzle. There were maybe a dozen others gathered on the soggy turf amongst the drooping daffodils. Huddled close together in their dark coats, she thought they resembled a small wet flock of blackbirds.

Most were from the club where Sunny worked—where she and Abby both worked, actually, although Abby's gig was solely that of cocktail waitress, being as how there wasn't much call for a dancer's talents in a small, smoky after-hours joint like Donovan's. It had been a good fit with Sunny's whiskey and cigarettes voice, though, and she'd been a popular feature on the nights she took over the mike. They'd passed the hat at Donovan's to help pay for Sunny's burial, and Abby thought she recognized most of those who'd contributed at the graveside today.

The police were there, too, she noticed. The two detectives assigned to Sunny's case, standing back and a little apart from the rest.

"Ironic, isn't it?"

Startled, Abby jerked toward the speaker, just in time to watch water drops cascade from the edge of her umbrella and splash onto his glasses. He took them off and wiped them matter-of-factly on the trailing ends of his neck scarf. Pauly Schulman was—had been—Sunny's agent. And still was Abby's. Both his head and his body were egg-shaped, and the beret that sat askew on his bald head topped Abby's shoulder by a couple of inches. In addition to the maroon beret and matching scarf, he wore a black trench coat today, and since he didn't seem to have an umbrella, Abby shifted politely so as to offer him a share of hers.

"Thanks," he said, then replaced his glasses and glanced up at her. "You know what I mean? Burying somebody like Sunny on a day like this." He gave a bleak one-shoulder shrug. "It's wrong. With her looks and her name. Just seems… ironic."

Abby nodded, but personally she thought the weather was kind of fitting, and that it was actually Sunny's *name* that was ironic. Because in spite of all that golden hair and a smile that could light up a room, all anybody had to do was look in her eyes to see that down deep she was anything but sunshine. Surely, Abby couldn't be the only person to have seen the sadness in Sunny's eyes, the darkness that reflected the places in her soul where no light could ever reach.

"Nice turnout, anyway," Pauly observed, gazing at the knot of watchers half-invisible beneath their glistening umbrellas. "Sunny had friends."

Again, Abby only nodded. But she was thinking: *Friends? Coworkers, customers, neighbors, maybe, but hardly friends.*

Where were they, she wondered bitterly, those people Sunny had called "friends," the ones who had been with her at the party the night she died, the ones who had let her walk home alone? Where were they now? Abby couldn't imagine any of them caring enough to make the effort to come to a cemetery in the rain.

At least you had me.

Only...am I any better than they were? I wasn't there for you that night, was I? I was working late, and got home too tired to bother to check to see if you'd made it home safely. Though probably even then it would have been too late. By that time you were already dead, lying in that alley, cold and alone.

The knot of watchers was breaking up, people beginning to drift away in ones and twos in an aimless way, as if they weren't quite sure they should. The two cops had already disappeared.

"Can I give you a lift?" Pauly was looking at her again, light reflecting off his glasses so she couldn't see his eyes. But there was a crease between his eyebrows, and it occurred to Abby that he was actually a kind man. Either that, she thought more realistically, or he'd just had a soft spot—or the hots— for Sunny.

"No...thanks," Abby said. Kind or not, she didn't feel like making polite conversation with him. Or anybody. "Thanks anyway." She gave him a lame smile and started to walk away.

"Wait..."

She turned to look at him, her smile fixed but growing tenuous. He was reaching inside his trench coat, pulling out his wallet. Reflexively, she held up a hand to stop him, but he took out several bills and thrust them at her with one of his apologetic half shrugs.

"Come on—at least take a cab. You'll catch your death."

She actually hesitated for a moment—purely out of an old

habit of pride—before accepting the money with a muttered, "Thanks."

"Use the rest for…you know." Pauly tilted his head toward the cemetery workers now methodically tamping mud over the box containing Sunny's ashes. "Expenses and…whatever."

"Thanks," Abby said again. She looked away, then back at Pauly and made a lousy attempt to smile. "I don't suppose you've got anything coming up…."

He shook his head and gave a grimace as if he felt a sharp pain. "Wish I did. Hey, it's the slow time of year, y'know? Later in the summer…new shows'll be hiring for the fall openings. Check back with me then, okay?"

She nodded and said, "Sure."

He hesitated, shifted awkwardly, then muttered, "Take care, kid." Head down, hands in the pockets of the trench coat, he went trudging down the grassy slope to where a few cars were still parked, lined up along the curving drive.

Abby watched him go, then turned to look back one more time. Pain sliced unexpectedly through her chest, but she refused to give in to it, and instead threw back her head, and with eyes closed, lifted her face to the rain. As if letting the sky do her weeping for her.

After a moment, she took a deep breath, whispered, "Bye-bye, Sunshine." And walked away.

It was very quiet when she let herself into the tiny apartment she and Sunny had shared. The neighbors were most likely at work—or maybe just avoiding her because they felt guilty about not doing more to help. Some of them had contributed to Sunny's burial fund, but none had made it to the cemetery. Abby didn't really blame them. A lot of the people in the building were elderly, and the others had to make a living, after all.

Pay the rent.

At the thought, she felt a cold squeezing sensation in her chest. Her rent was a week past due, and she'd cleaned out her bank account and maxed out her only credit card to pay for Sunny's burial.

She propped the umbrella next to the door, closed the door and locked it behind her. As the last lock clicked, a fluid shape leaped to the arm of the chair closest to the door, then to the top of the backrest, uttering a trill of welcome.

"Hey, Pia, m'baby." Abby reached to pet the cat and got a small wicked bite for her trouble. "Witchy-cat. Bad cat," she muttered, as the cat went bounding away to disappear into the closet-size bedroom that had been Sunny's. *Should've left you in the woods where I found you.*

Not that she could have. The kitten had simply demanded to be heard...to be found. To be rescued.

What else could they have done? When they'd first heard the cries, during a rare outing last fall in the Adirondacks, Abby had thought it was a bird. It was Sunny who'd said, with absolute certainty, "That's not a bird." They'd followed the sound to a shallow trench at the base of a rocky cliff, filled, at the time, with newly fallen leaves. Abby had reached down into the leaves and come up with her hand full of gray tiger-striped kitten, no more than a few days old, eyes shut tight, squalling its head off.

She remembered the way she and Sunny had stood there, staring at each other, asking each other what in the world they were going to do. "What are we going to do with it? We can't keep it," Sunny had said, and Abby had replied, "Well, we can't leave it here. We'll have to find a home for it. There must be somebody who...I don't know, rescues animals like this?"

Yeah, right.

Full of optimism, they'd taken the kitten—still squalling—back to their motel, where the nice man at the front desk had directed them to a pet supply store in the next town. There a nice lady had supplied them with kitten milk replacer and a kit that included a bottle, several nipples of various sizes and a cleaning brush. "You know the mother cat licks their little bottoms to make them go to the bathroom," the lady had told them. "You will have to do that, or the baby will die." She'd laughed at the looks of horror Abby and Sunny had given her, and added with a smile, "But, warm water and a cotton ball works very well."

And it had. And a good thing, too, because they'd soon discovered no shelter would accept a kitten so young; they'd have to raise it until it could eat—and go to the bathroom—by itself. Roughly eight weeks, they were told. By which time, of course, both Abby and Sunny had fallen in love with the kitten, in spite of—or maybe because of—the fact that she was rapidly turning into a hellion with paws. They'd named her Pia. Sunny told everyone it was short for Pain-in-the-Ass.

"That's what you are," Abby yelled after the cat, as she unwrapped her scarf and unbuttoned her coat. "You're a pain in the ass, and it will serve you right when we're both out on the street. What are you going to do then, huh?"

What am I going to do then?

She stood in the middle of the living room, absently rubbing the back of her hand where the prick of Pia's teeth stung but hadn't quite drawn blood, looking around at what amounted to everything she owned in the world. What did she have that was worth selling?

Other than the futon that doubled as her bed—she still couldn't bring herself to take over the one bedroom Sunny had won in a coin toss—most of the furniture had already been secondhand when they'd gotten it. The pictures on the walls they'd bought on eBay for a song. The books—mostly dog-eared paperbacks—had come from the library's once-a-year used book sale. The television was the big boxy kind that no self-respecting burglar would even bother with. So was the computer, its operating system probably way beyond obsolete. It did work, but she couldn't see getting rid of it. It wouldn't bring much, and she needed some kind of computer, didn't she? How could anyone get along these days without email?

What do I have that I could sell to raise enough money to pay the rent?

The obvious answer to that question was…

Nothing. Not one thing. No old jewelry, no silver baubles, no family heirlooms. A person didn't collect many of those bouncing from place to place in the Minnesota foster care system.

Which left…Sunny's things.

Dreading what had to be done, Abby went slowly into the bedroom and sat on the bed. Everything was neat and tidy, the way Sunny always left it; the police hadn't spent much time here, probably having already written off Sunny's death as a random mugging. Tears stung Abby's eyes and as always she fought them off, not even sure now whether the sorrow she felt was for Sunny, or herself.

She took a deep breath and looked around.

So. This is what nobody tells you about. What you do when somebody close to you dies. Is murdered. After the police and the questions. After the funeral, after the sympathy cards and flowers.

How did you go about cleaning up after a life? Tying up the loose ends of someone's existence on this earth? As far as Abby knew, Sunny had had no family. She'd told Abby she'd been on her own since she was fourteen, when she'd come home one day to find her mother dead of a drug overdose— suicide, the police had said. Sunny said she'd split that day and never looked back, preferring to take on the world on her own terms rather than let herself be swallowed up by the system. Smart girl.

Now Sunny was gone, and all Abby had to do was figure out a way to get along without her. Without her friendship, her company, prickly as that had sometimes been. Without her share of the expenses.

She hitched in another breath, rose to her feet and began methodically to go through the dresser drawers, the closet, making a pile of clothing, shoes and odds and ends in the

middle of the bed. Some things she would keep; she and
Sunny had been the same height and had sometimes borrowed
each other's clothes, even though their tastes had differed considerably. Sunny had had way more curves than Abby, and
had liked to show them off, whereas Abby's tastes ran more
to jeans, vintage jackets and boots. For sure none of the shoes
would fit her; Abby's feet were bigger—she had a dancer's
ugly feet. Still, there would be a few things she could use, and
she was sure Sunny would want her to have them. The rest
she would take to the women's and children's shelter down
the street.

When the drawers and closet were empty, she stood for a
moment surveying the shoebox-shaped room—windowless,
its walls covered with vintage posters and playbills from
Broadway plays, most of which had come from eBay. The
single bed and dresser took up nearly the entire room, and it
occurred to Abby that with space so limited, no storage possibility would likely be wasted. With that in mind, she dropped
to her knees on the bare wood floor and looked under the bed.
Sure enough, there was a flat plastic box there, and a suitcase.
Abby assumed they'd both be full of summer clothes, things
that wouldn't fit in the closet.

She was right about the storage box. She hauled it out from
under the bed and dumped its contents onto the pile of clothing on top of the mattress, then put the box itself aside. *That,*
she could definitely use.

Next, the suitcase. It was old and shabby; Abby remembered it from the trip to the Adirondacks, the only time she
could recall Sunny ever using it. She pulled it out…opened
it. And for a moment just sat on her heels, staring at the contents of the suitcase, not quite taking it in.

It was neatly packed, not with hot weather clothes, but as
if ready for a trip tomorrow, with an assortment of under-
wear and socks, tops and pants, shoes, toiletries, a jacket.
Lying on top of the folded clothes was an envelope, the card-
board the red, blue and white kind used for priority mail. It

was addressed to Sunshine Blue Wells—Sunny's actual full name—and the return address was a law firm in Beverly Hills, California.

Slowly, clumsily, as if there was a faulty connection between her hands and the brain that controlled them, Abby turned the envelope over and shook it. Several items fell out.

She drew a shaken breath and settled herself more comfortably. Then, cross-legged in front of the open suitcase, she picked up the items, one by one.

A heavy white business envelope embossed with the law firm's return address, covered with the official forms and stamps and tags that designate a letter as certified, registered, return receipt requested. It, too, was addressed to Sunshine Blue Wells.

A second, similar envelope, this one with only Sunny's name handwritten on the front.

A Visa card, stamped with the law firm's name.

A wad of small bills, mostly ones and fives. Almost one hundred dollars worth, Abby discovered as she counted it. She wondered if Sunny had saved the money from her tips at the club.

She opened the registered, official-looking envelope and took out several sheets of folded paper. She placed the papers in her lap, wiped her hands on her thighs, then took a deep breath before she picked up the first one and unfolded it.

It was a hand-written letter, on old-fashioned lined notebook paper, the kind with holes punched on one side. The writing was shaky and hard to read, and after a moment Abby put it down and picked up the second sheet. This was heavy, expensive-looking paper, and on it was what appeared to be a typed translation of the hand-written letter. As she began to read it, her breath stopped. Her skin prickled.

My Dear Sunshine,
My name is Sam Malone, though for some reason many

have preferred to call me by the nickname, Sierra, and I happen to be your grandfather.

I am a very old man now, and I've lived a full and interesting life, during which I managed to amass a considerable fortune and squander the love of three beautiful women. As a result, I was not privileged to know my own children, including your mother, a fact that I deeply regret. But this is not the time for regrets, and I can't change the past anyhow.

Since I have outlived all of my wives and my children, it is my desire to share my earthly treasure with my grandchildren, any that may chance to survive me, and it is this last wish that has led me to write this letter to you. If you are not too dead-set against me and would care to come to my ranch to collect your inheritance, I do not believe you would be sorry.

My lawyer will no doubt include with this letter the information you need to contact him to make the necessary arrangements.

Yours very truly,

Sam Malone

Cold, numb, hands shaking, Abby fumbled through the remaining papers and managed to scatter most of them onto the floor before she found the one she wanted.

The letter from the attorney—no, that one was only the cover letter for the hand-written one and its translation.

There must be another one. Yes—there it was, the second one. Dated just two weeks ago.

Dear Miss Wells,

Thank you for your email in response to your grandfather's letter. We are pleased you have decided to accept his invitation to visit him at June Canyon Ranch. Since circumstances make it advisable that you come as soon as possible, and you have indicated that you have no restrictions on your time, I have taken the liberty of booking a flight for you. Enclosed you will find your itinerary, which includes your reservation. This along with your photo I.D. is all the ticket you will need. However, since you will no doubt encounter additional costs, such as baggage fees and ground transportation to the airport, I have included a credit card for your use. Please use it with discretion, as its funds are limited.

If you require more time, please feel free to change the reservation to fit your schedule. If I do not hear from you to the contrary, I will assume the itinerary is to your satisfaction, and upon your arrival in Bakersfield, you will be met and transported by car to Mr. Malone's June Canyon Ranch.

I hope you enjoy a safe and uneventful flight, and I look forward to meeting you in the very near future.
Sincerely yours,
Alex Branson, Attorney at Law

Abby uttered a sharp cry, quickly stifled it with a hand clamped over her mouth. Then she began to shake with silent sobs. Sitting cross-legged on the floor, she wrapped her arms across her stomach and rocked herself back and forth as all the tears she hadn't been able to shed in the past weeks poured down her cheeks, mimicking the rain cascading down the windowpanes.

Hearing strange sounds emerging from her mother, Pia came running and jumped into the suitcase with a questioning chirp. Receiving no immediate reassurances, she stood on her hind legs, placed her front paws on Abby's chest and bumped her forehead against her chin. When even that failed to produce the soft words and ear rubbings to which she was accustomed, she began to lick Abby's cheek with her little sandpaper tongue. Tasting the salt, maybe. Or...offering comfort the only way she knew.

For the rest of that day and most of a sleepless night, Abby pondered the contents of the suitcase, the envelopes, the letters. A futon didn't allow much room for tossing and turning, especially with Pia curled up somewhere in the vicinity of her knees, and God knew she didn't want to disturb the Cat-from-Hell in the middle of the night, so mostly she stared at the darkness and thought. And by the next day she still hadn't decided what she should do about any of it. At times she felt all but smothered by the overload of the incredible, the unexpected, the unimaginable. She hardly knew where to begin to dig out and try to make sense of a senseless mess.

One thing that struck her almost as soon as the wave of overwhelming grief had passed was the irony of discovering that Sunny did have something of value—a first-class ticket to California would almost certainly be worth enough to cover the rent with some left over for next month. Except that, not counting the pitiful wad of cash, none of it was of value except to Sunny. The airplane ticket was in Sunny's name and evidently nonrefundable. The credit card? No matter how many times Abby looked at it longingly, picked it up, turned it over in her hands, she always put it back in the envelope with a sigh. It, too, was meant for Sunny. If Abby used it, surely that would be stealing, or at the very least, fraud. And anyway, according to the letter, the funds available were "limited"—whatever that meant. So, no—nothing in the envelope was of any help to Abby in her present financial situation.

And, of course, of no use to Sunny, now, either.

What kept Abby awake in the cold, lonely darkness listening to the night sounds of the city and the relentless rain outside her windows, was the thought that played over in her mind like a stuck phrase of a song: *Sunny had a family.*

She has *a family.*

One of the things that had brought them together from the

very first moment they'd met at that audition—Abby fresh off the bus from Minneapolis, Sunny a veteran of the New York theatre scene, both hungry and determined—had been the fact that both of them were pretty much alone in the world. Once they'd determined they weren't in direct competition with each other—Sunny was a singer, mainly, whereas Abby had a voice like a lovesick crow—they'd become not only friends, but each other's family. They'd looked enough alike to be sisters—and they'd fought like sisters, too. It had been an unlikely alliance from the beginning, but somehow it had worked.

But now…

Sunny has a family. Did she know all along? Why didn't she tell me?

Was she going to tell me? Ever? Or was she just going to leave, and not say anything?

She was like my sister, *dammit!*

She lay wretched in the wee hours of morning, thinking of Sunny abandoning her without any explanation, while self-pitying tears ran cold down the sides of her face and into her ears. It only made her feel worse knowing she was being selfish and horrible, feeling sorry for herself when it was Sunny who was dead and wasn't **ever** going to get to see the family she hadn't known she had.

Then, somewhere along toward sunrise, it hit her.

Somewhere out in California, there's a grandfather, and… who knows who else. A grandfather, at least. An old man who is looking forward to finally meeting his long-lost granddaughter. And now…

I have to tell him.

How am I going to tell him she's dead? Murdered. Strangled to death and left in an alley like so much trash.

Several times over the course of the next day she tried to do it. Picked up the lawyer's letter and her cell phone, held one in each hand, heart thumping while she tried to gather

her courage to make the call. Once, she actually did punch in the numbers, but broke the connection before the call could go through. Telling herself, *Maybe if I wait a day or two, until the shock has a chance to wear off, it will be easier.*

Hungry for more information, she searched the computer she and Sunny had shared, looking for the email the lawyer's letter had referred to. She finally found it in the computer's unemptied trash bin, Sunny's brief response to the letter from her grandfather, saying only that yes, she would come to California to meet him. Typically Sunny, no emotion, no excitement, just…sure, yeah, okay, might as well. Whatever.

Never let 'em see you sweat, right, Sunny?

Abby tried to imagine how Sunny must have felt, reading the letter for the first time. *What was going through your mind, Sunny?*

And why didn't you tell me?

Naturally, she ran an internet search on Sierra Sam Malone. After reading through the first half dozen entries—including the one from Wikipedia—out of many millions, she shut down the computer and sat for a long time staring at the blank monitor screen.

Apparently, the man—Sierra Sam Malone—was some kind of a legend. He'd gone from being a hobo during the Great Depression and a stuntman during the Golden Age of Hollywood Western movies, to become one of the richest men in the world. According to Wikipedia old Sam had indeed been married three times, had had three children and had outlived them all—the letter seemed to have been right on that score. At one time, during his marriage to his third wife—from a socially and politically prominent family—he'd even been talked about as a possible presidential candidate. Then, following the tragic death of their son and daughter-in-law and the subsequent collapse of that marriage, Sam Malone had completely dropped out of sight. Supposedly he'd retired to his ranch in a remote valley in the Sierra Nevada mountains, rarely to be seen in public again. Howard Hughes without the weirdness, it would seem.

As near as Abby could figure out, Sunny would have to be the descendent of Sam and his second wife, a Hollywood starlet named Barbara Chase, who had supposedly committed suicide when her daughter, Sunny's mother, was still an infant.

Wow, this can't be real.

Was that why Sunny hadn't mentioned it? Had she been afraid it was all some crazy joke, an elaborate scam, simply too far-fetched to be true? Maybe she was planning to check it out personally before allowing herself to buy into it?

It sure did seem real. Abby checked out the law firm, too, of course. It looked about as legit and respectable as anything possibly could. A bit staid and stuffy, even.

The credit card and plane ticket were real, too. So was the packed suitcase. There was no getting around the fact that, for better or worse, before she'd gotten herself murdered, Sunny had been planning to go to California.

Abby went to work that night, even though her boss had told her to take the rest of the week off if she needed it. But she'd had enough of sitting alone in her apartment with only the internet, the Cat-from-Hell and her own tortured thoughts for company. She figured even the club would be an improvement.

And besides, she needed the money.

It seemed strange, being in the club, everything looking the same, doing the same things, seeing the same people, the same faces, knowing it wasn't ever going to be the same again. The weirdest thing was, it actually *felt* the same, as if any minute Sunny would come gliding in, wearing the skintight black pants and black halter top that were her trademark, the golden mane of her hair tumbled over her bare shoulders as she picked up the mic and the room fell into a hush of anticipation.

"Seems impossible she's gone, doesn't it?" Elton, one of two bartenders on duty tonight, placed a pitcher of dark brew on a tray with four glasses, then turned a lopsided smile on Abby.

She gave him the same smile back as she picked up the tray. She was an actress; she could smile and pretend with the best of them.

She delivered the pitcher and glasses to a table near the dance floor—four well-fed guys wearing expensive haircuts and even more expensive suits. As she was pouring, one of the guys hitched forward and waggled a folded-up fifty between two fingers.

"Hey, Sunshine, sweetheart, the beer's nice, but my friends, here, we've been waiting all night to hear you sing. When are you gonna give us a song?"

Abby's smile froze on her face, but she didn't jerk or spill a drop of beer. She finished pouring, then flashed the smile at the man with the fifty. "I'm sorry—Sunny's not here tonight. I'm Abby, and trust me, you don't want to hear *me* sing."

The man looked confused for a moment, then gave her a long, narrow-eyed look and shook his head. "Sorry—I thought sure... If you don't mind my saying so, you sure do look alike. Sisters, right?"

Abby stretched out her smile and murmured, "That's okay, I get that a lot."

"Those guys giving you trouble?" Elton asked her when she took back the tray.

She shook her head. "No...just asking for Sunny." She took a deep breath. "I didn't tell 'em. Don't want to ruin their evening. Look, could you and Trisha cover for me for a few minutes? I'm gonna go...um..." She gestured vaguely toward the ladies' room.

Elton said, "Sure, no problem."

She pushed away from the bar and ran.

Thank God the restroom was empty. She checked the stalls, then went to the sink and turned on the water. Wet her fingers and patted her hot cheeks. Then stood and stared at herself in the wood-framed mirror.

You sure do look alike. You're sisters, right?

How many times had she heard that? She'd always thought it was just a superficial likeness. Sure, she and Sunny were the same height, approximately the same weight—if you didn't count the way it was distributed. Both were blond and blue-eyed, although Sunny's hair was darker and had more body, more curl. And her eyes were a deeper shade of blue, that dark violet that seemed to hide so many secrets, so much sadness. Abby had typical Nordic coloring, with blue-green eyes and straight, pale blond hair. She usually wore it twisted in a knot at the back of her head, because she was a dancer and that style made her neck look longer. More elegant.

Now, with her heart beating fast and hard, she lifted a hand to pull the elastic bands from her hair. It uncoiled in a way that seemed almost angry and slithered down her back, and she shook her head to make it fall forward over her shoulders. Tilted her head so that it covered one eye, the way she'd seen Sunny do so many times, particularly when she was singing some hot, sexy number.

Her image gazed back at her from behind the curtain of hair, cheeks flushed, lips pouty.

She looked…sexy, hot.

Like Sunny.

In a half daze, she went back to the bar and told Elton she didn't feel well and was going home. In the back room she took off her apron, gathered up her jacket and purse, still barely conscious of what she was doing. Outside, with a sweet spring breeze blowing and the sidewalks filled with people making the most of the balmy night, she searched through her purse for subway fare and found the money Pauly had given her at the cemetery.

What the hell, she thought, giddy with a mixture of exhilaration and fear, as she stepped to the curb and hailed a cab.

She was out of breath and her hands were shaking as she

unlocked the door to her apartment. Inside, ignoring Pia's chirp of welcome and barely flinching or altering her stride as the cat leaped from the back of the futon to her shoulders, she made straight for the kitchen, where the envelope the police had given her containing Sunny's personal effects lay unopened on the counter.

With Pia watching curiously from her favorite perch on Abby's shoulders, she opened the envelope and shook the contents onto the decades-old tile. It was a pitifully small pile—some things, anything with blood on it, she imagined—had been kept by the cops for evidence. She picked up Sunny's I.D. card. Hands clammy, she held it...stared at it...dropped it...picked it up and stared at it again.

It's true. I could do it.

I could pass for Sunny.

Chapter 2

So? What if I could pass for Sunny? The question is: Should I?

Why shouldn't I? It's not like I'm trying to steal her identity. It would just be for a little while. Just so I can use the plane ticket. And the credit card. To go to California. To tell her grandfather what happened.

Abby went back and forth with her conscience, which, annoyingly, didn't seem inclined to give in.

It's still wrong. Not to mention illegal. As in...stealing?

Not if I pay it back. Then it's only borrowing. And anyway, what good is the plane ticket to anybody else, if it's nonrefundable? It would just be going to waste.

Her conscience was silent, but intractable.

I have to tell them about Sunny. Wouldn't it be better to do it in person, instead of a phone call or—God forbid—email?

Very kind and considerate of you.

Sarcasm? Seriously? From her own conscience?

Okay, look. I said I'll pay it back. Maybe they'll let me

work it off. They have a ranch; there must be something I could do. How about if I could work for room and board to pay them back?

Stubborn silence on the part of her conscience.

Hey, I'm about to be homeless here! Worst-case scenario: I can be homeless in California. It has to cost less to live there than here.

And for darn sure, the weather's better.

So...I don't care if you don't like it, I'm using that plane ticket. I'm going to California. To tell them. In person. After that...I guess I'll just have to see what happens.

That's it. End of arguments.

Taut with excitement, stomach aquiver with butterflies, she sat down at the ancient computer and before she could change her mind, fired off an email to Alex Branson, Attorney at Law:

FORGOT TO MENTION. IS IT OKAY IF I BRING A CAT?

"You've gotta admit, the girl's got—what do your people call it..."

Sam Malone's lawyer raised his eyebrows. "*My* people? I assume that would be...Jewish?"

"Yeah. What's that word—great word, means *cojones*—balls. Which I can't use since she's a girl. You know the—"

"Chutzpah?"

"Yeah. That's the one." Sam gave a cackle of laughter. "The girl's got *hutzpa,* that's for sure."

Naturally, old uptight Alex didn't crack a smile. Just looked him in the eye and got straight to the point. "What do you want to do about her?"

Sam narrowed his eyes and scratched his chin, just to give his lawyer the notion he was thinking it over. Truth was, he was feeling damned excited. Happy, even, for the first time since he'd gotten the terrible news from New York. There was an itch under his skin he recognized and remembered from his considerably younger days, an itch that said there was adventure afoot. A challenge. Hell, he never had been able to resist a challenge.

"Cards have been dealt," he growled. "I'll be curious to see how she plays hers. Won't you?"

The lawyer raised his eyebrows again, but only said mildly, "Are you going to want to meet her?"

"I might."

"When—"

Sam waved a hand impatiently. "When the time's right." Damn lawyers always had to pin things down. "For now, just...tell her to go ahead and bring the damn cat. Then we'll wait and see."

Alex closed up the computer and tucked it into his briefcase. "Don't wait too long," he said, as he slid the briefcase off the wood plank table and headed for the door. He gave a nod and a wave as he went out, leaving the door open.

Sam grunted and went to shut it, hobbling a little. Damned legs—still feeling the effects of that crazy stunt he'd pulled a few weeks back, he supposed. He sure did hate being old. Simple thing like riding hell-for-leather across a meadow shooting at helicopters with a deer rifle wouldn't have bothered him a bit, back in his stuntman days. Woulda been all in a day's work. Nowadays, he paid a heavy price for such foolishness.

Sure was fun, though. He cackled with pure glee, remembering how it had felt to bring down that chopper along with the man who'd shot and wounded his ranch foreman and tried to kidnap his baby great-grandson. *I may be old,* he thought, *but I ain't through livin' yet.*

Instead of pulling the heavy pine plank door closed, he stood in the cabin's doorway and watched his lawyer stride through the meadow grass and swing himself into the waiting helicopter. Nice to be that young, he thought with an inward sigh.

Good man, Alex Branson—way too serious and buttoned-

up for a youngster, but they don't come any more honest or
loyal. Which, for a lawyer, is saying something. Yeah...he's a
good man. I shouldn't jerk his chain like I do.

But damned if it ain't fun.

Sam watched the little blue chopper lift off and bank away
toward the mountain ridge—looked just like a dragonfly, he'd
always thought. He watched until he couldn't see it anymore,
then turned and hobbled back into the cabin, closing the door
behind him. He made his way to the table and picked up the
black-and-white photo that was lying there. He stood for a
long time gazing down at the photo, an eight-by-ten glossy—
what they used to call a studio headshot—of a woman.

"Ah...Barbara. My God, but you were lovely." He no longer
cared that he spoke aloud when there was nobody but himself
to hear.

A wave of sadness swept over him, and after a while he
slid the photograph back into the manila envelope where it
had been kept for more than half a century. That was the best
place for it—the past. The past was dead, done with. The past
was nothing but sadness and regrets.

He shook himself, shaking off the sadness. And he grinned.
He couldn't wait to see what the future was going to bring.

Sage leaned one shoulder against a support pillar and
watched the first passengers from the New York flight make
their way toward him down the glistening corridor. First-
class passengers first, of course: businessmen with cell phones
glued to their ears; an older couple looking annoyed—he wondered if that was because it had been a rough flight, or if it
was just their normal way. An elderly lady towing an oxygen
bottle. A very tall black man wearing a suit Sage was pretty
sure had cost more than his pickup. He waited patiently and
watched them all go by, not the least bit concerned he'd have
trouble spotting the passenger he'd come to meet. How many
young, blond women carrying a pet crate could there be on
one flight?

Turned out, she'd have drawn his eye even if he hadn't been there specifically to pick her up. She was that kind of woman, tall and slim, with long legs that looked even longer in the skinny jeans and knee boots she wore. She had on a sleeveless top made of some kind of slithery material the color of old brandy, in a style that had the look of another time, and carried a black jacket thrown over one arm—the right. She carried the crate in her left. As he watched, she halted in the middle of the walkway, set the carrier on the floor and slipped the jacket on.

He couldn't blame her for that. Like most places where the weather could get hot, Bakersfield had a tendency to overdo the air-conditioning.

Then his breath caught.

He could see now that the jacket was of roughly the same vintage as the silky top, with padded shoulders, fitted in at the waist and flared out over the hips. From that point upward, with her blond hair tumbled all around her shoulders, she looked like a 1940s movie star. Looked, in fact, exactly like the pictures he'd seen of Sam's second wife, Barbara Chase. Not so surprising, though, he thought, considering Barbara would be this woman's grandmother.

Realizing the woman was just standing there looking around her—looking for him, no doubt—he pushed off from the pillar and moved purposefully forward.

"Sunny?"

Her gaze jerked toward him and her mouth opened; he could hear her suck in air. The look on her face made his stomach clench. Not because she was the most beautiful woman he'd ever seen, although she was, but because she looked absolutely terrified. Not the way most people look when they're scared, but like an animal with nowhere to run. He'd never had a woman look at him that way before. He had to say, he didn't much like it.

He smiled—he hoped in a reassuring way—and held out

his hand. "Sunny Wells? Sage Rivera. Welcome to California."

"I'm, uh… Thanks." She let out the breath and a smile flashed, although the wariness didn't leave her eyes. Striking…mesmerizing eyes. Silvery blue eyes, with just a hint of green.

She thrust out her right hand, and he saw it was bandaged—a fact she seemed to remember at the same moment, because she jerked it back with a little shrug and a breathless, "Um… hi, nice to meet you."

As he answered the shrug with one of his own, he realized he was experiencing something he wasn't used to. Which was awkwardness. He felt uneasy in his own skin. He didn't like that much, either.

Feeling a need to be doing something, he bent to pick up the cat carrier. A low growl issued from its depths. He looked at Sunny and raised his eyebrows.

"Meet Pia," she said darkly. "Otherwise known as the Cat from Hell."

He nodded toward her bandaged hand, which, he now realized, did look very white and fresh. "That what happened to your hand?"

She made a sound that wasn't really a laugh—more like a snort. "Yeah. They said I could take her onboard as my carry-on. They forgot to mention they were going to make me take her *out* of the carrier going through security."

"Ah." He dropped to one knee beside the carrier and placed his hand on the wire door. The growl from inside rose in pitch and volume. Okay, fair warning. He laughed softly. *Can't say I blame you, kitty cat…don't care much for flying myself.*

"Freaked her out," Sunny said with a breathless laugh. "I mean, totally. You should have heard her. Actually I'm surprised you *didn't*. The whole terminal heard her. Hey, what was I supposed to do? I couldn't very well let go of her."

"I'm surprised you don't look more beat-up than you do," Sage said, picking up the carrier and beginning to walk alongside her as they headed for the baggage claim area. She had a long, graceful stride, he noticed. And was nearly as tall as he was, in those boots.

"I had her wrapped in my jacket," she explained, sounding out-of-breath, although they weren't walking that fast. "I thought I could handle her. And except for the noise, it was kind of okay, at first. It was just when I tried to put her back in the carrier. That's when she really chomped me."

He gave a low whistle. "*Chomped* you? Sounds like a pretty bad bite. Think maybe you should see a doctor?"

She shrugged dismissively. "I don't know. It bled like crazy, which I think is good, right? They took me to this first aid place in the airport and put antibiotic stuff on it and bandaged it, so I think I'm good." She swore under her breath, fairly mildly, he thought, under the circumstances. "Stupid cat. She's bitten me before, lots of times. But never like this. I don't know, maybe I shouldn't have tried to…" Her voice seemed to wobble, and she took a breath and held it.

"She's just upset and scared. She'll get over it," Sage said.

She exhaled in a gust. "Yeah…I'm sure." But she didn't sound convinced.

They joined the cluster of people waiting at the baggage carousel. Sage set the cat carrier on the floor. And then… there it was again, that unfamiliar unease he couldn't define and didn't know what to do about. Some part of it—maybe a *big* part—he put down to plain old ordinary sexual attraction. Which wouldn't have been surprising, considering the woman standing next to him was chock-full of sex appeal, except she wasn't the type he would normally be attracted to. Tall, Nordic, blond city girls? Not even close. Not in the same hemisphere.

There had to be something else going on here. What, he didn't know, and that meant he was on guard and meaning to stay that way.

It occurred to Sage that she was looking at him, in a sidelong kind of way that made him wonder if she was as wary of him as he was of her.

She had the grace to look embarrassed, at least, when he met her gaze and said, "What?" in a challenging tone. There was just a touch of color in her cheeks that made her eyes almost seem to shimmer. And made him a little dizzy.

"You're not—" She stopped, but didn't look away, and the way she was studying him, a little frown between her eyebrows, appraising….

He got it. And felt a sinking in his belly he hadn't in a very long time. His skin grew hot.

"Yeah, I am," he began, quietly but with a touch of attitude, but before he could go any further she was shaking her head, looking confused.

"But…you can't be—" she said, at the same time he said, "I am Indian."

There was a moment of utter silence. Then she said dryly, "Well…I was going to say, 'the lawyer.'"

"Ah." His momentary spurt of anger died as quickly as it had risen, leaving him off-balance once more, and a little ashamed of himself. He stretched his lips in a smile. "No. That would be Alex Branson. Like I said, my name is Sage. Sage Rivera-Begay. I manage the ranch."

She went on gazing at him, and the off-balance sensation grew. He felt as if he were falling into her eyes. Then she smiled—really smiled—and his breath stopped.

"So, you are Indian… And if you're the ranch manager," she said, "that would make you also a cowboy, right?"

He gave a short bark of surprised laughter, and somehow found himself smiling back at her, the defensive belligerence stuffed back in the bottom drawer of his past where it belonged. She didn't deserve it.

She's not Heather.

"I prefer Native American, but yeah, I guess it does. Half and half, actually. My mother's people are local Tubatulabal and Navajo. My father was white."

She was still looking at him, chewing on her lower lip in a way that made him wonder whether she'd even heard him. Once again, he asked, "What?" without the defensiveness this time, smiling wryly.

She shook her head. "I didn't expect... I thought the lawyer would be picking me up—Mr. Branson...."

The carousel beeped a loud warning and started to move. She stepped up to the edge, and Sage moved with her, leaving the cat carrier unattended. The way he figured it, if someone wanted to snatch the cat, good luck to him.

"Alex?" he said. "He lives in Beverly Hills. Sorry to disappoint you. You got me."

She threw him a quick look. "I'm not...disappointed. It's just...you're not what—you're not *who* I expected." And there was that *something* in her eyes again, something he couldn't figure out. Uncertainty? Vulnerability? Fear?

She watched a line of suitcases make its slow, wobbling way toward them, then glanced at him again and said, "Am I what you expected?"

That was unexpected. He tried a smile. "What kind of question is that?"

"Just wondering." She gave a one-shoulder shrug and turned from him, in a way that made her seem isolated and alone, there in that crowd of people.

And it occurred to him suddenly that she could very well be scared, and that she had every reason to be. She was a New York girl—a city girl—who'd come all the way to the wild California mountains to meet a grandfather she'd never seen, never knew existed until a few weeks ago, on the strength of a letter from a lawyer she didn't know from Adam. And she was met by someone she'd never heard of, who could be anybody, in fact. So, no wonder she was edgy, he thought. His chest warmed with sympathy for the woman as he took his cell phone out of his jacket pocket and handed it to her.

"You're exactly what I expected," he said to reassure her, and he was thinking, *That's a lie. I didn't expect you'd steal my breath, make me feel like a newborn calf. Like a boy, not a man.* "But I understand if you need to make sure I am who I say I am. Here—you can call Alex yourself. He's number three on speed dial, or you can punch in the number he gave you if that makes you feel better."

Abby stared at the phone, at the strong work-worn hand that held it, her thoughts in a dizzy whirl.

What should I do? He obviously thinks I'm Sunny. I should tell him. But…I don't know who he is, what he is to my—to Sunny's grandfather— to this Sam Malone. I can't just blurt out to an employee that she's dead. Can I? I have to tell him— Sam Malone—personally. Or at least the lawyer, Alex Branson.

She shook her head, refusing the cell phone. "No—that's okay. I'm sorry, I'm just…" She tried to laugh, the shrugged. "Hey, what can I say, I'm a New Yorker. We don't trust that easily."

"I guess a little paranoia's probably a good thing to have in the Big City." He said it like it was in capitals. He was smiling at her, his teeth white in his dark-tanned face.

She said, "Yeah." And laughed again, though she barely had breath.

She hadn't expected *that.* A man who took her breath away.

Abby moved in a world of beautiful people, beautiful faces, beautiful bodies. Beautiful men, beautiful women, every single one of them desperate to turn that beauty into a career, or at the very least, a paycheck. It was a world where physical beauty was a commodity, something to be jealously guarded and tended. She wondered if what made this man, Sage, so different was that he didn't seem aware of the fact that he was gorgeous. Or if he was, simply didn't consider it important.

He wasn't all that tall, barely taller than she was—his cowboy boots had modest heels, similar in height to her own—but the light blue shirt and Western-style leather jacket he wore couldn't disguise the width and power in his shoulders and chest. His hips were slim in comfortable-looking jeans, and the leather belt at his waist had a silver buckle inlaid with turquoise in a Native American design. He moved with a natural and unself-conscious grace most of the dancers she'd known in the world of New York City theatre would have given anything to possess.

But it was his face that captivated her in a way she found almost hypnotic. His skin was flawless, the richest, warmest shade of brown she'd ever seen, and lay smoothly over bones that were strong and proud as some magnificent sculpture. His cheekbones were high and broad, his nose slightly hooked, his chin strong and masculine. But his mouth was sensual, with lips as beautifully shaped as a woman's, and when he smiled his teeth showed white and even. His eyes were black as coal, set deep beneath straight brows and shaded by straight, thick lashes, and even when he smiled, their gaze remained somber and mildly appraising. His hair was glossy black, swept sleekly back from a high, smooth forehead, twisted into a thick rope and knotted tightly at the back of his head in a style she thought might be traditional Navajo. She found herself wondering how long it was, and whether he ever wore it hanging loose. The image that rose in her mind at that thought made her breathing quicken.

She wanted to go on looking at him. Found it hard to tear her gaze from his face. Which was not only unnerving, but embarrassing and probably rude, and no doubt why he kept asking her, *"What?"*

She really did have to stop staring at him.

"I guess one of these must be yours?" His voice seemed to come from a great distance.

She jerked her attention back to the carousel, and to her predicament. "Oh—yes—I think that's it—the sort of greenish gray one without wheels…" *Sunny's suitcase.* She watched it slide toward her, her vision suddenly shimmered and fogged by unexpected tears. *I have to tell…if not him, then someone. But how? And when?*

What am I going to do?

Sage snagged the suitcase and swung it effortlessly to the floor. "Do you have anything else?"

"Just a backpack—it's dark blue with black trim. I think that might be... No, wait..." His sleeve brushed hers, and she flinched as if a torch had narrowly missed setting her ablaze. Embarrassed, she stood miserably next to him, watching other people's luggage drift past, wondering what he must think of her reaction. Her insides vibrated and her jaws cramped with tension. She felt more nervous than she'd ever felt before a performance, waiting in the wings, listening for her cue.

Then she thought: *A performance. That's what this is—a role. I'm playing Sunny. I have to, for now. For just a little while longer. I need to remember that.*

"There—that one." She pointed, and Sage snatched the backpack from the carousel one-handed and swung it onto his left shoulder. With his right hand he picked up the suitcase, then set it back down with a soft grunt and gave her a wry grin. "No wheels, huh?"

She shrugged an apology. "I know—sorry. It's all I had. I thought about getting a new one with the credit card Mr. Branson sent, but I wasn't sure if I—"

"Hey, it's okay." He drew himself up, flexing his arm, and his smile grew pained. But he shook his head and reached again for the suitcase. "I was kidding."

He tipped his head toward the cat carrier, standing alone in the diminishing crowd. "If you'll bring your kitty cat—"

She picked up the carrier and fell in beside him. "You mean, The Beast."

He chuckled, and the sound was like warm fur on her shivering nerves. "My truck isn't too far away."

"Truck? As in...pickup?" She hefted the cat's carrier and raised her eyebrows, asking a silent question.

He didn't look her way, but a smile teased the side of his mouth. "Don't worry, it's got a backseat." Then he flashed her an appraising look. "It's not far to where I'm parked, if you don't mind walking."

"Hey, I'm a New Yorker," she retorted, and was rewarded with that soft laughter. She laughed back. It felt good, and she began to relax a little.

I'll tell them when I get to the ranch, she told herself. *He'll probably be there—Sunny's grandfather. Sam Malone. To meet me—*her. *Of course he will.*

I'll tell him then.

"I can't get used to all this...this *space,*" Abby said, waving a hand in the general direction of the hills rolling by outside the windows of the late-model white pickup truck.

"The Basques still graze sheep on these hills. I haven't seen them in a long time, though."

The compulsion to look at him became too much for her willpower. She gazed at his profile, dark against the moving scene, and something stirred inside her chest. "The Basques? What about your—um." She stuttered to a halt and looked away again, not wanting to say the wrong thing. The politically incorrect thing. Wondering why that should be, when as a New Yorker she was used to blurting out whatever was on her mind, and if someone had a problem with that...tough.

"My *people?*" He sounded amused rather than insulted. "The native people here were hunter-gatherers, not sheepherders. There weren't any sheep or cattle before the white men came."

"It must have been very different. Before—"

"When the first white men came to this valley, they found the native peoples camped on the shores of a lake. There was plenty of food—elk and deer, ducks and geese, and fish. They gathered the reeds that grew in the shallows to make baskets."

"Your people?" she asked when he paused.

He shook his head. "No, they were Yowlumni-Yokuts—a different tribe. The Tubatulabal were from the valley to the east of here—up the river, where we're going. Anyway, the white men thought this looked like a good place to live, so they built a city." Now there was no mistaking the amusement in his voice.

"Only trouble is, they weren't wise in the way of this land, like the native people. They didn't know that in the springtime when the snow melts in the high country, the water comes here—to fill the lake. For the native people this was no problem, they just packed up and moved to higher ground. Kind of hard to pack up and move a city."

"So, what happened? I'm guessing it got flooded?"

"Sure did." He glanced at her. "After it happened to the white men's city a couple of times, the Army Corps of Engineers came and built a dam. So, instead of flooding the city of Bakersfield, they flooded the valley upriver."

"The valley of your people."

He shrugged. "By that time the valley belonged to the white cattle ranchers, so it didn't really affect the Native people that much. It flooded some of the old village sites." His tone was neutral, and a smile played around his lips as he looked at her again. "It's still a beautiful valley. And a beautiful lake."

"And...how do we get to this beautiful valley? Don't tell me—we have to go over these mountains?"

"Not over—through." He nodded toward the windshield, where the mountains loomed ahead like a wall, growing ever closer.

"I don't see— I mean, *how?*"

He chuckled. "Follow the river."

Then she saw it—the mouth of the canyon, like a giant fissure in the earth—or a hungry maw waiting to swallow them. She gasped.

"I hope you don't get carsick," he said, as the pickup slowed abruptly, then swept into the canyon, past rock cliffs that seemed to hang directly above their heads, close enough to the side of the car to scrape the paint. "If you do, the trick is to find a focal point—"

"Hey—I'm a dancer, I know about focal points, okay? How do you think we keep from getting dizzy when we spin?"

It was false bravado; what she wanted to do more than anything was shut her eyes, squeeze them tight so she couldn't see Death coming. But she was damned if she'd let him see how terrified she was. And damned if she was going to get sick in his car. Or pickup truck.

Oh, Sunny, she thought as she gripped the door's armrest and silently prayed. *What have you gotten me into?*

To Sage's relief, she didn't get sick, though he couldn't help but notice she had some trouble remembering about the focal point. She kept craning her neck to look up, or hitching forward in her seat to look past him, over the side to the river below. And while he couldn't very well look at her to confirm his suspicion, he would have sworn more of her suppressed gasps had to do with the vision of wildflowers cascading down the canyon walls than with the roller-coaster twists and turns of the road.

"It's beautiful," she said finally, sitting back and evidently trying once again to focus her eyes on the pavement ahead.

Just that, and it pleased him way more than it should have. Why did he care one way or the other what Sam's granddaughter thought of the part of the world he'd chosen to make his home?

Because Sam cares.

Then, because he wasn't in the habit of lying to himself: *Because it's your home, too.*

And because she reminds you of Heather.

Damn. There it was. And he had no idea why. This granddaughter of Sam's with the improbable name of Sunshine Wells looked nothing like Heather Whitlock, and there was no reason in the world why he should suddenly find himself thinking about the woman…

…that got away?

But she hadn't "got away." He'd let her go. *He'd* walked away. Big-difference.

Broke your heart, then?

Had she? What did a broken heart feel like? It had hurt, sure, leaving her, but he somehow thought a broken heart would be a deeper kind of hurt, the kind that couldn't be gotten over as easily as he'd gotten over Heather. And he *had* gotten over her. Of that much he was certain.

Oh, yeah? Then why did this woman—Sunny—trigger all your old defenses? Guilt, maybe? Or...regret?

Guilt...maybe. Although, the last he'd heard, Heather had married her law partner and was living happily ever after in Boston, so evidently her heart hadn't been broken beyond repair, either. And as for regret...no. He'd made the right decision. Staying together would have been disastrous for both of them. He shook his head. *I did the right thing.*

"What, you don't think so?"

He realized Sunny was looking at him, her expression disbelieving.

"How can you not?" she went on, while he was bringing himself back from his unexpected stroll down memory lane. "I've never seen anything like this—ever. It's just...amazing."

He gave a little grunt of apology. "Sorry...I was thinking of something else. Beautiful? Sure, I think it's beautiful. It's my home."

Home. She was silent for a moment, and the word seemed to echo in the space between them—as it had that day so long ago when he'd spoken it to Heather. The day he'd realized the place that was part of him, body and soul, would never— *could* never—be *her* home.

"Have you always lived here?"

"Except for when I was away at college, yeah." He braced himself for the next question: *Do you think you will always live here?* Prepared to answer her as he'd answered Heather: *It's where I belong.*

But she only said, "Where was that?"

"Yale, for a year. Then back to California. Cal Poly—San Luis Obispo."

"Yale? Wow."

This time, her little gasp of surprise only amused him, since he'd expected it. "It was Sam's idea, and since he was the one paying for it, I went along to please him. A year was enough, though. I was glad to get back to California."

"So, what's your degree in?"

"I have two, actually. Business and agriculture. That was Sam's idea, too. I was working on my master's in business, but then Sam needed me, so...I came home."

"Sam...um, m-my grandfather—you said he paid for your education? Why? That seems..."

"Well...he practically raised us—my sister and me." He heard her waiting silence and hitched a shoulder. "My mom started working for Sam before I was born. My sister was just two...almost three. My mom runs the house for him," he explained, tossing her a glance.

"So...she lives there? At the ranch."

He nodded, then waited for more, and he could feel her looking at him, all thought of focal points evidently forgotten. "You probably have questions," he prompted gently. "It's okay to ask."

She gave a small laugh and faced the front again. "Yeah... okay. So...who all is there now? At the ranch, besides your mother, and, I assume, your sister, and..."

"Not my sister. Cheyenne's...away." He shifted uncomfortably, because he knew what she was really asking. *Who will I be meeting? When will I get to meet my grandfather?* "At the moment," he said on an exhalation, "there's just Rachel, and—"

"Rachel?"

The eagerness in her voice made him smile. "Your cousin—another one of Sam's granddaughters. Then there's her baby, Sean, and—" He glanced over at her then. "Okay, I don't know how much Alex told you..."

"Not very much. Only that…m-my grandfather wanted to meet me, and that if I wanted to meet him, I should come to the ranch. That's all. That…and the letter Sam wrote."

He heard that note in her voice again, and wished he wasn't driving so he could see if the fear he heard was in her eyes, too.

While he was thinking how to begin to fill her in on what she was walking into, she burst out, "It's not about the money. That's not why I came. It's *not*."

"I believe you," he said gently, and he could almost feel her vibrating with tension, clear across the width of the truck. He wondered if that's all it was, that she was afraid he'd take her for a fortune hunter. She had no way of knowing he wasn't about to judge her, or any of the others, either. The way he figured, they all had their reasons for answering Sam's summons—one way or the other—and whatever those reasons were, they were no business of his.

Chapter 3

Abby settled back and once more focused her eyes on the twists and turns of the road ahead, willing herself to relax. Reminding herself that Sam Malone's granddaughter, Rachel, was Sunny's cousin, not hers. Sunny's family, not hers.

More family, looking forward to meeting Sunny. And instead...I have to tell them she's dead.

"So, tell me," she said, clearing her throat, "about Rachel."

"It's kind of a long story." He glanced her way, then tilted his head toward the windshield as the asphalt ribbon of highway abruptly straightened and widened out to multiple lanes. "You can probably forget about focal points from here on in. It's freeway from here—until we get to the valley, anyway."

"Thank God." She shifted abruptly in her seat, half facing him as she prompted, "So...this cousin..."

"Rachel." He nodded, then was silent for a moment as he seemed to gather his thoughts and absently massaged his right shoulder. He let out a huff of laughter. "Well, for one thing, she's about as different from you as I guess it's possible to be and still be related by blood."

Abby felt a jolt of alarm. *Does he suspect? Am I that different?* "What…do you mean?"

Again, he seemed to choose his words carefully. "Her grandmother was Sam's first wife—Elizabeth. Their son, Sean, Rachel's father, was killed in Southeast Asia when Rachel was a baby. Rachel's mother was from Vietnam—a refugee. They'd met in the Philippines. After she died, too, Rachel's grandmother, Elizabeth, brought the child to America—she was about four by that time—and raised her."

He paused, and Abby cleared her throat and nodded. The tension inside her eased a little as she saw where this was going. "So, that would make her half Vietnamese. I'm guessing she's tiny and dark, and I'm—"

"Definitely not, yeah." She heard amusement in his voice as he finished it for her, although the half of his face she could see remained impassive. "Don't let her size fool you, though." He rubbed his shoulder again, and threw her a quick, wry smile. "Rachel is one tough lady."

Which I'm not so much, Abby thought. *Don't let my size fool you.* Aloud, she said, "And she has a baby?"

Sage nodded. "Sean—he's a little over a month old now. Cute little guy."

"Is his father there, too? At the ranch?"

"No." She saw the corner of his mouth tighten. "Rachel's husband was the son of a big-time gangster down in L.A.—head of the Delacorte Cartel. After the son got himself killed in a shootout with federal agents, the father—Carlos—kept Rachel pretty much a prisoner. She was pregnant and afraid her father-in-law was planning on killing her and taking her son. She managed to escape from him, but got stranded out in the desert. Then…she went into labor."

"My God," Abby breathed.

He nodded again. "Fortunately, a deputy sheriff from San

Bernardino found her in time to deliver her baby in his patrol car."

"Oh, my God."

"Yeah. That's what I mean about her being tough. Anyway, afterward…the sheriff—his name's J.J. Fox, by the way— brought her and the baby to the ranch, thinking they'd be safe there." Once more he paused, and the corner of his mouth lifted intriguingly.

Gazing at him, Abby found herself fascinated once more by the play of muscles over the strong bones of his face. She said, "I'm guessing…they weren't?"

"They are now," he said softly.

He went on, then, to tell her about the day Carlos Delacorte had come for his grandson, leaving out the part Sam himself had played in bringing down Carlos's chopper and saving Rachel from being kidnapped—or worse.

"You were *shot?*"

The sting of horror in her voice brought it all back, but he didn't like to talk about that. Didn't like remembering the *thump* of impact that had spun him around and dropped him like a rag doll, and the fear he'd felt, the helplessness…but oddly, no pain. Not then.

"A flesh wound," he said with a shrug, resisting the urge to rub again at the still-healing scar on his right shoulder where a Delacorte gunman's bullet had torn through muscle but miraculously missed hitting bones and vital organs. "J.J. was the one who got the worst of it." He stretched his lips in a smile. "Not counting the bad guys."

"J.J.—that's the sheriff, right? So he was…what, protecting Rachel?"

"Well…it started out that way, because she was a witness to the shootout where her husband and those two feds were killed. But…" He smiled, then, for real, the warmth of it going all the way down to his belly. "Let's just say it's a whole lot more than that now. He's there with Rachel and the baby, in fact, and probably will be, for a while."

"At the ranch?"

He nodded. "While his leg heals, at least. High-powered rifle bullet took out a section of bone in his leg—they almost took the leg off, but Sam wouldn't hear of that. Told the docs to do whatever they had to do to save it, no matter what it cost or whether insurance would cover it. J.J.'s had a couple of surgeries on the leg already, and looking at more before they're done. They're taking bone from his thigh to graft into the gap the bullet left."

"Wow," Sunny said faintly.

Sage glanced at her. "I guess it's a lot to take in."

She gave an uneasy laugh. "It's like something out of a movie. It doesn't even seem real."

"Yeah," he said, with a soft laugh of his own, "sometimes it seems that way to me, too. Like it happened to somebody else, you know? A long time ago."

She didn't answer, although he could feel her eyes on him. He didn't look over at her; didn't want to risk direct eye contact. He'd already given away more of himself than he ever did with strangers. Than he had in a good many years, anyway—since he'd learned better.

Since...Heather?

"Trust me," he said dryly, "it's not like that, most of the time. Normally, ranch life is pretty dull stuff."

She settled back with a soft huff of laughter. "To you, maybe. To me it's like another world. I mean that literally—like an alien planet."

He nodded. "I can see how that would be."

Then she was silent for a long time. He'd begun to wonder if she'd fallen asleep when she suddenly said, "Are there any more? Besides Rachel, I mean."

"Sam's grandchildren?" She nodded. He could only throw her a quick glance, not long enough to interpret the look on her face, only long enough to get an impression. What he felt was a sense of profound *hunger* that reminded him of a little kid looking in a candy store window. He smiled at that notion, because he could guess how hard it must be to get her mind around all this—finding out she had a bunch of relatives she hadn't known about. "Besides you and Rachel, you mean." Again, she didn't reply, and after a moment he went on. "Yeah, there are a couple more from Sam's third wife, but we haven't heard from them yet."

There was another silence, not quite as long as before, and then: "Do you have a family?"

"You mean, am I married? Kids?" He shook his head. "No, but I've got a lot of family—on my mother's side, anyway. Don't know anything about my father's. More relatives on Mom's side than I know what to do with—they have a big family reunion every few years. People come from all over, bring their campers...stay all weekend."

He heard the hiss of an exhalation. "I can't even imagine what that's like. To have family. I've never—"

He threw her another glance but her head was bowed and he saw only the curtain of her hair. Something twisted oddly inside his chest. He said softly, "But you do now."

She'd been nervous, had butterflies before, of course she had. In her business, they came with the territory. She'd even been so nervous before a performance, she'd thrown up—oh, many times. Nearly every performer she knew got stage fright to one degree or another, whether they were rookies or old-timers. And not one of them, including Abby, would trade the business they were in for something less stressful. It was like the song: "There's No Business Like Show Business."

But this—this was something different. Exciting, yes, but not in a good way. This was feeling anxious and fearful and helpless and...small.

Small. Yes, and as she sat beside Sage in his big white pickup truck, peering through the windshield for her first glimpse of the place she was coming to, the place that was supposed to—that *might*—be her new home, it hit her. She was a child again.

She was…oh, maybe six, and she was riding in the back-seat of the social worker's car, being driven to yet another foster home. Shivering inside, trying desperately not to wet her pants, hands knotted tightly together in her lap, staring at her feet in a brand-new pair of sneakers. Her feet were sticking straight out in front of her, jerking rhythmically up and down. And her thoughts were a pitiful prayer: *Please let them be nice… Please let them like me… Maybe this time they will keep me.*

It infuriated her to be thrust back to such a time and place, to feel again like the wretched, miserable child she'd been then—except for the part about wetting her pants, thank God. But as angry as it made her to feel such vulnerability when she'd thought she was long past that, she knew there was nothing she could do to change the way she felt. As a therapist had told her long ago when she was still in the system, angry and rebellious about the way it had failed her: *Feelings can't be controlled, Abigail; only actions.*

That day, she'd set about learning how to control her actions—in a word, to *act.* It had probably saved her life.

She hoped it would save her now.

"Almost there," Sage said, because it had been a long time since either of them had spoken.

She settled back with an exhalation, a breathy laugh. He glanced at her and she looked at him and smiled. And again he felt that odd turning inside his chest. "Nervous?" he asked. And then: "You shouldn't be."

She gave a little snort of laughter. "Easy for *you* to say."

He acknowledged that with a nod and a half smile. He felt her eyes resting on him. After a moment she asked, "Have you ever been to New York?"

"The city?"

She nodded, still intently watching him.

"Yes, I have—several times. When I was at Yale."

"How did you feel the first time you saw it?"

He gave a soft laugh. "Overwhelmed." He shook his head

and added, "But it's not the same. For one thing, I was with a bunch of friends."

"Well, that makes a big difference."

"It does." He threw her another glance. "But on the other hand, I didn't have people waiting for me with open arms, ready to welcome me into the family."

She was quiet for a moment. Then she looked away. "Maybe that's part of the problem."

"Why's that?"

She gave another of those little snorts—laughter without amusement. "Oh, like, no pressure, or anything."

"Pressure? Why? You don't have anything to prove."

"Don't I?"

He glanced at her remembering she'd said she was a dancer. "It's not like this is an audition. You've got the job. You're Sam's granddaughter—nothing can change that."

She fell silent, and in the silence was something he couldn't name. It reminded him of the way the forest goes quiet when the predator walks. And it made him wonder about the woman sitting beside him…wonder why so beautiful a woman should be so insecure, so fearful. Made him itch to know the Sunny Wells she didn't let the world see, made him burn to ask questions his ingrained reserve would not let him ask.

He drove in silence as deep as hers, disturbed in ways he didn't understand.

"So, this is it," Abby said, as they turned left onto a paved but unlined road.

Sage nodded. "June Canyon Road. The ranch is a few miles farther up."

She didn't answer, but her heart quickened as she gazed at the granite peaks that lay ahead, seeming to block their path. An illusion, as she'd already discovered. There would be a hidden canyon, a winding road leading to…what?

What lies ahead…for me? What will happen when I tell them about Sunny? Will they hate me? Blame the messenger?

Oh, God...I hope they'll understand.

The paved road arrowed straight between barbed wire fences bordering pastures where dark-colored cattle grazed, then entered a swamplike wilderness of trees Abby didn't know the names of, many fallen and rotting, some half-submerged in water. They swept across a bridge over a small, sluggish river, and there were more fields, some freshly plowed, some filled with green grass and wildflowers. Then the road began to climb a slope covered with rocks and brush and small rounded evergreen trees.

"Over there—that's tribal land." Sage pointed as the road wound upward. "Some of my mom's family live there."

"Tribal land." She frowned with the effort to corral her wandering thoughts. "You mean like a...reservation?"

The side of his mouth lifted in what she somehow knew was not a smile. "No. The word *reservation* implies restrictions—kind of has a bad history with us, if you can understand that. When I say tribal land, I mean just that. It belongs to the tribe. As it always has—it's the site of one our historic villages. It was called *yitiyamup,* in case you wanted to know." He nodded toward the windshield. "There's another old village site where the ranch is now."

"Where the ranch—Sam's ranch—is now? Doesn't that...I don't know...bother you?"

He smiled—a real one, this time. "No, it doesn't bother me. What would be the point? It's the past. And besides—no one can own the land. People come and go. The land goes on forever. We only borrow the use of it for a while." His lips twisted and the smile became wry. "Hopefully, we leave it in as good condition as we found it."

"Yeah...right."

He lifted one shoulder. "All we can do is try."

The road twisted and turned and became a dirt track, then twisted and turned and dipped and climbed some more, seemingly forever. Around them the plant life began to change, trees appearing now in the spaces between rocks, tall, gray-green pines of some kind—like nothing she'd ever seen in the lush forests of upstate New York. She was sure Sage would know what they were, but she didn't ask; her mouth was too dry for conversation.

They had left all signs of human habitation far behind when the pickup bumped to a stop. Sage nodded toward the window on his side and said, "That's it over there—Sam's place."

Abby leaned toward him and bent down to see what he was talking about...and was somehow closer to him than she realized, until she felt the heat and caught the scent of his body, unlike anything she'd ever known before. She couldn't place it, but if she closed her eyes she could see green grass and tall pine trees and soft brown earth, and feel the warmth of sunshine on her cheeks...

"See it? In those trees, the red tile roof..."

Her breath caught, and she opened her eyes and struggled to bring the vista beyond the window into focus. "Yes—okay, I see it." Her heart was racing, her voice airless and small.

"It's okay," Sage said softly.

She jerked toward his voice and found his eyes so close they seemed to eclipse everything else; his eyes became her world, black as night, but warm as summer. Somehow, she managed to whisper, "What?"

"To be scared."

"I'm not scared," she lied.

"Then why are you shaking?"

"I'm not." She sat back abruptly, and from that safer distance, glared at him. "I'm a little nervous, okay? I already told you that. No big deal."

"That's right." He smiled in his enigmatic way and the truck moved forward.

A little farther on, the road turned sharply to the left, dipped down a bank, crossed a creek with several inches of water running swiftly over a rocky bed, threaded through a willow thicket, then angled up the other side. And now, across a landscape strewn with boulders and bristling with those wild-looking pine trees and rampant gray-green shrubs, she could see, stretching away to steep mountain slopes, lush green meadows where dark cattle rested in the shade of huge old trees.

She let out her breath slowly, silently, not wanting him to know.

The road became a T-intersection at the meadow fence. Ahead and a little to the right, Abby could see a cluster of trees and buildings.

"What's that?" She pointed. "Who lives there?"

"I do," Sage replied. "That's the original June Ranch. The house is the original adobe. Sam's place is this way. We call it the hacienda."

As he said that he turned left, and the road, though still dirt, was now smooth and wide. It meandered between towering evergreen trees and some others she didn't know the names of—poplars, maybe? In patches of sunshine between clusters of trees were beds of roses and irises in full bloom. Those, at least, she knew.

They passed a long building of white-painted stucco with a red tile roof, and Abby caught her breath.

Sage threw her an amused look and said, "Garage." She gave a low whistle, and he chuckled.

Then, around a last stand of trees, suddenly there it was— the hacienda, sprawling across the top of a hill like a sentinel keeping watch over the valley far below. The drive became an open area paved with flagstone, with wide curving flagstone steps leading up to a set of massive double doors, arched and carved from heavy wood, stained dark.

As the pickup truck pulled to a stop below the steps, two dogs came from somewhere to meet them: a shaggy black-and-white dog like the sheep-herding dogs in the movie *Babe*, bounding and twisting eagerly; and at a much more sedate pace, an old hound with wrinkled face, long droopy ears and sad dark eyes.

Abby's heart turned a huge flip-flop; as a child she'd

dreamed of having a dog. But, like family photos and heirlooms, pets didn't often happen for a child in the foster care system. At least, they hadn't for her.

She opened the door, and before she could even get her legs out of the truck the black-and-white dog came bouncing joyfully, wriggling into the space offered by the opening door, trying his best to climb into her lap, it seemed, in order to lick her face.

Breathless and overwhelmed, laughing helplessly, she heard Sage say, "Freckles—*down*." The dog backed away, but hovered, whining and all but vibrating with excitement. "You'll have to forgive him," Sage said dryly. "He's just a people-lover."

"It's okay—really. I like dogs." She slid out of the truck and dropped to one knee beside the quivering animal, murmuring the kinds of baby talk things people say to dogs. She put her arms around him and he took up licking her face where he'd left off, though in a slightly more subdued way.

Emotions she'd never felt before sizzled and shimmered all through her and threatened to leak out. *Careful—don't lose it now,* she cautioned herself. *Be strong.*

"He knows better," Sage said. "But he's young."

She rose abruptly, brushing at herself, and nodded at the old hound, who was sitting a little way off, panting slightly. "I'm guessing this one's not." She went toward the other dog slowly, holding out her hand. The hound sniffed the hand, then gazed solemnly up at her.

"Don't really know," she heard Sage say as she lightly touched the dog's wrinkled head. "She's J.J.'s—the sheriff's—dog. Her name's Moonshine."

Abby squatted on her heels and some impulse made her put her arms around the old hound's neck. "Hello, Moonshine," she whispered, and tears came unexpectedly to burn her eyes.

"He says she just wandered into his place one day," Sage said. "So he decided to let her stay."

"Good thing I did, too, or these two might not be here

now." The voice was deep, scratchy and Southern, like something out of a Western movie.

She froze, nerves twanging, heart thumping, nervous as a thief caught red-handed, as Sage called out, "Hey," greeting someone she couldn't see. She felt his hand touch her back as she rose, and resisted the impulse to reach for it…cling to it.

"Speak of the devil." Sage kept his hand on her back, barely touching but somehow supporting, and she turned with him to meet the three people coming down the wide flagstone steps.

The hound dog, Moonshine, went shambling over to meet them, too, and parked herself at the bottom of the steps to watch them descend, like a sentinel, Abby thought. Alert, now. Standing guard.

"Sunny, this is Sheriff J.J. Fox, and Rachel," Sage said, nodding at each in turn.

The man with the voice like a Western movie star looked like one, too, except for the fact that one leg was encased in a protective blue boot, and he was leaning heavily on a pair of crutches. He was tall and rangy of build, with keen blue eyes and wavy, sandy-blond hair that brushed his collar. The woman, Rachel, moved carefully beside him, both because she was carrying a baby and out of obvious concern for the man on crutches. She was exactly as Sage had described her: petite, with dark, almond-shaped eyes and long dark hair pulled back in a ponytail. Except Sage had neglected to mention the fact that she was exquisitely lovely. Possibly one of the most beautiful women Abby had ever seen—which, again, considering the business she was in, was saying a lot. She looked entirely too delicate and fragile to have borne the baby she was holding in her arms, but Abby remembered Sage had said she was tougher than she looked.

Abby said, "Hi," and lifted her hand in a wave, because she couldn't very well shake hands with a man on crutches and a woman carrying a baby, even if her own hand hadn't been bandaged. She was about to offer something more by way of a polite greeting when a hideous undulating yowl came from directly behind her.

She jerked around just as Freckles, the black-and-white dog, uttered a "Yike!" of pain and leaped backward, away from the cat carrier that was sitting on the bottommost step.

She clapped both hands over her mouth and gasped, "Oh, God—I'm sorry—" at the same time the sheriff was saying, "Holy… What've you got in there—a cougar?"

Sage picked up the carrier and said to the dog, "Yeah, I guess you learned a good lesson, huh, boy?" He gave Abby a crooked smile. "All the farm cats are his buddies. He's not going to know what to think of this one."

Abby was wondering what to say next when the big front door flew open and a woman burst through and came trotting down the steps, arms held wide.

"Ah," said Sage. "Here she is."

Abby had time to notice that the woman was short and round—solidly built rather than fat—and wearing blue jeans and a pink plaid blouse, and that her hair was thick salt-and-pepper cut in a short, becoming style, and that she was smiling, though her round cheeks were flushed and her dark eyes bright with tears. That was all, before the woman came to a halt on the next step up from her, and Abby was swallowed up in a huge, warm hug.

Such a thing had never happened to her, that she could recall. Never in her life before.

"Sunny," she heard Sage say in a dry tone, "meet my mother, Josephine."

The woman drew back to smile fiercely through tears. "*Josie.* You call me Josie. This is your *home.* Oh—welcome home, Sunny."

Abby was both shocked and mortified when she, too, burst into tears.

Chapter 4

Abby felt as if she'd been beaten. Not physically, on the outside where it would show, but on the inside. Her emotions felt bruised. Battered. Like a punchy boxer, she didn't know quite where she was. Or what to do next.

She was finally alone, in the room Josie had shown her to after a brief tour of the hacienda. The house was built in the Spanish style, a rectangle arranged around a central courtyard. The arched front doors opened onto a foyer larger than Abby's entire apartment in New York, with a high ceiling with dark wood beams and glistening tile on the floor. Across from the entrance, double French doors stood open, allowing the scent of flowers and the sounds of running water and birds' song to drift through the house.

Through more open doors to the left of the entry, Abby caught a glimpse of walls covered with shelves filled with books, and a large desk with a computer, and massive, comfortable-looking chairs, before Josie led her through matching doors on the right, into a living room that seemed roughly the size of Grand Central Station. In spite of its size, the room seemed warm and welcoming, with a huge native stone fireplace and cozy groupings of comfortable couches and chairs and Navajo rugs on the Spanish tile floor. This room didn't open onto the courtyard, but instead had large windows that overlooked the valley and the mountains beyond.

Next to the living room was the dining room, which was almost as big as the living room, with the same tile floor and spectacular view, a table that looked able to seat at least twenty people, and buffets and cabinets that looked ancient and would have dwarfed a normal-size room. Beyond that was a modern kitchen that would have done a five-star restaurant proud. Here, instead of windows overlooking the valley, double French doors opened onto a flagstone patio bordered by a low stone wall just the right height for sitting. Several round tables were arranged around a central fire pit, filled, now, with flowering plants in various size pots.

From the kitchen, a door opened into a bedroom wing, one of two, Josie had explained, each with four bedrooms, including private bathrooms. All of the bedrooms were accessible by a long hallway that ran the length of the wing, with windows high in the outer walls, and lamps in recessed alcoves across from each door.

Josie bypassed the first two doors, opened the third and ushered Abby into a room that was large and comfortable, light and airy, with a queen-size bed, a desk, comfortable chairs and double French doors that opened onto the courtyard.

"I hope this is all right," she said as she stood just inside the door, sounding breathless. "Rachel and J.J. have the two next to you—although…" She smiled and shrugged. "Well. I hope you'll be comfortable here."

Momentarily incapable of speech, Abby set the cat carrier on the floor and let her backpack drop beside it. Her suitcase, she saw, had been brought in and placed on a low wooden chest at the foot of the bed.

"It's lovely," she said as she turned slowly, enveloped in a fog of wonderment. She'd never had so much space all to herself in her entire life.

"Well," Josie said, looking rosy-cheeked and bright-eyed with happiness, "I'll leave you to unpack…settle in." She backed through the door and closed it gently after her.

Unpack? Settle in? How long will they let me stay here, I wonder, after I tell them about Sunny?

Do I have to tell them right away?

You know you do.

Seriously. What would it matter if I waited…just a day or two?

Don't even think about it. The minute you meet Sam Malone, it's all over. That was the deal.

How long she stood motionless in the middle of that lovely room with those thoughts swirling through her mind, Abby didn't know. It took a piteous chirp from the cat carrier to finally shake her out of her daze. Murmuring apologies, she knelt and opened the wire door. Pia stepped tentatively out of the carrier, stretching and looking bad-tempered and suspicious, but somehow lost and bewildered, too.

At which point, Abby realized she'd neglected to ask Sage to stop somewhere so she could pick up cat food—also, kitty litter and a pan to put it in.

Seeing no other option for the moment, she opened the door to the courtyard and crooned invitingly, "Come on, kitty… want to come out? It's nice…see? Mmm…sunshine."

Pia stalked to the threshold and paused there, head raised, eyes half-closed, sniffing the sweet evening air. Abby waited patiently while the cat took first one step…then another… cringed at some unseen threat, then ventured a few more steps. Like a space explorer, Abby thought, setting foot for the first time on an alien planet. Which, in a way, for Pia it was, she supposed, since the cat hadn't set foot on actual earth since the day Sunny had scooped her out of that pile of leaves.

When Pia began to dig industriously in the mulch at the base of a huge climbing rosebush, Abby exhaled a relieved sigh and went back inside, leaving the door open. Still unable to bring herself to unpack, she left her suitcase sitting unopened on the chest, picked up her backpack and sat on the bed with it in her lap.

Okay, what now?

She felt desperately lonely and scared, regretting the idiotic journey she'd embarked on and now didn't have a clue how to get herself out of.

She began digging through her backpack. *Toothbrush? Probably safe enough to take that out, surely they won't mind if I just brush my teeth.*

She took out the free magazine she'd taken from the plane, and the tiny package of pretzels she'd been too nervous to eat, and her cell phone. Realizing she hadn't turned her phone on after the flight, she did so now, and found she had four voice mail messages and two texts, all from Pauly. *Pauly? Why would he be calling me, unless...*

And wouldn't that be ironic, she thought, *if the minute I leave town he tells me he has something for me—an audition, maybe even a job interview.*

She tried to call voice mail, tried to return the call, but evidently there was no service. She checked the text messages. The first said, Where are you? The second, Call me!

Yeah, right. Would that were possible here on the dark side of Nowhere.

She was weighing her options and trying to decide whether she had enough nerve to ask to use a landline phone, when there was a knock on the door. She went to open it and found Josie standing there with a tray, on which were a moisture-beaded pitcher of iced tea, a glass, a long-handled spoon, a dish containing packets of assorted sweeteners and another with wedges of lemon. She also had a large manila envelope tucked under one arm.

"Hi—sorry to bother you again," Josie said as she breezed past Abby to set the tray on the desk. "I thought you might be thirsty—I know airplanes can really dry you out."

"Thanks...that's very nice of you," Abby said faintly. She took a deep breath. "Um...I was wondering—" But before she could ask about using a telephone, Josie held out the envelope.

"I brought you this. I don't know if you've ever seen a picture of your grandmother—Barbara Chase." She gave Abby one of her rosy smiles. "You know, you look just like her." Her smile vanished and she shrugged an apology. "I don't have a picture of your mother. We... I wish I did. Do you..."

"No—sorry," Abby said, and her voice was edgy and strained. She took the envelope and held it, staring down at it through a blur of tears. Because the realization had just struck her that there had been no photos whatsoever among Sunny's things. She wondered whether she'd destroyed them after her mother's suicide, or whether she'd ever had any to begin with. Whether in her case, as in Abby's, the past had been a place she didn't care to revisit.

"I'm sorry," Josie said, gently touching Abby's arm. "I don't mean to upset you."

"You didn't." Abby lifted her head, tossing her hair back over her shoulders. She forced a smile and it hurt her face. "Thanks—this is so nice of you." She stared hard at the envelope in her hands, frowned, and pulled words from somewhere. "What about my grandfather? Sam Malone? Is he here? When will I meet him?"

Josie's eyes slid sideways. "Oh, Sam—Mr. Malone—he's unpredictable, you know. It's hard to know when he'll show up." She gave an uncomfortable little laugh. "Well—I should go. I just wanted to tell you dinner will be ready in about half an hour, if, you know, you'd like to freshen up before then."

She turned to go, then paused, and her smile blossomed

as she looked past Abby. "Oh—look, so this is your terrible kitty. Hello there, pretty one…"

Abby looked over her shoulder in time to see Pia come stalking in through the open French door as if she owned the world. "Oh, God—I'm sorry," Abby said, clapping a hand to her mouth as Pia leaped gracefully onto the bed. "She had to go to the bathroom, and I didn't want— I hope she didn't—"

Josie laughed. "Oh, my goodness, don't worry about it. I think my flower garden will survive one kitty cat. You will need a litter box, of course—I imagine Sage has one he can spare. I'll have him bring one up. And some cat food, too." She turned to the door, and again, paused.

"You know," she said, studying the cat who was now lying in the middle of the bed, staring back at her, sphinxlike, motionless except for the tip of her tail, "except for the color she is like a very small…*tuugakut*—that is the word for cougar— or mountain lion—in Pakanapul. The language of the Tubatulabal."

She threw Abby a smile, said, "See you at dinner," and went out.

Abby looked down at the envelope in her hands, expecting to see it trembling. To her bemusement, it appeared steady, so all the shaking she felt must be deep inside. She tossed it onto the bed, and Pia chirped and dipped her head, graciously consenting to be stroked. Abby obliged, murmuring sweet nothings but fully alert, knowing from experience Pia's hellcat nature could assert itself at any moment, compelling her, for reasons beyond Abby's understanding, to bite the hand that petted her.

She reached for the backpack, opened it and took out the zip-locked plastic bag of dry cat food she'd packed for the trip. Pia rose, stretched, and sniffed with apparent disdain at the bag while Abby opened it and poured a small pile of the kibble onto the bedspread. Then, while Pia sat herself down and began crunching away, Abby closed up the plastic bag and picked up the manila envelope. She stared at it for a moment, then opened it and took out the single black-and-white photo.

She held the photo in both hands and gazed at it, while the envelope fluttered unnoticed to the floor. Slowly, mechanically, she sat down on the bed, without taking her eyes from the face in the photograph. She touched the image, and although it was only a black-and-white photo of a woman long dead, she could almost feel the warmth of real flesh beneath her fingertips. She could almost hear the whisper of a sultry whiskey-and-cigarettes voice coming from the vivid lips. The eyes, gazing up at her from behind thick lashes and a curtain of near-white hair, were dark, and filled with secrets and sadness.

Sunny's face.

And I look like Sunny, so I guess it's no wonder they think I look like her, too.

"So, she's there?"

"Yep."

"Well, what do you think of her?"

"What does it matter what I think of her?" The edge in his voice surprised Sage almost as much as it did Sam, who greeted the question with a telling silence. Sage drew a breath and sought self-control. "It's what you think of her that matters. She keeps asking about you. When is she going to meet you…you know."

There was a mild grunt, then more silence. Then, "Son, I asked you what you think of her because I really want to know what you think."

Sage pulled in another breath. He stared out the window at the spring-green meadow dotted with yellow flowers and the horses grazing there, and all he could see was a curtain of pale gold hair falling across one green-gold eye.

"What does she look like?" Sam prompted, when Sage remained silent. "You can tell me that much, can't you? I know you ain't blind."

No, he wasn't blind. "Well, she's pretty," Sage said, realizing even as he uttered the word that it didn't do her justice. "Tall... Blond hair..." He paused, then gave a kind of half laugh. "You want to know what she looks like, I tell you what. You go look at a picture of your second wife. Her grandmother. She looks just like her."

"What? You telling me she looks like Barbara?"

"The spittin' image."

"No foolin'?" The old man's voice had faded almost to nothing.

"Why are you so surprised? I've heard of family resemblances skipping generations. Happens all the time."

"Yeah...sure." Sam coughed, cleared his throat in the way he had that sounded like a love-struck bullfrog, and when he went on his voice still sounded like somebody being strangled. "So what else? What's the girl like? That's what I want to know. And don't tell me I ought to come down there and see for myself. I'll come down when I'm damn good and ready. I want to know what *you* think of her, gol-dammit."

Sage rubbed his knotted-up forehead, as if that might somehow smooth out the jumbled thoughts inside. What did he think of Sunshine Wells? He wished to God he knew. He exhaled, finally, and words came with it. "I don't know... there's something..."

"Yeah? Like what?" The tension in the old man's voice vibrated across the miles.

"It's kind of like...almost like she's afraid. Of us, I mean. Like she's not sure of herself—like, maybe whether we'll like her, or something, you know? Which seems kind of funny, for someone that looks like she does." He paused. "Just seems like a woman that beautiful ought to have more self-confidence."

Sam chuckled. "Listen here, son, you watch yourself, now, you hear? It's been my sad experience that you shouldn't ever trust a beautiful woman *too* far."

The shower proved too great a temptation for Abby to resist, even if she didn't feel right about unpacking her suitcase. She fully expected to be tossed out on her rear the minute Sam Malone showed up, but in the meantime it had been a long day of travel and her body clock was still on Eastern time, and she really could use the chance to "freshen up" before dinner.

The bathroom wasn't large or fancy, by any means—just a bathtub and shower combined, a toilet, a sink with plenty of counter space, but compared to the one she'd been sharing with Sunny, it was beyond luxurious. And when she turned on the shower and found it not only had an abundance of pressure but a seemingly limitless supply of hot water, she sighed with pure bliss. Still, mindful of her pretender's status, she did turn off the faucet to conserve water while she undressed and twisted her hair and pinned it high on her head. She'd like to have shampooed it, but knew it would never dry before dinner and decided she'd rather not appear at her host's table with wet hair.

The feel of hot water sluicing over her body made her ache with pleasure, and with longing. *It's all so beautiful here...I can't let myself get used to this...*

Enveloped in warmth, with her eyes closed she saw it all again like a montage of movie clips played at fast-forward: a brown-skinned man with jet-black hair, standing like a tree in the flowing stream of people, waiting for her; grass-covered hills folding into wild blue mountains, and flowers cascading over looming rock cliffs that whizzed by too fast to really see; black cattle and brown horses grazing in a sea of meadow grass and wildflowers; a dog with long ears and soulful eyes; a woman with salt-and-pepper hair and a welcoming smile; back to the man again, now with questions in his jet-black eyes and his big strong hand warm and steady on her back.

A shudder passed through her, and she drew a deep breath and willed the sadness away. *Remember it's only make-believe. Like a play I'm privileged to have a role in, for a little while...*

She turned off the water reluctantly, dried herself and

dressed quickly, envisioning the family gathered around the dining room table, waiting patiently for her to make her appearance. Not being sure how formal an occasion dinner was in this household, she chose a tunic and calf-length swirly skirt, both made out of some sort of velvety, stretchy, clingy material she didn't know the name of. She'd found both in a secondhand store. The skirt was coppery brown, the tunic a shade of sea foam-green that brought out the green in her eyes.

The air felt so good on her bare neck and shoulders, she decided to leave her hair pinned up in its usual style, even though she knew she looked less like Sunny that way. What did it matter? They would know soon enough anyway.

She replaced the bandage on her hand with a much smaller one she found in a box in the medicine cabinet, then left the bathroom and was about to step into a pair of brown sandals when she froze, senses on full alert. *Something* wasn't right. She held her breath and looked around the room. Then it hit her: the courtyard door was open a few inches. And Pia was nowhere to be seen.

Her heart lurched into emergency mode and she crossed the room in two strides. She'd closed the door, she was sure of it. She *remembered* the cold metal shape of the handle against the palm of her hand. Which left only two possibilities: someone had come into her room while she was in the shower—a scenario that made her skin crawl but was so ridiculous she instantly discarded it—or...Pia had opened the door herself. Which may have sounded far-fetched to anyone else, but Abby remembered how the cat had tried to open the doors in her apartment, stretching herself full-length until she could put both paws around the doorknob. It was only her lack of opposable thumbs, Sunny had once said, that kept her from being able to open doors.

But this was a *handle,* not a doorknob. And the door opened outward. All it would take, Abby realized as she experimented with it, was for Pia to reach up and pull down on the handle. Her weight would be enough to push the door open.

Now what? She stood with one hand clamped to her forehead and blood pounding in her ears, gazing out on the now-silent courtyard garden. The sun had already gone down behind the towering mountain to the west; the air had cooled and the hum of insects had ceased. Abby held her breath and listened for the slightest telltale rustling, the faintest chirping call. But there was nothing. So different from the unrelenting din of New York.

"Hi."

Soft and pleasant though it was, the voice made her jump, coming from out of the silence and deep shadows. She couldn't stop a small gasp.

"Sorry." Rachel was smiling as she rose from a rocking chair a short way down the veranda with her baby in her arms. "I didn't mean to startle you."

"Oh—that's okay." Abby waved a hand at her wide-open door and the courtyard garden beyond. "I was just looking for my cat. She got out…somehow. Now she's out here… somewhere. And she's not used to being outside. At all."

"I'm sure she'll be all right. Why don't you leave the door open for her? She'll probably come back on her own." She shifted the baby to the crook of one arm and made adjustments to her blouse, then smiled again at Abby. "You look lovely. What a fabulous outfit. I would give anything to look that slim again."

"Thanks," Abby said, unexpectedly touched. She was searching for the words to tell the other woman she looked pretty darn fabulous herself, and that she didn't need to be any slimmer than she already was, when the big blond sheriff appeared in the doorway, minus crutches and holding on to the door handle and frame for support.

"Hey, honey," he called softly, in his Western movie star drawl, "you 'bout ready to go?"

Rachel said, "Coming," in the breathy voice of suppressed

excitement, the kind that comes only from being in love. She swiveled and smiled at Abby past the little head, fuzzy with straight black hair, now resting on her shoulder. "We're just going in to dinner. Would you like to come with us?"

Abby said, "Sure," and found her voice was husky with emotions she hadn't known she was capable of.

The big blond sheriff held the door, and Abby followed Rachel past him into the room, noticing as she did so that Sunny's cousin's head barely came to the sheriff's shoulder. She wondered what it would be like to be so tiny. *A doll I can carry...* Wasn't that a line from a Broadway tune? One from way back when, and probably totally politically incorrect now.

She watched as Rachel carefully laid her sleeping baby in his crib without waking him and turned on the monitor, while the sheriff—J.J.—collected his crutches. Rachel gave Abby another warm, inclusive smile, and they left the room together.

As she walked with the couple down the long corridor, Abby discovered the butterflies were back.

Dinner was not served in the huge dining room, but outside on the patio overlooking the valley, which was rapidly sinking into the blue, purple, lavender and indigo shadows of twilight. There were five seated around one of the large round patio tables. Abby was directed to a chair between Rachel and Josie, which meant she was more-or-less across from—and could hardly avoid looking at—the two men. Not that she would normally have considered that a hardship, given that Sheriff J.J. was an attractive—though somewhat imposing— man, and she'd already acknowledged Sage as being one of the most beautiful human beings she'd ever seen. But these were not normal circumstances, and evidently in her case a guilty conscience trumped sex appeal.

A nervous shudder rippled through her. With a smile she turned it into what she hoped would be taken for breathless excitement and exclaimed, "Oh, what a lovely spot."

"It is, isn't it?" Josie placed a huge bowl of salad in the middle of the table and, with a smile and a gesture, invited Abby to help herself. "We eat out here quite a bit when the weather's nice," she added as she took her place on Abby's right, in the chair nearest the kitchen. "Or, in the kitchen, if it's too windy. When it's just us." Her nod took in Sage, J.J. and Rachel. "When we have a work crew here, we use the big dining room."

"A work crew? *Here?*" Abby was trying to imagine that elegant formal room filled with men in spurs, chaps and cowboy hats.

She caught a glimpse of a smile on Sage's lips, but it was Josie who answered.

"Oh, sure. This is a working cattle ranch, you know. Right now, the men are busy in the fields down in the valley, and since most of them live nearby, they go home for lunch—or dinner. That's what we call the midday meal—at least we used to. This would be supper." She paused for a small chortle of laughter, then shook her head and went on. "But next month they'll start moving the cattle up to the high meadows. They'll be branding and vaccinating over at the old place where the chutes and corrals are. And, since this is where the kitchen and the cook—which is me—are…" She smiled and shrugged. "It makes much more sense for them to come here to eat than for me to take the food to them."

"Oh, sure," Abby murmured, nodding.

She helped herself to a generous heap of salad, then waited for everyone else to do the same. A pitcher of what appeared to be freshly made ranch dressing began to make its way around the table. As Rachel was about to pass it to Abby, she hesitated and said, "If you'd rather have something lighter— a vinaigrette…"

"This is fine," Abby said, taking the pitcher and pouring a generous amount of dressing over her salad.

"I just thought—since you're so slim…" Rachel sighed. "How do you do it?"

Abby's glance lifted involuntarily and encountered Sage's unreadable black eyes gazing back at her. She cleared her throat and muttered, "I don't— I mean, it's never been a problem…"

"Well, I envy you."

"Oh, Rachel," Josie began, but J.J.'s deep rumble overrode her.

"Honey, you're nursing a baby. You don't need to be worrying about getting thin. I keep telling you, you're just fine." The way his blue eyes smoldered as they looked at Rachel, it was obvious he thought she was a lot more than "just fine."

Watching him, Abby felt a flutter in her chest that felt surprisingly like envy. She didn't think she'd ever had a man look at her like that in her whole life.

"Maybe it's because I'm a vegetarian," she said, with a shrug of apology.

The table went silent. Everyone looked at each other. Sage ducked his head to hide a grin, and Josie simply looked dismayed. Rachel murmured, "Oh, dear."

J.J. dug into his salad, then looked up at Abby and said, "You know this is a ranch, right? As in…beef cattle?"

"It's all right," Josie said in a comforting tone. "We'll find you something." She paused, then asked hopefully, "Do you eat eggs?"

"Please don't go to any trouble," Abby mumbled, poking at her salad. "This is fine. Really."

Josie subsided into troubled thought.

There was a little silence, and then Rachel said brightly, "What do you do in New York, Sunny?"

Abby put down her fork, wiped ranch dressing from her lips and cleared her throat. "I'm a dancer."

"Oh, wow." Rachel's dark eyes were bright with interest. Her smile was wry. "Okay, I guess that explains a lot."

"Yes, well…I'm an actress, actually. *And* I dance."

"Do you sing, too?"

Abby shook her head. Then panic seized her. *How much do they know about Sunny? Do they know she's a singer?*

She looks scared to death, Sage thought. It was the same impression he'd gotten at the airport. She'd reminded him then of a cornered animal, and he sensed the same panic in her now. *Why? I wonder...*

"I've been wondering about Sam—I mean...my g-grandfather," Sunny said, changing the subject.

Her voice was a little too loud, a little too bright. And was he the only one who heard the desperation in it? He stole a glance at J.J., who he thought ought to be tuned to false notes as much as anyone. But then, as usual, the sheriff had eyes—and evidently ears—only for Rachel.

Rachel had put her hand over Sunny's, and her voice was soft with compassion. "You have trouble saying the word, too, don't you? *Grandfather.* I know just how you feel."

"It seems so unreal." Sunny was staring down at her plate, so her voice was muffled. Then she seemed to gather herself, smiling too brightly as she turned to Rachel. "Have you met him? What's he like?"

Rachel gave a laugh that sounded like a musical note. She looked at Sage first, then J.J. "Well...sort of. I mean, not *really.* Not officially."

Sunny's confused look sought Sage; he held both hands up and shook his head. Damned if he was going to explain the man.

Sunny shifted the appeal to J.J., then Rachel, who cleared her throat and said, "It's kind of a long story." J.J. shifted in his chair. Rachel glanced at him, then continued, "Okay. Well...I was out walking one day, and this old man came riding—"

"Oh! Speaking of riding," Josie interrupted, turning abruptly to Sunny. "Do you like to ride?"

There was a moment's shocked silence, and nobody was more surprised by the interruption than Sage. Obviously, his mother was as anxious as he was to steer the conversation away from the subject of Sam Malone, but he thought she might have been a little more subtle.

Sunny gave her head a shake and her voice, faint with confusion, broke the silence. "R-ride?"

"Horses." Rachel had turned to Sunny, all pink-cheeked with enthusiasm. "Oh, please tell me you do. It would be so nice to have someone to ride with."

"Oh, God, no." Sunny's voice had gone husky, and the expression on her face was something close to horror. "I'm a city girl, remember? Uh…New York?"

"That's okay," Rachel said, giving J.J. a nudge with her elbow, "J.J.'s a city boy, too, and he's learning. Or, he was, before he got hurt."

"Yeah," J.J. drawled, "it was a pretty extreme way to get out of riding, but hey—it worked."

Rachel smiled and nudged him again with her elbow. Josie said, "Maybe you could teach Sunny to ride, too, Rachel."

And Sage heard himself say, "I might have some time." He looked up at Sunny and found her staring at him. He didn't look away. "If…you're interested."

Her eyes seemed to shimmer—or was it just him? Something weird that happened in his brain when he looked at her. Whatever it was, it made him feel slightly dizzy. He opened his mouth to say something—to take the offer back, at least make some sort of qualification—and at the same time, her lips parted as if words were trying to decide whether or not to come out.

But before either of them could say anything, his mother jumped up, grabbed the salad bowl and headed for the kitchen. Then, naturally, Rachel jumped up and asked if she needed any help, and so did Sunny.

"Oh, no, that's okay, you just sit down," Josie said.

She was all smiles, but Sage knew better. His mother's voice was tight…clipped. Something was bugging her, and he figured it was most likely Sam—or his absence—since if anybody had cause to be fed up with Sam Malone's disappearing act, it was Josie.

He shifted in his chair, thinking maybe he ought to go in and ask her what was on her mind. Which he knew would be pointless because his mother wasn't going to talk to *him* about personal stuff, particularly anything having to do with Sam.

And while he was considering, his mind half elsewhere, he heard Rachel say something about Sunny's cat.

He jerked his attention back to the table, just as J.J. remarked, "Well, you shouldn't have let her out so soon."

Sunny shook her head. "I didn't. She was out earlier to go to the bathroom, but I live in an apartment, so she's never been an outside cat. I left her in my room with the door closed and went to take a shower, and when I came out, the door was open and she was gone."

J.J. made a sound that pretended to be laughter, the kind of sound a cop makes when a suspect tells him stories he doesn't believe. "Oh, right," he said as he forked up a bite of salad, "so I guess she opened the door all by herself."

"I believe she did," Sunny shot back, not a bit intimidated.

Sage had to hand it to her; the sheriff could be a pretty intimidating guy. When she went on, her voice was low and vibrant, with a resonance that seemed to find corresponding harmonies in him, the way a cat's purring sometimes made his chest hum.

"She's tried to, before. She can't manage a doorknob, but the French doors have those handles you just pull down on. Anyway." She lifted her head and stared him down. "Who else could have opened it?"

"Maybe," J.J. said equably, pushing back his salad plate, "you only *thought* you shut the door."

"I *know* I shut it." She held up her bandaged hand. "I know my cat. And I'm not stupid."

Watching her stand up to the sheriff like that, looking like a queen with her head high on that long graceful neck, and her eyes sparking like flint on steel, he felt a rush of something that was almost exhilaration, like a fine cool spray of water on a hot day that could make him gasp and whoop with the sheer pleasure of it.

He heard his own voice say, "I'll help you find her. She's somewhere in the courtyard. She'll keep until after we eat."

Josie came through the door just then, juggling a platter heavy with roast beef and vegetables and a small bowl containing cheese and deviled eggs for Sunny. He got up to help her, so he didn't see Sunny's face as she murmured a breathy, "Thank you."

But the sound was like warm fur on his ears.

The evening had turned unexpectedly cool, after the heat of the day. A breeze had come up, carrying with it the scents of growing things Abby didn't recognize and making the long arching wands of climbing roses dip and wave as if they danced to music she couldn't hear.

She stood on the veranda, hugging herself and rubbing her arms, thinking again how *quiet* it was. Though not silent; there were sounds: the shushing of wind through distant trees, the rustling of leaves closer by, the musical trickle of water in the central fountain, the mooing of a cow somewhere far away. The rhythmic chirping of some sort of creature—frogs, crickets—how would *she* know? But these sounds were soft... gentle...peaceful, so different from the sounds of a New York City night. There, the night would be noisy with the muted roar of traffic, the wail of a siren, horns honking, someone's radio thumping, people shouting—angry, impatient, hurrying, frantic sounds. She felt a sudden wave of homesickness for the craziness of the city—and how did that make sense, when she so did *not* want to go back to it?

She heard a light tapping at the door to her room and went to open it. Sage loomed, silhouetted against the light in the alcove behind him, seeming bigger, somehow, than she knew he really was. Her heart quickened.

"Hi," she said, her voice breathless.

"Hi," he replied, his voice soft. "She come back yet?"

"No." She stood aside to let him in. "I thought she'd come if I went out there, but…I even tried calling her, not that she ever comes when I call."

Sage's laugh blended well with the gentle night sounds. "If I call 'kitty-kitty,' cats come running from all directions with their tails in the air."

"Yeah, well, maybe you've noticed, but Pia's not exactly a normal kitty." She glanced back at him as she stepped through the door onto the veranda. "Josie said she looks like a…tooga—something? A small mountain lion."

"Ah—*tuugakut*. Yeah, I can see that. Small head, long body, long tail…those little tufts of hair on the tips of her ears. Wrong color, though. She's more like a very small gray leopard. Or a stretched-out lynx cat with a long tail."

He followed her onto the veranda, and she felt his closeness like a humming below the level of sound. It made her edgy with awareness, and why should that be, she wondered, when in New York there were strangers invading her personal space constantly—in subways, buses, elevators, sidewalks, crowded hallways and dressing rooms. But no stranger had ever set her senses on alert the way this man did.

"It's so dark," she said, gesturing toward the shadowy courtyard. "I thought there would be lights, or something."

"Like in the city, you mean." She could hear rather than see the smile in his voice. "Yeah…I remember that about the city. It's never dark." He moved to stand beside her and she felt his body's warmth. "There are lights out here. But if you turn them on, you can't see the stars." He was looking at her; she could tell by the way his voice sounded, though she didn't dare turn to see. "Look—there's no moon tonight. You can even see the Milky Way." His arm lifted, and brushed hers as he pointed.

She couldn't seem to find words to answer him. Dutifully, she tipped her head to follow his direction, and felt a tickling in her scalp as her hair touched his shoulder. Her skin prickled as if all the stars in that black sky had come inside her.

"That's…amazing." Was that her voice?

She moved away from him, stepping resolutely into the shadowy courtyard. "Here, Pia…come on, Pia-Pia." Even she could hear the note of desperation in her voice. "Here, kitty-kitty—"

Hands came to rest on her shoulders, fitting warmly over the rounded parts, and Sage's voice, close to her ear, murmured, "Hush." And it was the voice more than the hands that held her in utter stillness, listening to the sound of her own beating heart.

When she heard a familiar chirping sound, her heart gave a hopeful leap—until she realized it had come from Sage, not Pia. He made the sound again, and again they waited in absolute stillness, while Abby tried not to breathe.

Once more he made the little trilling chirp, so much like Pia's Abby wouldn't have believed it had come from a human throat if not for the tickle of breath blowing past her ear.

They waited. She thought she could hear *his* heart beating, not quite in sync with her own. And then, as she was about to speak, to ask, from far away…came a tiny answering chirrup?

"I hear—" Abby cried, half turning.

"Shh." His hands tightened just a little on her shoulders. "She's on the roof." He made the trilling sound again, and after a moment the answer came, from above but closer than before.

"Stay here. I'll get a ladder." He slipped soundlessly into the shadows. Her shoulders felt cold where his hands had been.

Chapter 5

The evening was chilly, and she'd begun to shiver by the time he returned no more than a minute or two later, though it seemed like hours had passed while she waited alone in the darkness. Hugging herself, she uttered a tiny whimpering sound of relief as she watched him come toward her, a shadowy form moving in a way she realized had already become familiar to her.

Wordlessly, he moved past her. She heard a soft creak and a muted click, then a scuffling, crunching sound as he set the ladder firmly in the soil of a flower bed.

His voice came out of the shadows. "Come here and hold it steady for me."

She moved toward him and his hand reached for her before she could see it, slipping around her upper arm and drawing her close to him. The sensation of safety that came to her then was as profound as it was unexpected. Even more so was the feeling of longing she suddenly felt…longing to keep walking another step or two, straight into his arms…to slide her arms around his waist and put her head down on his shoulder.

It's been a long and trying day, she thought. *I'm just tired, is all. Any place to lay my weary head would seem like heaven to me now.*

"Hold it here—just like this." His hands covered hers, guiding them. Then for an instant his body brushed hers, quickly there and then gone, and it was as if someone had waved a lighted torch over her, close enough to singe her skin. She gave a small gasp—she couldn't help it, and he murmured, "Hold steady, now."

She managed a breathless "Okay," and leaned her weight against the ladder. She felt it sink as he put his weight on the first step, and then he surged upward, catlike himself. He paused, and she felt the rough denim fabric of his jeans brush her cheek. His voice drifted down to her.

"I'm going up another step. Can you hold it?"

"Yes. Okay." She braced against the ladder and felt his weight shift upward. There was a long silence before the suspense got to her and she had to ask, "Is she there? Do you see her?"

The only answer was some low *chirring* sounds—Sage's, she thought, though who could be sure?

"Be careful," she said, laughing nervously. "Remember, she bites."

Again, she heard his voice, speaking low in a language she didn't understand. Her heartbeat was thunder. She leaned her forehead against the cool metal of the ladder and pressed her lips together. She would *not* ask again.

A sudden creak, his weight on the ladder shifted, and a moment later Sage stood beside her, holding Pia in his arms. *In his arms.* Miraculously, the cat wasn't growling, biting, hissing, clawing or turning herself into a furious bundle of rage.

"How did you do that?" Her voice was a squeak that ended in a sobbing laugh. "What are you, a cat whisperer?"

"She was just scared...recognized a savior, I guess." He was facing her room, and the light spilling from the open

French doors highlighted his crooked smile and reflected in the cat's eyes, turning them into round iridescent buttons. "Didn't you, little one?"

Fascinated, Abby watched while he gently scratched between the cat's ears, and Pia turned her head in a quick, open-mouthed way, as if trying to catch his fingers. Abby reached toward the cat, then nervously pulled her hand back. "She won't let *me* carry her. I've never seen her let *anyone* carry her. You must have done *something*."

He shrugged and began to walk slowly back toward her room, still cradling Pia in his arms. "Like I said, I have a bunch of cats."

She found herself walking beside him. "So, that means... what? You speak their language?"

He looked over at her and smiled. "Kind of. I guess."

He stepped over the doorsill, into her room. She followed and pulled the door shut behind her. Safe inside, Pia vaulted from Sage's arms onto the bed, where she turned her back on her rescuers and began industriously washing herself.

Sage watched her for a moment, then shifted his gaze to Abby and said, "How did you come by such a wild thing, living in the big city?"

Her room that had seemed so airy and spacious before now felt warm and close. She moved away from the source of the heat, looking for a patch of air that didn't hold his clean, masculine scent. Odd, though... it seemed to follow her, making her think again of warm breezes blowing off sunlit meadows, even though she'd never experienced such a thing in reality before.

"We...found her in the woods. My r-roommate and me." She took a deep breath. *Be careful...be careful! Remember who you are now.* "She's my roommate's cat more than mine, actually." He waited, not asking the obvious question, except with his eyes. She hitched in another breath, this one to ease the tightness in her throat, then shrugged. "She, um...she died, so I guess the witch-cat is all mine now."

"I'm sorry." Sympathy creased his forehead, but his black gaze didn't waver. "Recently?"

The familiar pain gripped her chest. *I won't cry. Sunny wouldn't cry.* She nodded and tossed her head, defying the grief, and hardened her voice and her eyes. "Yeah—three weeks ago. She was murdered."

"Wow." In contrast to hers, his voice was soft, little more than a whisper. "That's... Wow. How? Have they found the one who did it?"

"No..." came on an exhalation that helped a little to ease the ache in her throat. She went on in a more normal voice. "She was, um...strangled. In an alley. The police think it was a random thing. The chances of finding the killer are pretty slim. So they tell me."

He reached out a hand and touched her arm, the kind of thing people do out of sympathy. The kind of thing a lot of people had done, in the days after it happened—friends of hers and Sunny's, coworkers, neighbors—touches on the arm, pats on the back. Hugs. Lots of hugs, some even from almost-strangers. She hadn't flinched then, and didn't know why she flinched now, when Sage touched her. Ashamed and appalled, she tried to hide it by turning away from him, and it was only when she felt his hand fall away that she realized what she really wanted was to turn *toward* him, have him put his arms around her. Hold her.

What craziness is that? I don't even know this man.

"I'm sorry," Sage said again, stiffly, this time. There was a pause, then, "But it's good you're here. I'm glad you're here."

She heard the words he didn't say: *I'm glad it wasn't you—Sunny—who was murdered.*

Hearing the voice, so rich and vibrant, so full of compassion, she wanted to close her eyes and wrap herself up in it, to let herself accept the solace it offered. But how could she?

I'm glad it wasn't Sunny *who was murdered.* That's what he was saying.

But of course...it was, wasn't it? It was Sunny who died.

This is becoming complicated. Too hard. I can't do this anymore. I have to tell someone.

Sage?

Maybe... Why not? He seems like a kind man. Would he understand? Can I tell him the truth? Do I dare?

It would be such a relief. Over and done with. At least I could move on.

She turned to him, the words of her confession poised on her tongue, but before she could utter a single one, he lifted a hand in an awkward little gesture and moved away from her, a smile stiff on his lips.

"Well. So...you've got your *tuugakut* back, safe and sound..."

"Oh—yeah." She made the same kind of gesture, then hugged herself. "Thanks a lot. You know, for—"

"Not a problem. Well, I'll just...let you get... You must be tired—"

"Yeah...kind of. On East Coast time...you know how it—"

"I do. Sure. Well, then. See you tomorrow."

"Yeah...see you."

With his back to the door, the doorknob in his hand, he paused. "Good night..."

"'Night." Her smile hurt her face. He opened the door and backed through it. She called out, "Thanks again—" as it closed.

She sank onto the bed, her breath coming in tiny whimpers. Pia came with her usual interrogatory trill, climbed into her lap and crouched there, eyes half-closed, paws tucked under her and tail twitching.

Sage strode down the hallway, head down, fists clenched in a way that was familiar to him, though he hadn't felt like this since he was a boy. Since before he'd learned to let the small slights and insults aimed at his ethnicity roll like water off his skin. To not let them touch who he was inside.

She's afraid of me. What the hell is that? She flinches whenever I touch her even accidentally. As if...as if—

He halted and ran a hand over his face. Took a deep breath.

Get ahold of yourself, man. It's probably not even about you. She's afraid, all right, but it's not you...exactly. Something in her. Something going on with her. Just back off, give her some space.

Be patient.

She was like a wild creature—like that cat of hers. Wary. Distrustful. But he knew how to deal with wild things.

Like most theatre people, Abby wasn't an early riser. So, when she woke up on a California ranch at her usual New York City time, she was surprised to find she hadn't even missed breakfast.

"I'm not used to this," she admitted to Josie as the housekeeper set a mug in front of her and filled it with steaming hot coffee. Even though the sun was up and shining, the weather had turned cool and windy, so breakfast was being served in the kitchen rather than outdoors on the patio.

"I'm happy to do it." Josie smiled over her shoulder as she returned the carafe to its place. "You're our guest—but family, too. It's such a pleasure to have you here."

After a momentary bit of confusion, Abby laughed. "No, no, I don't mean being waited on—or...well, that, too, actually." She picked up the mug, took a sip, then lifted it toward the housekeeper in a little salute of appreciation. "Umm... great coffee—thanks." She put down the mug and ran her hands over her hair, which she'd twisted again into its customary knot at the back of her head. Her own style, not Sunny's. Why not? It seemed everyone here was eager to accept her as family anyway, no questions asked, and she felt more comfortable in her own skin. "No, I meant mornings. I'm not used to being up this early."

"It's the time change," Josie said, nodding, and her dark eyes crinkled at the corners with her smile.

Sage's eyes.

Abby shifted in her chair and tried to shake off the image

that seemed to find every possible excuse to pop into her head. "I guess," she said. She drank more coffee, then cleared her throat. "So…what do people do with mornings, anyway? Where is everybody?"

"Well, Rachel and J.J. left already—they took the little one for his checkup out in Ridgecrest. And of course, Sage is down at his place doing chores."

"Okay…so…guess I'm not so early," Abby said with a wry smile.

Josie dismissed that with a wave. "You're fine. This is a ranch—we probably get up earlier than most people. Oh—and Sage brought you a pan and some kitty litter when he came for breakfast. It's out on the patio."

And Sam Malone? Where is he?

But Josie had turned back to the stove, and there was something defensive about the set of her shoulders, so Abby only said, "Thanks," and didn't ask.

"Where is that terrible kitty cat of yours this morning?"

"Shut in my room—with a chair in front of the door." Abby made a face, an apologetic grimace. "I'm so sorry—I let her out in the courtyard this morning, just long enough to, um… use the facilities." She hadn't wanted to, scared to death she wouldn't be able to coax the cat back inside, or that she'd climb up on the roof again. The thought of having to call on Sage for help made her heart do strange things inside her chest. The only thing worse, as far as she was concerned, would have been to have to ask Josie to clean up a mess in that beautiful bedroom.

Josie waved that off with another smile, and asked what she would like for breakfast. "I know you don't want bacon."

Abby smiled back. "Toast is fine. Honestly—please don't go to any—"

"How about some French toast, with fresh strawberries?" Josie asked.

Abby sighed and said, "I've died and gone to heaven."

And she thought: *No, that would be Sunny. Where I am I*

think is what Catholics call Purgatory. Otherwise known as... in limbo.

After breakfast, she took the litter pan and plastic container of litter back to her room and set it up on the tile floor in the bathroom. Then, feeling a need to work off the three slices of French toast heaped with sweetened berries she'd consumed for breakfast, she decided to go for a walk. She'd spent the previous day mostly sitting; her muscles needed limbering up.

"Oh—sure," Josie said when Abby mentioned it to her, "why don't you go down to the barns? Sage can show you the animals. There are lots of babies, you know, this time of year."

Did something flash in the woman's dark eyes, too quickly gone to identify? *Probably just my imagination,* Abby thought. *Paranoia playing with my head.* Because Josie's smile seemed as warm as ever.

Sage was finishing up the last of the milking when his dog told him he was about to have company. The border collie got up from where he'd been stretched out in the barn doorway in the sun and stood looking off down the lane with his tongue hanging out and his tail waving slowly back and forth. Sage took the milk bucket into the cold room and put it through the strainer, then went to see who was coming. Although he was pretty sure he knew.

She'd stopped beside the corral fence about halfway down the lane, and was doing some sort of stretching, warming up routine. He wasn't sure what made him do it, but when he realized she hadn't caught sight of him yet, he stepped back into the barn shadows and just watched her.

She was wearing jeans and athletic shoes, and a cotton knit zip-up thing with a hood hanging down the back, nothing that showed her body off, for sure. And yet, watching her bend and twist and reach and turn, stretching those long legs of hers, he felt stirrings in parts of his body that had been dormant for a long time. A lot longer than he'd realized.

Not good, he told himself. He didn't know what Sam would think of him having wicked thoughts about his granddaughter, but he was pretty sure he didn't want to find out.

He waited until she'd finished her workout and came on up the lane, and the dog went bounding out to meet her, then he moved into the sunlight. She saw him and lifted a hand in a wave of greeting. He watched her come closer, a tentative smile on her face, not out-of-breath, just flushed and wind-blown, strands of pale hair straggling out of the knot she'd made of it on the back of her head. He'd have sworn she didn't have on a speck of makeup, and yet, as he looked at her, his stomach coiled and made hungry noises, although it hadn't been that long since he'd had breakfast.

Sorry, Sam, he thought. He could curb his thoughts, up to a point, but there wasn't much he could do about his body's natural responses.

"Hi," she said.

He nodded back to her. "You're up early."

"Evidently not as early as everybody else around here." Her smile was wry.

He gave her back one like it. "You'll get used to it."

She made that scoffing sound. "Don't count on it. I've been a night owl for a long, long time."

"How's your little *tuugakut* this morning?" he asked, moving beside her as she ventured into the barn, looking around like a tourist venturing into a jungle.

She pulled her gaze back to him from the barn rafters, eyes still wide with wonder, and he had to catch his breath. Something different about her this morning, he thought. *Can't quite put my finger on it...*

Then she smiled—really smiled—and he thought: *I know what it is. She's not afraid.*

"She's fine, thank you. And by the way, thanks for the litter box."

"No problem."

She'd gone back to scanning the barn and everything in

it—a big stack of alfalfa hay and a bunch of spider webs and rusty tools, mostly. "Where are all the cats? You told me you have tons of them."

"Ah...well, they've already been fed," he said, "so they're pretty well scattered now. Hunting...hiding...sleeping..."

She looked disappointed, but only for a moment. Then she turned to him and her face lit up like an eager child's. "Well, Josie told me you could show me the animals, so...I've come to see animals."

He found himself smiling back at her, the change in her making him feel easier in her company. "You make it sound like a zoo or something. These are just your basic farm animals."

"Hey, I'm a city girl, remember? What do I know from farm animals?"

He laughed and said, "Seriously?" Then he realized she was. "You're telling me you've never seen farm animals? Not even horses...cattle..."

"Oh, well, I've seen horses, sure. The cops in Central Park ride horses. Hey, I've even petted one. Plus, they pull tourists around in these open buggies. Uh...that would be the horses, not cops," she added, and he laughed with her again. Then her forehead creased in a thoughtful way. He found it completely charming. "Cows...I've seen them, too. I saw lots of them just yesterday, remember?"

"Yeah," he said, making a challenge out of it, "from a distance. How about close up?"

"Are you nuts? No."

"Come here..." He touched her elbow and brought her with him to the barn's back door. No flinching this time. In fact, the warmth of her arm, even cloaked in cotton, seemed to melt and flow into his hand and from there into other parts of his body. Fortifying himself against the pull of physical attraction, he slid the heavy door open, and heard her gasp.

She halted and whispered, "Oh, my God."

He moved to one side and watched her—eyes wide and

brilliant as stars, strands of golden hair lifting in the wind, hands pressed against her mouth—and he couldn't have described what he was feeling if his life had depended on it. All he knew was, it felt like something bottled up inside his chest, looking for a way out.

"Go ahead," he said. "Pet one."

Her head jerked toward him. "Really? They won't...I mean—" she gave a breathless laugh "—my God, they're so big."

"No bigger than horses."

"Yeah, but horses don't have horns."

Though even as she said that in a fearful whisper she was moving slowly toward the stanchions, where the three cows he'd just milked were finishing up the last of their hay. The only one with horns had lifted her head, still munching, to study the stranger with lazy curiosity.

"That's Black Betty," he said, tucking his hands in his pockets and leaning against the barn door frame to watch her. "She's gentle." It felt good, being there with her, out of the wind, warm in the sunshine, senses filled with the sights, sounds and smells of healthy animals. *And a beautiful woman named Sunshine...*

Giving himself a mental head-slap, he straightened and went to join her at the stanchions.

Abby was determined to show no fear. Animals, she had heard, could *smell* fear.

"Uh...where, exactly, do I...you know—*pet* her?" she inquired, without taking her eyes off the beast, who was regarding her with apparent unconcern with eyes the approximate size and color of chocolate cupcakes.

"She likes to have her poll scratched," Sage said, in a lazy cowboy-type drawl.

"Her...poll."

"Her head—the part between the horns."

"Of course she does," Abby muttered and, pushing up her jacket sleeves, stretched out her hand to touch the recommended part of the cow's anatomy. The part between those enormous horns.

The cow sort of bobbed her head, but didn't appear annoyed.

Abby let out a relieved breath and burrowed her fingers into the tufts of coarse black hair. When that didn't produce a negative response, either, she gave the mound a tentative scratch. And from somewhere deep inside her, a smile seemed to blossom. It grew and burst onto her face, and she turned triumphantly to Sage.

"Look, I'm—" She got no further. The cow lifted her head and bumped Abby's forearm with her nose. Her very large, moist, rubbery nose. Abby jerked her hand back, but only a little, because the cow still didn't appear threatening in any way.

A long grayish tongue snaked out and lashed across her hand. Her breath caught, then stopped altogether. "Oh, my God," she whispered, "that is so cool." She looked up at Sage, and found his gaze resting on her, a quizzical half smile on his lips. Her breathing resumed with a little hiccup of laughter. "It feels like sandpaper."

His smile grew, and he shook his head and looked past her into the hazy distance. She could see his body shake with silent laughter, and her own body felt suddenly shaky, too, but with a warm and melty center.

"Hey, what can I say? I'm a city girl," she said indignantly to the cow. Who, having evidently decided Abby wasn't bearing anything good to eat, had already lowered her nose back into the pile of hay. Struggling to hide her own smile, not to mention the shaky, melty feelings, Abby scratched earnestly at the hairy mound between the cow's horns, then patted the broad flat space between her huge brown eyes where the hair seemed to grow in a whorl from a center point. "Yes...you are just a great big old sweetie pie, aren't you?" she crooned. "And so beautiful...Black *Beauty,* that's your name. You are beautiful—*big,* but beautiful."

Behind her, Sage cleared his throat and said in a gravelly growl, "Not so bad, right?"

She straightened and dusted her hands, striving for nonchalance. "Yeah, okay, but she's still awfully damn big."

"How about if I show you one in a smaller size?"

She cocked her head to look at him against the sun, shading her eyes with a hand. His black eyes seemed shadowed, brooding, mysterious...but his teeth showed white with his smile. Though she tried not to, she couldn't seem to help smiling back. "Little ones? Babies?"

"They're called calves," he said as he opened a gate in the wooden corral fence and held it for her.

"I knew that," she replied with a snort, and heard his soft laughter as she slipped past him.

Passing so close to him almost overwhelmed her senses: that warm, husky laugh...the musky scents of hay and animals and clean clothes and man...the rich brown tones of his skin, that somehow seemed to hold the warmth of the sun inside... the sleek black hair, like the glossy hide of a well-groomed animal. A panther, she thought. *Or a magnificent—*

She stopped herself there, shaken by her own thoughts. But she didn't regret them.

He closed the gate after her, then led her through a dusty passageway between two high steel fences. At the end of the passageway was another gate that matched the first, which he again opened and held for her.

"Watch your step," he warned as she slipped past him.

She nodded without really registering what he'd said. She was utterly enchanted. They stood in a large pen, with a wide gate at the far end that was closed, now, but could be opened onto that beautiful green meadow dotted with yellow flowers. The other end, close to where they'd come in, adjoined another barn, this one smaller than the one she'd just come through, with its high arching roof and stacks of baled hay. This one was painted red with white trim, like a barn in a child's picture book, and it had a big sliding door that stood open to a mysterious shadowy interior. In the adjoining pen, a half dozen or so baby cows—calves!—watched them with soft brown eyes.

"Oh…" Abby murmured, making the word a sigh, "just look at them. They're…*beautiful*."

Sage cleared his throat, laughed a little, and muttered, "Yeah, they are, aren't they."

He hadn't expected that word. *Beautiful.* Cute, maybe. That was what girls usually said. *Ooh, they're so cute.* Which for some reason always set his teeth on edge. But *beautiful?* He agreed with her, but hearing her say it made his chest go warm inside.

He stood with his arms folded, hands tucked against his sides, and watched her venture on her own, farther into the calf pen. Watched one little black guy with a white spot on his nose—the rejected twin he'd brought in day before yesterday—totter out to meet her, muzzle outstretched. Hoping for another bottle, probably, although Sage had been working with him trying to get him to suck Black Betty for two days, now. When the calf took the outstretched fingers Sunny offered and started sucking on them, and she laughed out loud, laughter came tumbling out of him, too. He began to feel as though his arms were holding back something that might be too big for him to handle if he ever let it loose.

She turned her face to him, eyes glistening in a way that made him think of rain. In a hushed voice, she said, "They look so shiny…like they're brand-new."

He drew in an uneven breath. "Well, I guess he is pretty new. Just about…three days old."

"Three days? So…where's his mother?" She'd turned her attention back to the calf, who was nuzzling hopefully at her pants leg.

"He's a twin—his mother rejected him."

She gave a shocked gasp and threw him a look of outrage.

He shrugged. "Happens sometimes." He waved a hand at the other calves, two of whom had come to see whether the tall, light-haired stranger had anything interesting to offer. "These are all leppy calves—means they don't have mothers, for one reason or another. That one there," he said, nodding at the brown bull calf that was regarding Sunny suspiciously, head down, front legs planted wide, "we found him down in one of the winter pastures in the valley. Who knows how long he'd been surviving on his own, stealing from whatever cow he could, fighting off coyotes... We never did figure out who his mama was. But he's a survivor, for sure."

She threw him a look and asked, "So, what do they do for food? Do you give them bottles, or what?"

"We usually have to start them on a bottle, but as soon as we can we like to get them to nurse one of our milk cows. Like Black Betty, there. She's got way more milk than her own calf can drink, so we put a couple of these little ones on her. She doesn't like it much—they don't like to let strange calves nurse—so we have to restrain—"

Just about then, the brown bull calf evidently decided the stranger looked more like trouble than she did food, because he suddenly charged and butted her hard in the side of her leg, knocking her backward, right into Sage's arms.

Chapter 6

He was glad he was there, in just the right place and at the right time to keep Sam's granddaughter from falling on her backside in the manure. He knew he couldn't have done anything else but what he did. Still, when he thought about it later, it seemed to him what it had done to his feelings, those things that had been rumbling around after being dormant in him for so long, was something like pitching a rock into a beehive.

When her body slammed into his, and his arms came around her as they pretty much had to do, needs and desires he'd thought he had under control, that he'd thought were sublimated to the daily responsibilities of the crops and animals in his care, awakened and erupted in a frenzied, stinging swarm. And when he felt her warmth melt into him, and heard breath gush from her lips along with laughter and a whispered, "Oops!" he knew it wasn't likely they'd be going back into the hive anytime soon.

"Wow. That was a surprise." Her voice was hushed. She tilted her head to look up at him, and her hair brushed his lips. Tickled his nose. "Did I do something to make him mad?"

He fought desperately against the urge to press his mouth against her hair, and his voice was tight with the strain. "Nah...told you he's used to fighting to survive. Hasn't got it in his head yet he doesn't have to anymore."

Her breasts were warm and firm against his arm, and he felt the nipples harden even through the soft knit thing she wore. The urge to run his hands under her sweater and cup those warm firm breasts in his palms was a pain he felt from his belly to his groin.

Sage, listen to me, man. Put her down, let her go. Step... away...from...the beautiful woman, Sage.

He set his teeth together, clenched his jaws tight and slowly lifted her until she was standing upright on her own feet. And even then he couldn't seem to make his arms unwrap themselves from around her body. He wondered what would happen if she were to turn, just a little bit....

And it came to him, then: *She didn't flinch.*

He was touching her—in a fairly intimate way, in fact— and she hadn't flinched. Far from it. Pretty much the opposite; she seemed downright comfortable in his arms. And seemed no more eager to end that state of being than he was. Admittedly, he didn't know the woman that well, but he was pretty certain that if she *did* turn just a little bit, and if he were to, say...kiss her, she probably wouldn't object.

It was an exhilarating notion, and as it swept over him, he found himself laughing out loud, with the same kind of warmth and joy and thanksgiving he sometimes felt after assisting in the successful birth of a new calf. He knew now. His touch hadn't made her flinch before because she was afraid of him, or because she found it offensive, or repugnant. He knew now, with absolute certainty, that she'd flinched because she'd felt the same electric jolt he had.

She was attracted to him.

Which, he reminded himself, didn't change the fact that messing with one of Sam Malone's granddaughters was a bad idea. More than bad—unthinkable.

Still. His day felt brighter, somehow.

She was laughing, too, as she slowly eased herself away from him. One hand went to her hair, self-consciously tucking loose strands behind her ear. "Well...thanks. That wouldn't have been pretty."

"Glad I could help," he said.

Then, for a while, they just looked at each other, and it seemed to Sage all the warmth and colors of spring were right there in her face: golden hair, pink-flushed cheeks, eyes the soft blue-green of hills newly carpeted with grass. And he knew he didn't want her to leave—not yet. He opened his mouth to tell her there was a lot more he could show her, at the same moment she started to say something, so they both spoke at once.

"I guess you have better—"

"If you want to see—"

They broke off, laughed—and from somewhere on her person came the unlikely tinkle of music, a bit from a Broadway tune, if he wasn't mistaken.

She gave a start, jammed a hand into the pocket of her jeans and came up with a cell phone. "Oh, my God, I can't believe it's working!"

"It comes and goes," Sage said.

She stared at the phone in her hand for a moment, then lifted her eyes to him as she held it to her ear. "Pauly? Pauly— yeah, hold on just one sec, okay?" She covered the phone loosely, gave a shrug of regret and whispered hoarsely, "He's been trying to reach me. I kind of need to take this."

"Yeah, sure—that's okay. Go ahead." *Pauly?* A boyfriend, probably. Well, hell. What had he expected?

"Um...can I come back?"

"Anytime," he said, and there was gravel in his throat. As he watched her walk away between corral fences, head down, the damn cell phone pressed against her ear, he felt in every muscle, nerve and bone a lingering ache of regret.

"Where've you been? You didn't get my messages?" Pauly sounded about as crabby as she'd ever heard him.

"Gee, Pauly, you know, I didn't—except I got your text. But I haven't been able to call back because cell service is awful here. I'm really sorry—"

"Here? What do you mean, here? You out of town, or something? Not that I blame you, after everything. Probably good you could get away for a day or two."

"So, what's up?" she asked, just as he was saying, "So, where are you?" And they both said, "Go ahead," and then Abby said, "California."

There was dead silence for a moment or two, and then Pauly gave a funny little laugh and said, "California? So, what're you doing there? And they don't have cell service in California?"

Abby laughed, thinking she sounded about as sincere as Pauly. "Evidently not the part I'm in. At least not reliably. It comes and goes." She could hear Sage's voice saying that, and closed her eyes briefly as the image of his face formed crystal clear in her mind. A little spasm of regret and longing twisted in her chest, so sharply she almost gasped.

"So," said Pauly, "where is that, exactly?"

None of your business, is what she wanted to say, but didn't, because Pauly was her agent, after all, and sort of a friend besides, one who'd been kind to her after Sunny died. But she wasn't about to tell him the whole Sunny story, either, especially not the idiotic reasoning that had brought her here, pretending to be someone she wasn't.

"It's a long story," she said, and gave it a couple of beats, thinking it would be a really good time for the cell phone to cut out on her, and why did it have to be working so well right *now?* She let out a gust of breath. "I'm, uh, taking care of something for Sunny, okay? She, uh…didn't get a chance to—"

"You mean, that rich grandfather of hers?" Pauly's voice

tried to sound casual, but she had that ear for nuances, and she could hear that it had sharpened.

Then she heard—really heard—the words he'd spoken. She felt as if she'd been punched in the stomach. "She *told* you?"

"Yeah, well…sure. I'm the one who convinced her she should go check him out. I mean, she should at least see what was in it for her, you know?" There was a long pause, during which Abby prayed for the call to get dropped, or at least for the nerve to fake it. "A shame she never got the chance," Pauly said. "A real shame."

"Yeah," Abby said, and cleared her throat. *She told Pauly and not me? I was her roommate, her best friend. How could she tell Pauly but not me?* She closed her eyes, frowned at nothing. "Uh…so…Pauly, why did you call me? Did you have something—"

"What? No, no, I was just calling to check up on you. You know—see how you're holding up. I care about you—you know that, right? You and Sunny both. Always did." There was a pause. Abby bit her lip but didn't say anything; the knot of pain in her throat was too big. "So," Pauly said, in a tentative, careful way, "how did the old man take the news?"

Abby gave a sharp, painful laugh. "I wish I could tell you that, Pauly. I haven't met him yet, actually."

"Seriously? So, what—is he out of town or something? You'd think he'd want to hear about his own granddaughter, even if he is a gazillionaire."

"An *eccentric* gazillionaire. Don't forget that part." Pauly laughed. Abby closed her eyes and rubbed at her forehead. "Uh, listen, Pauly…I really should—before I lose you…"

"Right. Yeah. So…when are you—"

"I don't know yet. I'll call you when I know more, okay?"

"Sure. Okay…"

"Bye, thanks, Pauly."

She broke the connection, then stood in the middle of the dusty lane and stared at the phone for a moment. The battery was almost dead. Pity it couldn't have conked out five minutes ago, she thought. She tucked the phone into the pocket of her jeans, then looked over her shoulder at the cluster of buildings she'd left behind. The big barn with its stack of sweet-smelling hay, and out of sight behind it, the corrals with contented cows and adorable baby calves. To the right of the big barn, the dirt lane turned toward a cluster of giant metal buildings that seemed to hold equipment of various kinds, the uses of which she could only guess. And in the middle of the wide space between the barns and the metal buildings, shaded by huge old trees, stood a little white house made of whitewashed adobe with a Spanish tile roof nestled behind a screen of lilac bushes and rambling roses.

Oh, wow, she thought, and something leaped inside her chest. All it needed was a picket fence and a swing hanging from one of those big tree limbs, and it was the house she'd dreamed of as a child, the one she'd fantasized about living in, all those years she'd been growing up in those miserable foster homes.

A wave of longing swept over her, homesickness for a place she'd never known. For a long time she stood gazing at the house, imagining herself walking up to the front door—it would be blue, she thought—and Sage opening it and inviting her in.

But he and his exuberant shaggy black-and-white dog were nowhere to be seen, and after a moment she turned and walked on, back down the lane to the road that led to the hacienda, home of the elusive Sam Malone.

"She just left here," Sage said.

Sam snorted. "I didn't ask the question yet, wiseass."

"Yeah, but you were going to."

"Is that a fact. Well, I bet I know what you're going to ask me next. 'When are you comin' down to meet her?' Right? Admit it, smart aleck."

"Well, you'd be wrong," Sage said. "That question's been

asked and answered. So what would be the point in asking it again?"

That made Sam cackle with laughter. "You've got the gift of patience, son. Something I never had. That's a rare thing. Must have got it from your mother. There's a patient soul if ever there was one."

Sam waited a beat or two, hoping the kid would offer something without being asked. He should have known better. "So, you say she came down there to the old place? What for?"

"Said she wanted to see the animals. Guess Mom told her there were babies all over the place—you know how it is." The phone went silent again.

"And?" Sam prompted. "How'd she take to 'em? She's a city gal, you know."

That brought one of the kid's soft chuckles, the one deep down in his chest that always made Sam think of a horse whickering. "Well, she seemed okay with the cows and calves. More than okay—seemed to enjoy herself, I think...."

There was something about the way he said it that made Sam's ears perk up. "Son," he said, with some steel in his voice, "there's something you're not telling me, I can hear it. You still having some reservations about her? That it?"

"What? No. It's not—" There was a gust of breath, and then: "She was different, this morning. Relaxed. Happy. Nothing like yesterday when she seemed like she was scared to death. It's, I don't know, like she's two different people."

Like she's two different people.

Sam stood still and silent while the words echoed down the halls of his memory. He muttered something, he wasn't sure what, and disconnected the call. Didn't care if it made any sense; Sage would just chalk up any peculiarities to old age anyhow.

He made his slow way over to the desk by the window and hauled the handful of handwritten pages out of the drawer he'd dumped them in. They were in a mess, he knew that, scattered all over the place, some of 'em down at the hacienda, some of 'em up here. One of these days he was going to get them all sorted out and put in some kind of order. *Hopefully before I die,* he thought, with an audible snort. *But that ain't gonna be today.*

He hauled out a chair, hitched himself onto it, pulled the pile closer and lifted the first page.

From the memoirs of Sierra Sam Malone:

I always thought it was like she was two different people living in the same body. Back then they didn't have names for it, like they do now. And they sure didn't have medicines to fix it. Back then, you pretty much just took her as she was, made the most of the good times, and stayed out of her way when she was in one of her bad ones.

I knew that day was one of the bad ones before I even got to her trailer. I could hear her banging around and hollering, and things breaking in there, and my director was exiting about as fast as he could get through the door. He gave me a look and shook his head as he went by me, which was his way of telling me as far as he was concerned she was my problem, not his.

I went in with my hat in my hand, and there she was with her beautiful face and her sea-green eyes all drenched in tears, and makeup running like watercolors in the rain. "Now, Barbara, honey," I said, "what's all this about?"

And, being the queen of drama she was, she collapsed in a heap on the floor at my feet, sobbing as if her life was all but over. Which, I guess, to her way of thinking, maybe it was, considering how things were, back then.

I went down on one knee beside her and took her in my arms, but she fought me like a tiger. "I'm pregnant!" she screamed, and then she cussed me with language I'd never heard coming from such a lovely mouth. But it was what she told me next that made my blood run cold.

She couldn't bear it, she said, meaning the scandal, I

guess, rather than the child she was carrying. It would mean the end of her career, she said, and how could she go back to her folks in Omaha in disgrace? Then she gave me an ultimatum: Either I would find a way to "fix it"—that was the way she put it—or she would, even if it killed her. Which again, in those days, it might well have done.

Well, anyway, I had good reason to believe she meant what she said. And I thought of my son, who I hardly ever saw since his mother and I had become all but strangers to one another. And I knew what I had to do.

"Now, Barbara, honey, calm down, there's no need to do that," I told her, "because it's gonna be okay. I'm gonna marry you."

And that's what I did.

There was a scandal, of course. The movie gossip rags—that Louella Parsons woman, for one—heaped coals of fire on my head for leaving my wife and son to go and marry a starlet I'd been having an affair with. But then, when the baby was born they couldn't get enough pictures of Barbara Chase, looking radiant and happy, like an angel, holding her beautiful little bald-headed pink-and-white baby girl.

But she still had her dark times, Barbara did. And it was during one of those times, when I was off in Nevada shooting another movie, that she left the baby with her nanny and drove up Pacific Coast Highway to a lonely spot she'd always loved, and she left her clothes lying on the sand and walked naked into the ocean. Just kept on walking and never looked back.

Sam dropped the pages into the drawer and slammed it shut, then leaned back in the chair and stared out the window at the meadow stretching off into the morning sunshine. Looked nice out there, but a mean gust of spring wind was blowing a spattering of pine needles across the porch.

"Well, hell," he said to the wind, "what was I gonna do with a child? No more than a baby, and a girl-child, at that. Letting those Omaha folks take her—sure seemed like the right thing to do at the time."

The right thing? You mean, the easy thing—for you, anyway.

The wind skirled away across the meadow grass, leaving its accusing whispers behind in the pines.

Being a habitual late-riser, Abby wasn't used to having so many daylight hours to fill.

After returning to the hacienda to find her bed made and Pia curled up asleep in the middle of it, she went off to find Josie, intending to offer to help with the rest of the house-cleaning. Or laundry. Or fixing lunch. Or…whatever. But Josie didn't let her get the words out of her mouth before shooing her off with orders to "relax and enjoy" herself.

When had such a thing happened to her before in her whole entire life? Ever. Even that weekend in the Adirondacks with Sunny hadn't been what she could call relaxing; Sunny wasn't relaxing company.

She did give it a try. She went into the big study, or library, or den—the room off the front foyer with the desks and books and computers in it—and tried to figure out how the sleek, latest-model computer worked, having some idea that she should check her email. But it appeared to need some sort of order she didn't know how to give it, and since she didn't want to bother Josie, she figured she'd wait until Rachel and the sheriff got home and ask them to show her how to work it.

She browsed through the shelves of books and found one she'd been meaning to read, which she took back to her room. She stretched out with it on a comfortable lounge chair outside on the veranda with her head in the shade and her feet in the sunshine and the breeze rustling the leaves on the climbing roses above her head. But she couldn't seem to get into the book. Thoughts kept getting in her way.

Specifically, thoughts of Sage.

He kept sneaking into her mind, watching her with that little smile on his lips and his deep, dark somber eyes, leaning against a barn door frame in that graceful way he had, smiling as if he knew she was aware of him and amused by that fact. It probably should have annoyed, or at least concerned her that he could distract her so easily when she had so much on her mind and her situation here was so precarious. But when his smiling face came into her thoughts, all it did was make her want to smile, too. And if she closed her eyes she could feel his touch, his hand firm and sure on her elbow, his body solid and steady against her back, his arms wrapped around her, so warm and yet…she'd felt the prickle of goose bumps over every inch of her skin, and her hardened nipples almost hurt where they rubbed against his arm. Even now, remembering, she shivered as if a million tiny pinpoints of light were dancing over her skin.

Wow. It had been a long time since a man—or anything else, for that matter—had made her feel so alive.

Yes—alive. And that was the problem. Not that she was bored. Far from it. With everything so new and strange, she wanted to be out exploring it, wanted to see everything there was to see. Reading a book…she felt like a kid trying to concentrate on schoolwork when spring had sprung and the sun was shining and birds were singing outside the windows.

Only now, here, there was no teacher telling her she had to stay until the bell rang.

She closed the book and went to find Josie to let her know she was going out again. She could hear a vacuum cleaner humming somewhere far off down the hallway, but didn't like to venture into parts of the house she hadn't been shown, so she let herself out the front door and started off down the winding drive.

She walked quickly, at first, with her head down, as if she had someplace important to go, some appointment to keep— before it occurred to her that there was no need to rush for anything. She was accustomed to power-walking through the streets of New York City, but here she could simply stroll, if she wanted to. On the way to nowhere in particular, she could pause and look up at the sky to follow the flight of a huge black bird, or drop to her knees to examine a never-before-seen flower blooming in the grass beside the lane. Accustomed to always having appointments or work schedules to keep, here, if she wanted to, she could wander off on a quest to discover the source of that strange croaking sound and completely lose track of her original purpose—if there had been one. Accustomed to constant worry about things that seemed to pose imminent disaster, here all her worries seemed far away.

Even the fact that she was pretending to be someone she wasn't seemed not worth worrying about now. Until either Sam Malone or his lawyer contacted her, there wasn't anything to be done about it anyway, so she could just…put it out of her mind.

And that was easier to do than she could have imagined, in this place so far away and so very different from the world she and Sunny had shared. She was growing comfortable in the role she'd taken on. The role of Sunshine Wells.

Putting Sage out of her mind wasn't so easily done.

His face hung in her mind like a moon in the sky, seeming to follow her wherever she went, and if she let herself, she knew, she could pull the memories of that morning close again, until they touched even her senses. But what would that do but fill her with longing, that aching nostalgia for something she'd never had? What good would it do to daydream, when, like his home and his family, Sam Malone's ranch manager wasn't and could never be hers?

As much as she would have liked to go back to the barn and visit the calves again—he'd told her she could, anytime—she didn't feel strong enough to hold those longings at bay just now. So, to avoid encountering Sage she climbed through a barbed wire fence and struck out across the pasture where she'd seen the horses grazing. It seemed safe enough; she could see they were all far away down at the other end of the pasture and didn't appear interested in her in the slightest. And even if they were, she'd never heard of horses attacking anyone.

And unlike cows, they didn't have those giant horns.

As she made her way across the pasture she came upon a large patch of charred ground, and remembering what Sage had told her about Carlos Delacorte coming for Rachel's baby, his grandson, realized this must be where the helicopter had crashed and burned. She shivered in the warm sunshine, thinking about the fact that three men had died here on this very spot, even if they were, according to Sage, very bad men. Now, looking at the black blot on the lovely green meadow, she felt certain there must be more to the story than she'd been told.

But of course, that, too, was something she had no real right to. Especially if it involved Sam Malone. He and his family were actually none of her business. None whatsoever.

When she continued, making for the line of trees on the far side of the pasture, she discovered the horses were following her—at a distance. Evidently, they'd spotted her and come to check out the tall, yellow-haired trespasser. There were six of them, and although they were every bit as big as the ones she'd petted in Central Park, and running loose besides, she didn't really feel afraid. Her heart quickened, sure—whose wouldn't, in the presence of such magnificent beasts? But the horses seemed merely curious and wary, content to follow along to see what she was up to.

The sun was high and hot, and by the time she reached the trees she was grateful for their shade. Grateful, too, for the water in the little creek that ran chuckling softly through them, winding its way between banks that alternated between boulders and meadow grass and copses of willows. The water was icy cold, she discovered when she dipped her hands in it, but it felt good to bathe her face and neck even though it made her gasp.

She sat on a rock, remembering what Rachel had told her about going down to the creek and meeting an old man on horseback, and later finding out he was none other than her grandfather, Sam Malone.

Maybe he'll show up again, she thought. But of course, he didn't.

Refreshed and ready to move on, she thought about crossing the creek and climbing the rocky, shrubby hill beyond, but decided she didn't really want to get her shoes wet. So instead, she turned right and followed the creek upstream, and the horses stood in a tight little cluster and watched, almost, she thought, as if they were sorry to see her go.

After climbing through another barbed wire fence, she found herself directly behind the old farmhouse and barns, though screened from the buildings themselves by corral fences and an orchard of some sort. Beyond the ranch house, the meadow narrowed and became a ribbon of emerald-green that snaked upward between slopes dotted with boulders and shrubby trees, toward mountains where sheer granite cliffs interrupted the deep blue-green of pines. Here and there on barren slopes were splashes of brilliant orange, like spilled paint. Abby thought she'd never seen anything more beautiful.

Then, for some reason the scene in *The Sound of Music*— the movie, not the Broadway version—where Maria whirls around in the meadow on the mountain and bursts into song, popped into her mind. *Oh, if only I could sing!* But she couldn't, and so she closed her eyes and held out her arms and turned in a slow, rapturous circle while the music swelled gloriously in her head.

Except, she realized, the music wasn't only inside her head. Some of it was real.

She stopped whirling and stood motionless…poised… listening. Listening to a sound so soft and pure and sweet, it seemed almost to be part of the morning, the meadow, the mountains. It hovered in the air, balanced like a bird on the wind, a song without a tune, so haunting it made her throat ache.

She began to move again, led by the sound.

Chapter 7

She almost didn't see him at first. As the meadow wound upward it had grown increasingly narrow, hemmed in by the creek on one side and the steep mountain slope on the other, the swath of wind-rippled grass surrounding outcroppings of granite boulders like flood waters swirling around islands in their path. On one of these islands of piled rocks, Sage sat cross-legged, naked to the waist, his long straight hair loose down his back and blowing in the breeze. But for that slight telltale movement and the music he was making, he might have been part of the earth itself. She halted and stood rooted in the meadow grass, her breath stolen by the sheer beauty of him, and the sound of the wooden flute he played.

He had to have seen her; from where he sat his view of the meadow, the ranch and the valley below must have been all-encompassing. But the music of the flute continued as though she were no more an intrusion than the sun on his shoulders or the wind in his hair. So, after a moment she hitched in a breath and went on climbing, making her way toward him and the rock pile he commanded like a prince his castle. Her heart pounded harder with every step she took.

Sage watched her approach from beneath his lashes, eyes half-closed, a slow heat building in his belly and a sense of inevitability calming his mind. He'd taken his flute and time out in the middle of his working day to do just that—calm his mind and reconcile the burning attraction he'd been developing toward Sunshine Wells with the knowledge that she wasn't for him, for so many reasons. And it hadn't worked. Normally, playing his flute relaxed his body and cleared his head, but today, images of a tall woman with golden hair danced across the blank screen of his mind in perfect harmony with his music, and it became as seductive as a siren's song.

And then…the image in his mind became real. And the peace that had eluded him came and filled him like the warmth of a rising sun.

He waited until she was standing below him, then stopped playing and laid his flute across his lap. He didn't speak.

She said, "That was lovely. Please don't stop."

He shrugged, smiled a little. "The song was finished."

"Oh." Her face, her eyes were hard for him to read. There was something vulnerable about the way she gazed up at him, expectant…hopeful…but defensive, too.

Fully aware of the danger in doing so, he leaned over and held out his hand. She hesitated, her eyes resting on the healing scar that ripped across his upper arm. But she didn't remark on it, just gripped his hand and came up onto the rock beside him. She let go of his hand and for a moment balanced there, poised on the balls of her feet, eye-level with him, her face so close to his he could feel the warm flow of her breath across his lips.

The urge to bring her closer still…to tip her into his lap, say, and if she didn't object, kiss her senseless, was like an electric current running through his body. It took all his will to quell it, to keep himself still with his hands relaxed, cradling the flute that lay across his thighs.

The moment passed. She wiggled around and settled herself beside him on the rock and lifted her hands to hold windblown strands of hair away from her face.

"That's a Native American flute, isn't it? Can I see it?"

Wordlessly, he passed the flute over to her and she took it and held it with what seemed like reverence.

"It's beautiful." She looked up at him. "Did you make it?"

He shook his head. "Not this one. I have an uncle—great-uncle, actually, my mother's uncle—who makes them. But I guess I lack either the patience or the skill. Or both. I bought this one." He smiled. "Online, of course."

She smiled back. "Of course." Her gaze skipped across his scar and went back to the flute.

So did his, and he watched her fingers as they moved over the smooth length of carved wood, almost caressing it. Juices flowed in the back of his throat, as if he were a starving man gazing at a laden banquet table.

"How do you—" she asked, at the same time he said, "Would you like to—" and her face lit up and she whispered, "May I?"

"If you don't mind my germs," he said with a smile and a shrug. The thought was in his mind: *No more germs than you'd get from kissing me.*

Then he watched her lift the flute slowly to her lips, her eyes shining brightly as they clung to his, and he knew as surely as if she'd spoken out loud the same thought was in her mind.

Abigail, what are you doing? Voices of warning shrieked in her head. She ignored them all.

The instrument was warm, like a living thing. Warm from the sun, perhaps…or from *his* hands, his breath. Thinking of the way she'd seen him hold it, the way his mouth had formed around it, she closed her eyes and placed the mouthpiece against her lips and blew, expecting to produce the same lovely sound she'd heard floating across the meadow.

Not quite.

"Oh," she said, opening her eyes to regard him with dismay. "What am I doing wrong?"

His smile was gentle. "Nothing. It just takes practice, is all. Here…like this." He took the flute from her and raised it once more to his own lips, and in a moment the air was filled with that sweet haunting sound.

Tears sprang unbidden to her eyes; her throat ached. Her chest grew tight with so much longing, she feared there wouldn't be room for her heart to beat. She thought she'd never wanted anything so much as she wanted now to lean over, take the flute from his mouth and put her mouth where it had been. The desire to touch him was overwhelming, the desire to stroke that beautiful sun-warmed skin, trace the terrible scar that marred it with her fingers. To lay her face against his chest and breathe the scent of him deep into her lungs…into her very soul.

Appalled and desperate, she closed her eyes and turned her face away from him. The music ceased abruptly.

"Here…" his voice was a soft rumble. "Try it again."

She shook her head and smiled at him across her shoulder. Smiled through pain. "You go ahead. I'll just listen."

He shrugged and put the flute to his mouth, and again the music lifted into the afternoon sunshine, a melody without form or pattern, like the clouds floating across the sky, or the wind stirring through the meadow grass.

To keep her mind from returning to dangerous, forbidden paths, she closed her eyes and tried to let the music fill her empty places, as her body moved to its rhythms. But sitting beside him, so close beside him the heat and scent of his clean, masculine body seemed all around her, so close the wind-lifted feathers of his hair brushed her skin… It began to be agony. Unable to bear it any longer, needing to distance herself from it, she slid down off the rock and onto the grassy slope below.

The sharpness of the loss he felt when she left him both astounded and alarmed him. But he was strong, and forced himself to play on without faltering through the searing pain in his belly, the ache in his throat and the tumult in his mind.

Can't do this. Can...not...do this. God help me...

Then...instead of walking away, heading back down the mountain as he'd thought she intended, she paused just below the rocks on which he sat and began to dance.

Dance...but like no kind of dancing he'd ever seen before. He didn't think she meant to be seductive; she seemed completely unself-conscious, all but oblivious to his presence. It was more, he thought, as if she couldn't help herself, the music was inside her, part of her, and she simply had to move as it bade her.

Watching, he felt something swell inside him, something he'd never felt before and couldn't have put a name to if he'd tried. Fully aware that he might be caught up in some sort of spell, and that it could prove to be nothing but disastrous for him, he began to play again, reaching for her with his music, speaking to her in that language, touching her in a way he wanted to but couldn't allow himself to, not physically.

And though she never once looked directly at him, he knew from the movement of her body that she understood his language, and that she was speaking back to him in a language all her own. Using only her body she created patterns of incredible beauty, patterns that interpreted his music in ways that made him think she must see inside his mind. The vision of a blackbird filled his mind, or a sunflower, or a lion or a doe, his flute painted it in sound, and he watched, fascinated, as the woman in the meadow recreated his vision using only the movements of her body. It was sorcery...magic.

He ran out of breath, and feeling as if he'd run a marathon, slowly lowered the flute to his lap. She turned once more and smiled at him, flushed and windblown.

"Nice," he said, fully aware of the inadequacy of it.

She held out her hand and made a beckoning motion with her head, winsome as a child. "It's fun. Come on, you try it."

He shook his head, knowing his smile had gone awry. "Dancing's not my thing," he said, but grabbed up his shirt as he slipped down from his rocky perch and went to join her anyway.

She waited until he was standing before her, then smiled into his eyes and murmured, "Chicken... I dare you."

He had a fleeting vision of the two of them, as if watching a snippet of film—a movie, or a music video. Facing each other in the middle of a grassy meadow, he the taller, mainly by virtue of being on the uphill side, he with his hair blowing free in the wind, hers pulled back in a chaste bun but with mischievous tendrils floating like feathers around her face. He could see himself lifting a hand to her cheek, bending his face to hers...could almost feel her hand touching his waist, feel its warmth on his naked skin. His belly writhed with wanting.

Hastily, he corralled his hair, twisted and clubbed it at the nape of his neck and secured it with the rubber band he'd placed on his wrist for that purpose. She watched him with shimmering eyes, lips slightly parted.

"Not chicken," he said in a husky growl. "Just wise."

In spite of the breeze the heat in that meadow seemed oppressive. He could see a pulse beating in her throat. His imagination wanted to take him there, wanted to see him pressing his mouth to that spot.

But if I take your hand...if I let myself touch you...can I make myself stop there? Can you...will you stop me there?

"Wise." Her gaze brushed his scar, then shifted to his chest, and she nodded.

He watched a shutter come down across her eyes, and the fragile skin around them fluttered. Beneath her flawless skin, vivid now with sun and exertion, he could see the muscles of her face tighten and draw up. She reminded him of a hurt child bravely determined not to cry, and his own throat ached with regret. He might have reached for her even then…was a heartbeat away from it. Then she looked away and laughed softly.

"Maybe so," she said, and her eyes slid back to him, teasingly now, "but you're still a chicken." She turned and started off down the hill, and the spell was broken.

"Maybe so," he said, catching up with her and matching his strides to hers. After a moment he added, "But so are you."

She threw him a quick, furtive look. And although he caught a glimpse of the old fear, now that he thought he knew its cause, it no longer troubled him. "Me? How?"

He shrugged. "You won't sing, you won't ride a horse. I have my reasons for not dancing with you. Can you say the same?"

She made that snorting sound. "Well, for starters, I can't sing. Seriously. I can't."

"Nonsense. Anybody can sing. What you mean, is, you don't sing *well*."

"Same difference."

He didn't argue the point with her. "What about horseback riding? Only reason I can think of why you wouldn't want to do that is fear." They walked in silence for a few paces while she stared at her feet. "Chicken," he prodded gently.

Her head came up and her eyes lashed at him, suddenly the deep slate-gray of storm clouds. Then just as suddenly she smiled, and he could see why she'd been given the name Sunshine. "Okay, if I let you teach me how to ride, how 'bout you let me teach you to dance?"

"Who said I *can't* dance?"

"You said—"

"I said it's not my *thing*. I never said I *couldn't* dance."

"Okay, now you're just waffling. Come on—you teach me to ride, I teach you to dance—the way I do, not the Texas Two-Step, or whatever they do out here. Is it a deal, or not?"

He tried to think about it, tried to think of all the reasons it was a bad idea. His mind was a blank. After a moment he nodded. "Okay. Deal." He halted and looked over at her while he shrugged his shirt on. "Shall we start tomorrow?"

She paused, too, and her eyes followed his fingers as they worked their way up the row of buttons. He knew he didn't imagine the hunger in them. "Why tomorrow? Why not now?"

Still buttoning, he jerked his head toward the barns, looming close below them now. "Chore time. Got hungry animals to feed."

There was a hiss of breath, and he saw her teeth dent the pillow of her lower lip. Couldn't help but notice how soft it looked…how inviting. "Can I help?"

He was silent while he buttoned the last button. "It's dirty work," he said as he walked on, leaving his shirttail untucked and flapping in the breeze, because no way was he going to unbuckle and unzip in order to tuck it in with her watching him. "Carrying hay, shoveling out calf stalls…"

She fell in beside him. "Hey. Do I look like a fragile flower? I can do that."

He smiled but again didn't answer her immediately, because he was dealing with some powerful and unexpected feelings. Tenderness, for one.

A fragile flower? Miss Sunshine, you may not know it, but that's exactly what you are. Like a sunflower…seems so tough and sturdy, but it's really so vulnerable to the whims of weather, to the turning of the sun and the buffeting of the wind. And the bigger and brighter it appears to be, the more it needs protection and support.

He finally spoke, but only said, "Okay, then, you're on."

Abby didn't think she'd ever had a shower that felt so completely wonderful. She stood naked under the deluge of steaming hot water and felt…exhilarated. Joyful. *Happy. That's what this is: happiness. I…am…happy.*

For the life of her, she couldn't think why that should be so. What was so joyful, so good about this moment…this day?

After chores, she'd come back to the hacienda with Sage just in time for dinner, with no time even to grab a quick shower first. They'd brushed themselves off, left their shoes on the front doorstep, washed their hands and faces in the kitchen sink and joined Rachel and J.J. on the patio, and nobody had seemed to mind that they were both sweaty and dusted with hay. Dinner was Mexican, with beans, rice and enchiladas—cheese for Abby, chicken or beef for everyone else. Except for Abby's brief description of her walk in the meadow—leaving out the part about dancing, or her deal with Sage—the conversation had mostly revolved around Rachel and J.J.'s trip to the doctor with Sean. He'd gotten his first shots, and was fussy now, running a slight fever.

After dinner, she was finally able to retire to her room and strip off her dirty, itchy clothes. She didn't think she'd ever been so dirty in her life. Or so tired. And yet, it had been one of the best days of her life.

If I'm not careful, I could get to love it here.

A small voice in her head said, *Too late. You already do.*

Pain lurked in that thought, and for some reason her mind called up images of Sage, inevitably returning there like a threatened creature to its den. Under the cascading water she smiled, remembering how happy she'd felt just working beside him, carrying chunks of scratchy hay—he'd told her they were called flakes—filling mossy murky water troughs, pouring buckets of grain into pans for eager cattle, or fresh warm milk into pans for a swarm of meowing cats. She remembered his face as he'd told her to be back at six o'clock in the morning. *Six o'clock?* An unthinkable hour, and yet all she'd felt—still felt—was a fluttery sense of anticipation.

I could easily get to love him, too.

And again the voice in her head whispered, *Too late.*

The pain she'd been trying so hard to avoid twisted in her belly like a knife.

She'd dated a lot of men—even had a couple of relation-ships that lasted as long as…oh, maybe a few weeks. But nobody…no one had ever made her feel the way Sage did.

A cliché popped into her head: *Where have you been all my life?*

Oh, God, why? Why did I have to meet him here? And now?

Just like that, happiness turned to despair. Blindly, she turned off the water and toweled herself dry, then crawled into bed and pulled the sheets up to her chin, shivering with misery rather than cold. Pia came and stood on her chest, chirping her usual question, and receiving no answer, bumped Abby's chin with her head and licked her nose with her sand-paper tongue.

In spite of her anguish, Abby was tired enough to go to sleep, and woke to the chiming of her cell phone alarm. She threw back the covers, dislodging Pia, who uttered a chirp of protest. She dressed quickly in jeans and T-shirt, twisted her tangled hair into its usual knot, grabbed up her hooded sweatshirt jacket, and all but sprinted to the kitchen.

But once again she was too late. Sage had already eaten and gone, Josie told her.

"Oops, well, I guess no waffles for me this morning," Abby said, hiding her disappointment with a smile as she accepted the cup of coffee Josie had poured for her.

"Oh, but you shouldn't skip breakfast. It's not good for you." Josie's forehead was creased with dismay.

"I know, but I don't want to be late for chores—Sage is ex-pecting me." Abby lifted her coffee cup. "Is it okay if I take this with me?"

"Of course. And here—take this." Josie tore a banana from a bunch in a big wooden bowl on the countertop and thrust it at her. "Oh—and these, too." She peeled the lid off of a plas-tic container and took out two large, flat oatmeal cookies. "Breakfast to go." She smiled, but her eyes looked worried.

"Perfect," Abby declared as she stuffed the cookies into

her jacket pocket along with her cell phone. "Thanks so much. This is great." She grabbed up the banana in one hand and her coffee cup in the other and all but skipped toward the door, where she paused and turned to wave the coffee cup with a reassuring smile. "Really—thanks. This will be fine."

But she knew Josie still wasn't happy about sending her off without what she considered to be a proper breakfast, and was shaking her head as she speed-walked down the lane. She was thinking the housekeeper's concern should have been annoying. So why, instead, was a warm spot blossoming inside her chest?

Once again, it was his dog that told Sage she was coming. This time, though, the border collie went bounding down the lane to meet her without hesitation, wriggling with joy as if the woman had been a prodigal daughter, returning from her travels.

"I see you made it," he said when she joined him in the barn, where he was stacking a wheelbarrow full of flakes of hay and pretending he hadn't been watching for her. He threw her a look, just a quick one, but it was enough to fill his mind with an image of pink cheeks and shining eyes and soft lips stretched in a radiant smile.

"What, you thought I wouldn't?" She was juggling a banana and a coffee mug in one hand while she brushed Freckles' footprints off her front with the other.

"Not this early." He nodded at the banana. "I'm surprised my mother let you escape without breakfast."

"She didn't, actually. She just sent it with me." She stuck her hand into her jacket pocket and pulled out a handful of Josie's special oatmeal cookies. "Want one?"

He smiled but shook his head. "Had my breakfast, thanks. You'd better hang on to those—you'll need 'em."

She shrugged, tucked one of the cookies back in her pocket and took a bite of the other one, while Freckles sat at attention and drooled. He watched her break off a piece of cookie and give it to the dog, who swallowed it in one gulp and then sat quivering in hopes of another handout. Which she gave him.

"Pushover," Sage muttered.

For a reply, she popped the last piece of cookie into her mouth and gave him a cheeky smile with her lips tightly closed. She chewed and swallowed, took a big gulp of coffee, then set her mug and the banana on the nearest hay bale and dusted off her hands in a businesslike way. "Okay, what do you want me to do?"

He nodded at the laden wheelbarrow. "Grab that and follow me." He picked up two grain buckets and headed for the barn door, wondering what she might have done if he'd told her what was really on his mind.

He worked her hard, as he had the night before. He kept thinking he'd find something messy and dirty enough she wouldn't want to put her city-girl hands in it, but she never hesitated, not once, just jumped in and did the job and asked what next.

Half of him was happy about that, the kind of happiness that filled him with warmth, like sunshine. Yeah, he knew he was thinking in too many Sunny metaphors, but he couldn't seem to help himself.

What worried him was that the warmth was having an effect on some dreams he thought he'd cast aside long ago. Turned out they'd only been buried, and the warmth of Sunshine Wells was making them poke their little heads out of the barren soil of his life and... *Oh, Lord, I have to stop this.*

That was the part of him that wasn't happy about the fact that Sam's city-bred granddaughter acted like she'd been born to farm. He knew he had to stamp out those newly sprouted hopes and dreams before it was too late, and he was becoming more and more afraid it might already be. He was beginning to think it might be like trying to hold back the rain forest with a hoe.

He tried not to pay too much attention to her, but even knowing it wasn't helping him any, he couldn't keep from stopping what he was doing to watch her with the calves. That seemed to be her favorite chore, and she was just so damn *watchable* when she let one suck on her fingers, or when she'd kneel down in the dirt and wrap her arms around a calf's neck and press her face into the warm hair, because, she said, it felt so clean and soft.

He watched her try to coax the ornery brown bull calf into letting her pet him—without much success, but at least the little devil didn't try to butt her again. Part of him almost wished he would, and that *he* could manage to be there to catch her again, because the memory of the way she'd felt in his arms was a constant temptation in his mind.

He tore himself away from watching her and went to milk out the cows, now that the calves were done. But his respite was short-lived, because she came and hunkered down beside him and watched him avidly while he milked, and no matter how hard he tried not to let her, she filled up his senses. She smelled of hay and cattle and sweat, but even that couldn't quite smother the scent of something sweet and flowery and fresh that came in tantalizing little whiffs, like the smell of apple blossoms from his orchard when the wind was blowing just right.

"Can you teach me to do that?"

Her face was so close to his, he could feel her breath when she spoke. He shoved back the milking stool and stood up, every nerve in his body vibrating with restraint.

"Another time," he said, and his voice creaked like a rusty hinge. "This morning we're going riding…remember?"

"Oh, damn," Abby said, "I was hoping you'd forgotten that."

Which was a lie. Not that she was any less leery of getting on the back of something so big and potentially troublesome, but she was willing to try just about anything if it meant she could spend a little more time with Sage.

For some reason, she thought about the time, in her younger days, when she and Sunny had found themselves in a New

York City cowboy bar, and Sunny had dared her to ride the mechanical bull. Naturally, she'd taken the dare. What she remembered most about the ride was that once it started, she couldn't let go. She knew she had to hang on until it was over, no matter what.

"I'll have you know I've ridden a mechanical bull before," she said in a voice loud with false bravado.

Sage laughed. "Then this should be a piece of cake."

She stood hugging herself nervously while he took two feedbags from a nail on the wall in the barn and filled them with grain. Then, with a sense of impending doom, she followed him through the gates and corrals to the meadow where the horses were grazing.

Their heads came up when they saw Sage with the grain, and they came at an eager trot, shaking their heads.

Abby had time to whisper, "Oh, God," before they were surrounded, and she felt all but buried by huge creatures that seemed to be made of pure energy, a flurry of stomping hooves and switching tails and snorting muzzles, all whickering and bumping each other, competing for grain. She held her breath and stood absolutely still in their midst, determined not to disgrace herself in front of Sage by whimpering and cowering.

She was awed by the way he moved so easily among the horses, speaking softly to them, giving each one a handful of grain, telling Abby their names as he patted and stroked them, reaching under their manes to brush dust and grass from their shiny hides. Then he slipped the feedbags over the noses of two of the horses, a reddish brown one with a white mark on his forehead he called Diamond, and a darker red one with a black mane and tail whose name, he told her, was Morning Glory. He tied ropes around their necks and gave the end of one to Abby.

"What do I do with it?" she asked in a whisper.

He smiled, but at least, she thought, he didn't fall down

laughing. "Lead her back to the barn," he said kindly. "So we can saddle and bridle her."

"But…" she swallowed, and her throat was so dry it made a sticking sound. "How do I— What if she—"

"She won't step on you. Just walk—she'll follow."

She took in a breath and let it out with a doubtful, "Okay." Hiding her terror, she began to walk toward the corrals, which now seemed a mile away. And just as Sage had said she would, the horse followed her, just ambling along, matching her pace to Abby's.

Fear left her and was replaced by wonder. Now, she couldn't seem to stop smiling. When the horse—Morning Glory—nudged her with her nose and blew a gust of breath into her hair, she gasped in delight and looked over at Sage, and when he smiled back at her she felt the warmth of it from the top of her head all the way down to her toes.

Back at the barn, he showed her how to brush and groom her horse before saddling her, to make sure there were no burrs or stickers or sores where the saddle would be.

"You touch her gently, like this," he told her as he demonstrated. "She can feel a fly when it lands on her, so you know how sensitive her skin is." And she nodded, watching his hands move over the horse's glossy red-brown hide like a lover's caress, and wouldn't have been able to reply if her life had depended on it. She was too busy trying to keep her imagination from feeling that same gentle touch on her own skin.

Next, he showed her how to put on the saddle and cinch it tight, how to slip the bridle bit between the horse's teeth and pull the strap up over her ears. His nearness while he did that made her heart thump and her breath catch and her skin prickle with goose bumps.

Then she noticed that while he was telling her how to put her foot in the stirrup, holding the reins and the saddle horn in one hand, he kept well beyond touching distance, and instead of showing her on Morning Glory, demonstrated on his own horse, Diamond.

With a mental sigh she thought, *He's noticed. I've scared him off, poor guy. I've got to have better control.*

Frowning in concentration, she watched him put the toe of his boot into the stirrup and swing himself into the saddle in one easy motion. Now, he seemed to loom far above her, until he leaned over the pommel of his saddle and smiled down at her.

"If you're waiting for me to give you a leg up…sorry. If you're going to ride, you'd better know how to get on and off your horse by yourself."

She tossed her head and gave him a scoffing laugh. "Hey, I'm a dancer, remember? I've got strong legs."

"Yeah?" He reared back with a taunting smile. "Then let's see 'em."

"Huh. Okay, smartass, watch this…" Shivery with excitement, she set her teeth, gripped the saddle with both hands the way he'd showed her, poked the toe of her left boot into the stirrup, and hoisted herself up. And it was easier than she'd thought it would be, because of course she *did* have a dancer's strong legs and supple body.

Once firmly in the saddle, she turned to give Sage a smile of triumph. He chuckled softly and turned his horse's head toward the meadow.

She's a natural, he thought, without surprise. He imagined it had a lot to do with having a physically fit body, as she'd said, but he thought it was more than that. The innate grace he'd noticed before, something in her genes, maybe—and why not? The way she sat on her horse like she was born to it, she reminded him a lot of her grandfather. As far as Sage was concerned, as old as he was, there was no better horseman alive than Sam Malone.

In any case, she seemed to have gotten over her fear pretty quickly, and when he asked her if she was ready to try a faster pace, she didn't hesitate—although he did hear a little bit of a gasp when Morning Glory first broke into a trot. But then he noticed she was bobbing up and down from her knees, lifting out of the saddle, trying to time the gait.

"No, no—that's the English way," he said, moving in closer to her, close enough that his knee brushed hers, though he hadn't meant it to. "Out here we ride Western style—butt glued to the saddle. Okay? Relaxed and easy...see? What you want is to be one with your horse."

"Easy for you to say," she muttered, her voice bumping with the jolting of the horse's gait.

He grinned. "Flopping up and down gets you branded a greenhorn. And I don't imagine the horse likes it much, either. How'd you like something heavy bouncing up and down on your back?" She threw him a dirty look, and he laughed and moved out ahead of her, leaving her to work it out by herself.

A few minutes later she rode up even with him, looking kind of mulish, and said, "How's this?"

He let his gaze drop to the place where her butt met the saddle—a mistake, probably, but the heat that spread through his insides felt good, and he didn't try to stop it. He brought his eyes slowly back to her face and drawled, "Lookin' pretty good...for a greenhorn."

"Hah!" He could see she was trying hard to hide a grin of triumph. "Okay, cowboy, what's next? Do we gallop, or what?"

Lord, but it was hard to tear his eyes away from her. He just wanted to go on looking at her, smiling and goofy as a kid. But he shook his head. "How 'bout we try an easy lope first?"

"A lope—sure. What's that?"

"Call it a slow gallop."

"Okay, I can do that."

"Yes, you can...ready?"

She nodded—game for anything, and his heart quivered with delight in her. But when he nudged Diamond into a lope and Morning Glory did the same, she wasn't quite so brave.

She uttered a little squeak of fear and grabbed the saddle horn. He dropped back to ride beside her.

"Let go of the horn, grip with your legs," he told her. "Find your balance. Find your rhythm. Just like a rocking chair."

She nodded again, a quick little bob of her head, but he noticed she still kept that death grip on the saddle horn. Her jaw looked rigid as rock.

"You can do this," he said gently. "Trust the saddle."

She flashed him a brave look that touched his soul, the way she seemed scared to death but determined to do it anyway. He gave her a smile of encouragement. Slowly, she uncurled her fingers from around the horn, though her hand still hovered nervously inches above the pommel. Again, he moved away from her, giving her some room. And when he saw a smile spread across her face—yes, like a sunrise—and she turned to him a face alight with purest joy, he felt something sweep through him like a pollen-laden breeze, making his nose tickle and his eyes burn.

"This is *great!*" she yelled a few moments later as they loped along together, side by side. Tentatively, she lifted a hand to the bundle of hair at the nape of her neck and gave her head one quick hard shake. The wind picked up her hair and carried it out behind her like a banner, and she laughed out loud, like a child.

Chapter 8

He'd never seen anything so beautiful. *God help me,* he thought. *I could fall in love with this woman.*

They rode down to the south end of the meadow, slowing to a trot, then to a walk to give the horses a breather while he gave her some tips to improve her form. Heading back toward the barn, he picked up the pace to a lope again, having decided he wasn't quite ready to let her go for a full gallop just yet. But he couldn't say he was all that surprised when Sunny passed him, leaning forward in her saddle and giving Morning Glory her head. As she left him in the dust, he heard her give a whoop that could have been either joy or terror.

He took off after her, swearing under his breath, thinking she was going to get herself either killed or hurt, and what in the hell was he going to tell Sam? But when he caught up with her, just before they reached the corrals, he saw she was laughing, and any thought of being mad at her for scaring him to death flew right out of his head.

Pasting what he hoped was a scowl of disapproval on his

face, he leaned over and caught Morning Glory's bridle and turned her into the corrals.

Sunny gave an indignant squawk. "Oh, no—really? We have to quit *now?*" Her eyes were bright with excitement. "But I was just getting the hang of it. Did you see me? That was a gallop, right? That was the most—" Then, evidently the expression on his face got through to her and she broke off with a guilty frown. "Oh, no—you're mad. Was I not supposed to—"

"I'm not mad." He let out a gust of breath. "Have you always been this foolhardy?" And he gave up trying not to smile. How could he stay irritated with her when she looked so damn happy?

She smiled back, radiantly, and raked her fingers through her windblown hair. "I didn't think so…" Laughter burst from her, as if it couldn't be contained another second. "Seriously— do we have to stop? Oh—I'm sorry—" She pressed fingertips to her lips. "Do you— I guess you probably have other stuff to do—"

"It's not me," he said as he dismounted, nodding toward her. "You're the one that's not used to this. I don't want you crippled up."

She made that snorting laugh. "As if. I told you, I'm a dancer. I'm in shape."

An understatement if he'd ever heard one. He rubbed the back of his neck and said patiently, "Yeah, you are. But you're not used to a saddle. Trust me. Riding uses muscles nothing else does. You don't believe me—" he caught Morning Glory's bridle and gave Sunny a nod "—try getting off your horse. Right now."

The look she gave him was arrogant, confident, disbelieving. But she got off her horse with fairly decent form and turned to him with a smug little smile.

"Now, walk," he said.

She took a step, still holding on to Morning Glory's mane. And halted. Her face crumpled into a frown of dismay that was almost funny—except he knew how she was feeling. "Oh, God. My legs don't work."

He just laughed and led the horses into the barn, figuring he could do her the favor of letting her figure out how to walk again without an audience. At least save her some pride.

"Well, that was embarrassing," she muttered when she joined him a few minutes later, still hitching and hobbling.

"Yeah...it's tough finding out you're human, ain't it?" He didn't look at her, because he didn't have a lot of confidence in his ability to keep his feelings off his face. He hauled Morning Glory's saddle off of her and carried it over to the rack, picked up a brush and brought it back with him.

"Here," he said as he handed it to Sunny, and his voice had turned thick and gruff. "Rub your horse down and turn her out, and then you can go home and soak in a hot tub. That'll help."

On the other hand, he was afraid the only thing that was going to help him was a cold shower.

He kept his eyes on Diamond and his concentration on getting the horses unsaddled and turned out, and by the time he'd finished with that and was standing with Sunny in the corral watching the two horses go galloping into the meadow to find a patch of warm dirt to roll in, he was pretty sure he had himself under control.

It had been a good day, he thought. And at least for the most part, he'd managed to keep his hands off of Sam's granddaughter.

He hadn't counted on Sunny all of a sudden turning to him and throwing her arms around his neck.

"Thank you," she whispered, her breath warm and close to his ear, "that was one of the best things ever in my whole life."

"Really?" he croaked, brilliantly. Which was about when it occurred to him where his own arms were and what they were doing.

Sage was pretty sure tightening his arms around a beautiful

woman who had just thrown herself into them would qualify as a reflex action on the part of a normal, healthy man. He was also pretty sure he knew what a decent man was expected to do with his arms once his thinking mind was back in charge. He knew what he *should* do. But damned if he could make himself do it.

So, his arms stayed where they were, wrapped around her, and her body fit against his as if she were the missing piece he'd been looking for all his life. She felt slim and strong and supple—all the things he'd seen and known she was already— but so much more. She was warm and surprisingly soft. Her whole body seemed to quiver and pulse with energy and life, and holding her made him feel as if he'd been plugged into the same power source. He felt bigger, stronger, fearless and mighty.

"Really," she murmured, pulling back to look into his eyes. She was touching his face. Her hand lay softly along his jaw.

He looked back at her and knew he would kiss her, now. And knew it was right and inevitable, and that it didn't matter if he'd only known her a couple of days, didn't know her at all, in fact, and that she was Sam Malone's granddaughter and heir. Kissing her seemed like the most natural thing in the world to do...like taking his next breath.

He tilted his head slightly and heard the sigh of a breath from her waiting lips...and then, from her pocket, came the tinkle of a Broadway tune.

"Damn," she whispered, and her body had gone rigid.

He was conscious of his hands, one on the small of her back, the other higher up, under her tumbled hair, almost to the nape of her neck. Her body felt hot against his palms, burning hot, like something forbidden.

Abby shuddered when he took his hands away from her, as if she'd felt a gust of cold wind.

He tucked his burning fingertips in his pockets and lifted his eyebrows. His smile felt crooked. "*A Chorus Line? Really?*"

She laughed without humor, at the same time frowning as she looked down at her cell phone. *Pauly, of course.* She hit the ignore button and shook her head. "Stupid thing only works down here, for some reason." She shoved the phone back in her pocket and tried to smile. "That's okay—I'll call him back." Oh, how she wished…

Can't we go back? Hit Rewind and go back to the place where you were about to kiss me, before the phone…

But of course, that moment was gone forever.

"Him?" Sage asked as they walked through the corrals, back to the barn. His voice sounded casual, only mildly curious.

She glanced at him, but he wasn't looking at her, and she could see a muscle working at the hinge of his jaw. Her heart began to beat faster. "Yeah…Pauly. He's my—"

"Boyfriend?" he said, just as she said, "Agent."

He did look at her, then, a quick hard glance, sharp and black as obsidian. "Agent?"

"Yeah…" She didn't seem to have enough breath. Giddy laughter tumbled inside her. "No boyfriend."

"Huh." He muttered something she couldn't quite catch as he turned his gaze upward, evidently finding something fascinating in the barn's rafters. She found that incredibly endearing.

Abby bit back a smile. One moment might be gone forever, but that didn't mean another might not be waiting in the wings.

"Pauly's a friend…but not like that. God, no. He was—" She stopped herself, heart hammering. She'd almost said, *He was Sunny's friend, too.* She hitched in a breath and finished it. "He was my roommate's agent—and friend—too."

Sage nodded. "The one that was killed."

"Yeah…"

Slowly, they walked through the shadowy barn and through the big open doorway, into the sunlight. The awareness that shimmered between them was almost visible, like heat waves.

In the lane, Abby paused and turned to him, shading her eyes with her hand.

"So…I guess you probably have things…"

With uncharacteristic awkwardness, he hooked his thumbs in his jeans' pockets and frowned at the ground. "Yeah…I do."

"So…can I come back tonight? To help with chores?"

His black eyes came up to meet hers; his smile spread slowly. "You sure you want to?"

"Yes!"

"Well, all right, then."

"Will you teach me to milk?" Why was her voice so breathless, so husky?

"Well, I guess we'll see how it goes." His voice, too, sounded deeper, slower than usual. The air between them seemed to have thickened.

"And…can we go riding again?"

"Uh…how 'bout tomorrow?"

She tried not to smile, but it was like trying to stop her heart from beating. "Okay."

He smiled, too, in that way he had that left his eyes grave and dark. "Well, all right, then."

"So—guess I'll—" Her phone tapped out the first bars of "One." *Jeez, Pauly, give it a rest.* She gave a frustrated laugh. "—Um—yeah, so, I'll see you later." She shrugged a mute apology for Sage and turned, thumbing on the phone and lifting it to her ear as she walked away and left him there.

"Yeah, Pauly, what is it?"

"Hey, what's with the attitude? I just called to find out how you're doing. You said you'd call and I hadn't heard…"

"Yeah, it's been what, a whole day?"

"Well, excuse me for caring."

Abby pressed her thumb and forefinger against her eyelids and let out a long slow breath. "Look, I'm sorry. It's just that… things are kind of awkward around here right now, okay?"

There was a pause, and then: "Still haven't told them about Sunny?"

"No! How can I? I haven't even met her grandfather. Nobody even seems to know where he is." She halted in the middle of the lane and cast a quick, guilty look around. Even though there obviously wasn't another soul anywhere near her, she lowered her voice. "Pauly, they think I'm *her*."

"What—you mean *Sunny?*"

"Yes." It was half hiss, half moan. She hurried on into Pauly's shocked silence. "I didn't mean for it to go on this long, Pauly, I swear I didn't. I just—well, the plane ticket was in Sunny's name, and it couldn't be transferred, so in order to use it I had to use Sunny's I.D., right? I was going to come out here and tell him in person—the grandfather, I mean. It seemed better than just blurting something like that out over the phone, or, God forbid, in an email. But then, he wasn't here, and nobody seems to know when he'll show up, and… the longer it goes on, them thinking I'm Sunny, the harder it's going to be to tell them the truth." An image rose before her mind's eye, Sage's smile, his somber eyes, and she squeezed her eyes shut in futility.

Pauly's silence seemed to go on forever. She heard him clear his throat. And then: "You sure you have to?"

She couldn't have heard him right. She whispered, "What?"

"Think about it. They've already accepted you as Sunny. Why do you need to tell them any different?"

"*Why?* Jeez, Pauly."

"I'm serious. The old man wants an heir, he's never met the real one, who happens to have been tragically murdered, so why not give him what he wants?"

She felt cold and sick. Like throwing up. "Why not?" Her voice was shaking. "B-because it would be a lie."

Pauly laughed. "You're an actress, kid. You lie for a living."

"That's different." She was trembling.

"Yeah? How?"

"Because the audience is in on it!" She was yelling now, one hand pressed against her forehead. "And it's not illegal!"

"Well," Pauly said, and his voice had a strange note in it

she'd never heard before, "looks to me like you've already committed fraud. Haven't you?" She said nothing. She felt cold...and for some odd reason, frightened. "Look," Pauly went on, and his voice was kind, now. Cajoling. "You're lying the way things are now, aren't you? What's the difference if you lie a little longer? Maybe get something out of it."

"They'll find out," she whispered.

"Who's gonna tell them?"

"Uh...DNA?" Abby was shaking so hard she could barely hold the phone. *Oh, God, Sunny...what have I done?* "Look, Pauly, I'm not doing this, okay? It's...it's just crazy."

"Come on, Abby, it's not crazy. Think about it. What's the old guy to you—"

"No!" She jabbed the disconnect button and turned in a desperate circle, wanting nothing so much as to hurl the phone into the bushes.

I have to tell somebody the truth, she thought, as she sniffed and dashed a tear from her cheek. *I have to. If Sam Malone hasn't shown up by tomorrow, I...I'll go to Los Angeles and find the lawyer myself. This has to stop. I'm not a liar. Or a fraud. I'm not!*

A small voice inside her head whispered: *Then, what are you?*

As it turned out, she didn't get to go back to the barn that evening. When she returned to the hacienda, she found that Josie had been waiting for her. She needed to go grocery shopping, the housekeeper said, and wanted to know if Abby would like to go with her. It would be a great opportunity, she said, for Abby to explore the valley. Rachel wanted to go, too, since J.J. had offered to babysit Sean, and they could take the long way around the lake, stop for lunch in Kernville, then go around through Wofford Heights and Isabella. They could show Abby where all the shops were, and have a nice outing, just the "girls."

Abby had mixed feelings about the outing. On the one

hand, she thought it would be good to be busy and distracted, so she wouldn't have to think about the predicament she was in, or that awful upsetting phone call from Pauly. On the other hand, being around these people was a strain because she had to remember to stay in character, maintain her pretense, play her role. It was also a strain because they were so *nice*. To her, their niceness was becoming a burden, and her awareness of the way she was lying to them a constant heaviness in her heart.

In spite of that, she enjoyed the trip. Since Sunny's death she'd been too wrapped up in grief and shock, first, and then in the impersonation of Sunny to realize how much she'd missed the company of friends. Female friends, in particular.

Of course, Josie and Rachel couldn't be called *friends*, could they? Not when she was lying to them every minute she was with them, simply by *being*.

In any case, by the time they returned with the back of the SUV packed full of groceries, the sun was going down behind the mountains and the chores had been done. Abby and Rachel helped Josie unload and put away the groceries and get supper on the table. Afterward, Sage said good-night and went back to his little adobe house, alone. Rachel and J.J. said they were going to watch an old John Wayne movie they'd just gotten from Netflix, and Josie retired to bed.

Abby went to bed, too. She tried to read the book she'd borrowed from the den but fell asleep and dreamed she was being chased by Sunny's killer, who wore heavy gloves and a hood over his face. As was typical in chase dreams, her legs felt heavy, leaden…it was so hard to keep running, even though she knew her life depended on it. When she woke to her cell phone alarm, she found that Pia was curled up asleep on her feet.

Sage found Sunny perched on a stool at the kitchen counter when he went in for breakfast. She smiled and raised her coffee mug to him in a little salute.

"You're up early," he said.

"Really?" she countered, lifting her eyebrows. "I thought you were late."

He kissed his mother's cheek, said, "Mornin', Ma," and slipped onto the stool next to Sunny.

There's something different about her this morning, he thought. Partly it was her hair, which she was wearing in a single braid down her back, which made her look more like a Nordic milkmaid than either a 1940s movie star or a prima ballerina. But it was something else, too, something in her eyes. A certain sadness, maybe, or a hint of the fear he'd noticed that first day. Seeing that look in her eyes again made him want to erase it, eliminate whatever it was she was afraid of. He wanted to see her face alight with joy again, the way it had been yesterday when she'd galloped Morning Glory across the meadow.

"I think I know your hairdresser," he said, tilting his head so his braid fell toward her across his shoulder.

She tilted her head the same way and looked sideways at him, and their eyes met across their two braids, hers the color of sunshine, his the color of midnight, lying side by side along their arms, their sleeves almost touching...

"Black and white," she murmured.

Yin and yang, he thought.

Then his mother was there, filling his coffee mug, and when he thanked her, he thought he caught a glimpse of a worried look in her eyes, just before she turned back to the stove.

Worried about me, Ma? I know Sam's granddaughter is off-limits. But he felt a flash of resentment.

Why, Ma? Why should Sam's granddaughter be off-limits to me? Do you think I'm not good enough for her? Would he?

He wolfed his breakfast in silence, then drained his coffee mug in a couple of gulps and slid off the stool. "Ready?"

"You betcha." She swallowed the last of her coffee and

stood up, aiming a challenging grin his way. "You going to teach me to milk today?"

"You betcha," he said, mimicking her, and she laughed and matched him stride for stride as they walked through the house and out the front door and down the steps to where he'd parked his truck.

Freckles came bounding up and she dropped to one knee to throw her arms around the dog's neck. J.J.'s old hound stood by, tail waving slowly, patiently waiting her turn, and Sunny hugged her, too. When she finally finished loving up the dogs and climbed into the cab beside him, Sage felt his spirits lift, and he realized it was because the fearful look in her eyes was gone.

"What's this stuff for?" Abby eyed the jar of murky-looking ointment doubtfully.

"It's bag balm," Sage explained. "It's a lubricant. Protects the cow—and it's not bad for your hands, either. Help heal up that cat bite."

"Ah." She poked a forefinger into the jar and scooped out a glob and rubbed it briskly over her palms. "Hmm...not bad. Feels kind of nice, in fact. Okay, what now?"

She could see Sage was trying to hide a smile, but who could blame him? He must think she was nuts, going giddy with excitement over milking a cow, for God's sake.

Better to have him think that than know the truth, which is that it's he *who makes my heart pound and my hands go damp.*

"Okay, come on over here. Sit right here, on this stool."

"Yeah...okay." She cast a quick, wary look to her left, but Black Betty's head with its sweeping horns appeared to be firmly locked into the stanchions with a metal bar. The cow was placidly munching hay, seemingly without a care in the world, just switching her tail at flies from time to time. Abby gingerly settled her butt on the stool—and found that her knees were now on a level with her chin.

"Get comfortable," Sage said, and she threw him a *yeah, right* look, which he ignored.

He hunkered down beside her and placed a stainless-steel bucket between her knees, and sort of under the cow.

"Now," he said, turning his head to look into her eyes, "you can set the bucket on the ground, like this, but it's better if you can manage to hold it between your knees, so you can move it out of her way if she decides to kick or put her foot in it."

He was so close she could see herself reflected in the tiny twin mirrors of his eyes. She tried to swallow, but her mouth had gone dry as dust. Lines deepened around his eyes, and she nodded and hurriedly looked away.

"Okay, you've seen me do it...you know what to do." His voice was soft and deep, and very close to her ear. So close she could feel his breath stirring wisps of her hair that had been left out of the braid.

She gave a nervous little laugh. "Yeah, but I'm pretty sure it's not as easy as you make it look. Like playing the flute, remember? I couldn't make that work, either."

There was a pause. She could hear her own heart beating. She imagined she could hear his. He let go a sigh of breath and reached for her hand.

"Okay, here..." He took her hand and held it, then separated two of her fingers and encircled them with his hand. "It's like this...you don't tug, you don't yank. Just a gentle downward squeeze. Feel it?"

Feel it? It seemed incredibly, unbelievably erotic. Somehow, she managed to nod.

He smiled into her eyes. "Now, you do it. Here—take my finger. Now, squeeze..."

Laughter bumped around in her chest, and yet, weirdly, she felt like bursting into tears. *Why is this so terrifying? It's milking a cow, for God's sake, not jumping off a cliff.*

And yet...for some reason, that was exactly what it felt like.

"That's it, you've got it," he whispered in her ear as he took hold of her waist and turned her back toward the cow. "Now, try it on her."

She nodded, and he held her steady with his hands on her shoulders while she leaned forward and took hold of the cow's teat. Her forehead rested on the great beast's flank, which was warm and smelled of...cow? Something earthy, anyway, and not at all unpleasant. She bit down on her lip, concentrated... squeezed the way she'd squeezed Sage's fingers.

A stream of milk shot out and hit the bucket with a satisfying percussive sound. Abby jerked back and gasped. "Oh, my God—I did it."

"Yep." He let go of her shoulders and drew back a little, giving her an encouraging nod as his forearm came to rest on one knee. "Now, let's see you try it with both hands."

"Oh, *both* hands he wants now," she grumbled, but she was all but bursting with self-confidence and pride. She could do this. She knew she could. She *was* doing it. *I'm actually milking a cow.*

She tried to imagine Sunny milking a cow, but it was simply beyond her.

Within a few minutes, after some fits and starts, she had two streams of milk swishing into the bucket in a slow but steady rhythm. She was surprised at how easy it was—except that now the muscles in her forearms were starting to cramp.

"Boy, speaking of muscles I didn't know I had." She paused to shake her hands, first one, then the other, not wanting to admit she was already getting tired.

Sage laughed softly. "You get used to it. Builds a nice little arm muscle for you."

She glanced down at his arm, at the shirtsleeve buttoned to his wrist, then lifted her gaze to his face. His smile was sort of goofy, actually, but it made something flip-flop inside her chest. Hurriedly, she returned her attention to her task, blinked away the lingering vision of that smile, and shot a few more milk streams into the bucket.

She was too warm, suddenly. Burning up—and how could

she not be, with Sage on one side of her, the cow in front, the sun beating down on her back. The air seemed dense and hard to breathe, and she felt as if her whole body was vibrating, deep down inside.

"It's foaming," she mumbled, staring blindly at the bucket, and her lips felt thick and barely able to form words. "Why does it foam?"

Close beside her, Sage shrugged one shoulder. "I don't know—just does."

She glanced at him. Licked her lips. "What does it taste like?"

He shrugged again, his eyes shining. "Milk."

"No, I mean…don't you have to do something to it, before you— Can you drink it just like this?"

"Sure you can."

"How—"

He reached one arm past her and she let her hand fall away from the cow's teat, and his take its place. Her shoulder was pressed against his chest. She didn't dare look at him now.

I know where this is going. And I don't care.

"Open your mouth," he said.

He knew it was a silly, showoff-y think to do, the kind of thing he might have done back in high school to impress some girl. And maybe that was why he did it, because he felt carefree and young, not like the shy boy he'd been back in high school, but one with all the confidence and self-esteem he'd earned as he'd grown into a man. Although, ironically, he no longer felt the need to impress anyone. Especially this woman.

The revelation came to him in a moment of thrilling clarity, taking his breath away. He would remember this moment, he knew, the way he remembered the first time he'd seen a bald eagle flying high against a deep blue sky, the first fish he'd ever caught. This…the moment he knew he could truly be himself with this woman. That with her he would never have to pretend to be someone or something he wasn't.

The moment he knew she was *the* woman for him.

"Open your mouth," he said again. And she did, and then she closed her eyes, too, and humbled him with her trust.

He aimed a stream of milk at her open mouth, and she caught it, laughing with sheer delight as the milk ran down her chin.

She was still laughing when he kissed her.

Chapter 9

He kissed her joyfully, with unreserved happiness, and she kissed him back the same way. He could feel her body trembling a little, and wondered if it was with the same profound relief and awe of discovery that filled him. He never for a moment doubted the rightness of what he was doing, and in fact would have defended with a fierce and primitive resolve against anyone—be it Sam Malone, or his mother, or the Fates—who challenged his right to this woman. The woman he had chosen.

Her hand lay soft and warm on his cheek, and he felt her lips form a smile against his. When he turned his face to press a quick, shaken kiss to the palm of her hand, she made a happy little humming sound deep in her throat. He smiled, too, and returned to her mouth, savoring its mysteries for as long as he dared before finally pulling back, just slightly. Their foreheads touched. They whispered and laughed softly together, like children sharing secrets.

"You taste good."

"Mmm…yeah. Like milk, probably."

"Nectar of the gods."

"More, please."

He obliged, and felt godlike, himself, as she laid her head back in the curve of his arm in complete and joyous surrender. The bucket of milk sat forgotten between her feet, and Black Betty munched on, oblivious, lazily switching her tail at the occasional fly.…

The milk stool tipped over backward. Sage wasn't prepared for the sudden shifting of the weight in his arms, and the kiss broke apart as they both tumbled laughing into the straw.

They couldn't stay there, obviously. Of course not, although Abby wished with all her heart the moment could go on forever.

Slowly, with some reluctance, they helped each other to their feet, brushing and tugging at clothing, laughing and exclaiming and apologizing. Sage retrieved the bucket and stool, while Abby brushed herself off. She straightened up and they faced each other, and the words and laughter died.

Sage reached out his hand and plucked a piece of straw out of her hair, then let his hand slide slowly down to cradle the side of her head. She closed her eyes and rubbed her cheek against his palm, like a cat being petted.

I've never felt like this before, she thought. *I feel…*

How did she feel? Shocked and frail and bewildered, as if she'd been hit by some terrible catastrophe…and yet, what kind of catastrophe could make her feel so *happy?* Desperately, painfully happy. How could such a mishmash of feelings be, unless…

My God, is this what it feels like to fall in love?

Sage was gazing at her, his mouth curved in a smile, his eyes no longer somber but burning with a strange dark light.

"Take the milk into the cold room," he said, his voice like a gentle rasp on her auditory nerves. "You'll see a pan and a strainer set up on the counter. Pour the milk into the strainer and just leave the bucket in the sink."

She nodded, licking her lips. There were so many things she wanted to ask him. And she couldn't make a sound.

"There's something I have to do." He brushed her lips with the pad of his thumb, and that seemed to her as erotic as a kiss. "Okay?"

She nodded again, and they turned to walk together into the barn. At the cold room door, Sage handed her the bucket, waited for her to step inside, then turned away. Just before the door closed, Abby saw him take a cell phone out of his shirt pocket.

Though still shaken, she poured the milk into the strainer the way Sage had told her. She set the bucket in the deep stainless-steel sink and ran some water into it, then went back to the door. It hadn't latched, and opened soundlessly when she gave it a slight push. Through the slowly widening crack she could see him standing almost where she'd last seen him, a few feet away from the door, with his back to her. His head was bowed, and his hand held the phone pressed to his ear. He wasn't talking, but obviously listening…waiting.

Then, abruptly, he lifted his head and let out an exasperated breath. He spoke in a deep, guttural growl. "Okay, look, I don't know where you are or why you're not answering your phone. I hope you get this message, because…well, something's come up. And, I, uh…I really need to talk to you. It's important." He paced a couple of steps, gazing up at the rafters, then spoke again with quiet urgency. "Okay, I guess you're still determined not to come down here, so…if the mountain won't come to Mohammed…" He gave a bark of frustrated laughter. "So…this is me—Mohammed—and I'm coming to the mountain. Okay? I hope you get this message, because I'm coming up there. Now. See you…"

Abby bumped the door loudly, then pushed it open. Sage turned as he was tucking the cell phone into his shirt pocket.

"Are we going riding today?" she asked, already knowing the answer but wanting to hear what he'd say. *I know you're going to find Sam. Please, please don't lie to me.*

His eyes, that a moment ago had been hard and black as flint, seemed to soften as they came to rest on her. "Tomorrow," he said gently. "I have…something I need to do today. I'll… There's someplace I need to go."

He hesitated as if he would say more, and Abby tried to find answers to the questions swarming in her mind in the bottomless depths of his eyes. *What just happened, Sage? Are we going to pretend it didn't? I don't know what it means, or how it makes me feel. Do you?*

His smile flickered briefly, and then he took a feedbag down from its hook and turned to the door. She watched him as he walked away, counting his footsteps with her own pounding heartbeats.

"Sage." He halted and turned in a pool of sunshine. "You're going to see him, aren't you?" He didn't reply, and she walked slowly toward him, joining him in the light. "My grandfather—Sam Malone." At arm's length away from him she paused, and gave a shrug of apology. He opened his mouth to say something and she rushed to get there first. "I, um…I heard you on the phone just now. That was Sam, wasn't it?"

"Voice mail." Sage gestured with the feedbag. "I was leaving him a message."

"Saying you're coming up to see him—I heard that. So you do know where he is."

He let out a breath and lifted his eyes to gaze at the mountains. "I know where he probably is, yeah. There's an old cow camp in one of the high meadows. He's got a cabin up there. It's pretty primitive, but he likes it that way. It's kind of like his hideaway. He goes there when…I don't know, just when he doesn't want to deal with…life, I guess."

"You mean, he doesn't want to deal with *us*. Right? His granddaughters. Why did he ask us to come, then, if he doesn't want to see us?"

"It's not that he doesn't want to see you." They were walking together, now, moving slowly toward the meadow where the horses were grazing in the early-morning sun. Abby was shivering, more with a surfeit of emotions than the chill in the air.

She glanced over at him. "What, then? Even Rachel thinks—"

He exhaled sharply. "He'd probably kill me for saying this, but if you want to know the truth, I think he's afraid."

She gave a snort of laughter. "Yeah, right. This is the ex-stuntman. The man who shot down a helicopter with a deer rifle. And…why would he be afraid of meeting his own grand-daughters?"

He was silent as they walked a few steps more. She watched a smile come and go. "Sam's…a hard man to under-stand, I'll grant you. He's probably the smartest, bravest man I've ever known, except for one thing. And that's relationships. Particularly with people he really cares about. People closest to him. Like family. He…well, let's just say he doesn't have all that great a track record in that department."

"He said that," Abby said. "In the letter."

Sage nodded. "He believes he's got one last chance, and that's with you—his four granddaughters. He doesn't want to mess this up, like he did with his wives and kids. That's what he's afraid of."

Abby's heart felt like a lump of lead. *Too late,* a voice in her head intoned, like a bell tolling someone's death. *Too late… Too late…*

"You said you needed to talk to him," she blurted out, touching his arm, tense with urgency. "I heard you—in the message you left. I need to talk to him, too. If you're going to see him, please—can I come with you?"

He paused and turned to her, and the look on his face stopped her breath. He touched her cheek. "It's you I need to talk to him about. Understand? You. Me. This. Whatever *this* is, between us."

She nodded, but couldn't speak. Her eyes, gazing back at him, began to burn and fill with tears. The kiss…the memory of it…was suddenly there between them, huge and inescapable, as if it were happening all over again, right then, at that moment. She licked her lips…saw his throat move as he swallowed.

He took a breath…looked away as he let it out in a ragged gust. "I don't know how he'll feel…you being his granddaughter. The thing is, Sam raised me. He's the closest thing to a father I've got." His voice sounded hoarse and raw. "I know he respects me—maybe even loves me. I know I love and respect him too much to go behind his back. So, I need to talk to him. Okay?"

All she could do was stare at him, wanting desperately to tell him what was in her heart. Terrified of what he would think of her if she did. *You know what? It's all right, Sage. And here's the irony. It's all right because once I tell him I'm not his granddaughter, he won't care.*

But the question is, will you still want me, once you know the truth about me? Once you know what a fraud I am?

"I really need to talk to him, too," she whispered. "To Sam. My grandfather. Please?"

He let his hand slip down to cradle the side of her neck, and his thumb traced the line of her jaw. His smile was tender. "Sunny, it's a long ride, even for me. Remember how stiff you were yesterday, after our short little jaunt? And, there's a storm coming in, too. Supposed to turn a lot colder." His lips brushed hers, and she caught a hopeful breath. "It's best you stay here…keep an eye on things for me. I'll try and convince him to come back with me. Maybe. I hope." His smile flashed, and then he left her.

She watched him slip through the gate and stride across the meadow, and the horses come trotting out to meet him. She watched him slip the feedbag over Diamond's nose and lead him back to the barn while the other horses followed just to keep him company. She stood by, miserably hugging herself, and watched while he saddled and bridled Diamond, then took a heavy denim jacket lined with sheepskin from the tack room and tied it onto the back of the saddle. Silently, she watched him take a handful of granola bars and a bottle of water from the cold room and tuck them into a leather pouch on the back of the saddle. And all the while, the aching knot inside her chest grew bigger and heavier.

Sage called to Freckles, and when the dog came, wriggling with eagerness, he snapped a small chain, the other end of which encircled one of the barn's big wooden support columns, to his collar. The dog sat on his haunches and whined softly, and his disappointment seemed to echo the heaviness in Abby's own heart.

"Stay, Freckles…good boy," Sage said, patting the dog's head. And then, to Abby, "You can let him loose in a little while, after I leave. This is just so he won't try to follow me."

She nodded but didn't try to speak. He gazed at her for a long moment, his eyes somber and searching. She thought he would kiss her again…and oh, how desperately she wanted him to, knowing it would probably be the last time he ever would.

But he didn't. Instead, he turned, gathered up Diamond's reins and led him through the barn door and out into the sunshine and a rising wind. He lifted himself effortlessly into the saddle, gave her one last wave and rode away at an easy trot, only breaking into a lope when they reached the open meadow.

Abby watched horse and rider until they vanished from sight behind the corrals, and she had seen that they were heading up the meadow toward the rocks where she'd found Sage playing his flute. Then she moved quickly and decisively, taking down a feedbag from its hook and heading for the meadow where the horses still dawdled, disappointed at being left behind. They came to her eagerly, now, since she was not only no longer a stranger, but also associated with that bag of tasty grain. Imitating Sage, she made sure all the horses got a handful before she singled out Morning Glory and somehow managed to get the bag over her nose and the straps over her ears.

As she was leading the mare back to the barn, the magnitude of what she was doing, the enormity of the risk she was taking, hit her like a buffeting wind. So did the adrenaline. Her limbs felt jerky and awkward, her body felt filled to bursting with energy. It occurred to her that it was like being backstage with the rest of the chorus line, waiting for the curtain to go up on opening night. *Pure terror. Pure excitement.* Her heart beating so fast she could barely breathe, and her legs so shaky she wondered how they could hold her weight.

But…on each of those opening nights, the curtain did go up, the show did go on. Abby did not stop breathing, and her legs did not fail her.

I'll be okay. I can do this.

In spite of fingers that didn't seem to do what they were told, she saddled and bridled Morning Glory exactly as Sage had taught her, while one of the barn cats wound itself around her legs and Freckles hungrily watched her every move. Imitating Sage's preparations, she looked in the tack room for a jacket, found a poncho made of some sort of thick woven material that appeared to be wool and looked as if it would be both warm and itchy, which she tied to the back of the saddle. She took the last of the granola bars from the cold room and broke two into a small milk pan, which she put beside Freckles along with a can of water. He whined when she knelt to hug him, looking as worried as it was possible for such a perpetually happy dog to look.

"You be a good boy," she said, burying her face in his neck ruff. "Okay? I'm sorry, but you have to stay here. Sorry…I'm really sorry…"

She rose quickly, dashed moisture from her cheek and took hold of Morning Glory's bridle. As Sage had done, she led the horse out of the barn before hoisting herself into the saddle. Muscles she'd abused the day before protested, but she was used to forcing muscles to do things they'd rather not, accustomed to working through pain and stiffness. After a few bends and stretches, she muttered between gritted teeth,

"Okay, Morning Glory, let's do this. Let's go find your buddy, Diamond."

She made a clicking sound with her mouth like the one she'd heard Sage use when he wanted his horse to *go*. Or go *faster*. She was beyond pleased when her horse seemed to understand what that meant, breaking first into a trot—which Abby bore stoically, though she winced with every jolt—and then, when they reached the meadow, into that nice easy lope. *Much better*.

She couldn't see Sage anywhere in the meadow, but she'd watched and knew which way he'd gone, and after all, how many trails could there be leading up into these mountains? She was sure she'd be able to figure out where to go when the time came.

Her nervousness—okay, *fear*—hadn't completely dissipated; it did occur to her that what she was doing might be foolhardy. A bit. Maybe. But she felt driven by a fear that was so much greater, so much more compelling, it made riding off alone into an alien landscape of towering mountains and granite cliffs seem no more daunting than taking a New York subway ride. The fear that kept her riding on into a vast unknown, a fear so great it chilled her to her very soul, was that her happiness had just ridden off into those mountains without her, and the only hope she had of keeping that happiness from riding right on out of her life forever, was Sam Malone.

If Sam Malone was up there in those mountains, then she was going to find him.

The last thing in the world he'd expected was that she'd try to follow him.

Because it was the last thing he expected, he ignored his horse's warnings—he, who prided himself on being so well-tuned to his horses, in understanding the secret languages of animals. In his own defense, he could argue he might have been distracted by the realization he was falling in love with an heiress—his boss and mentor's heiress, on top of it. But that didn't excuse his dismissal of his horse's behavior as just uneasiness about the incoming storm. When Diamond kept whinnying and wanting to look back down the trail, he should have known better.

He *did* know better. Horses whinnied for only one reason he could think of. They may whicker and snort and chuckle and squeal for any number of reasons, but a whinny, that from-the-belly sound people most associate with horses, is a call out to another horse in the vicinity. And he missed it.

But all those recriminations were in hindsight. As he rode through the early part of the day his mind was occupied with many things: the changing weather, the work he'd left behind, the man he was going to find, the state of the trail—which was much better than he'd expected considering it was the first time he'd been over it since the previous fall. Sam used the trail fairly regularly, of course, which would explain why it was relatively clear of debris and easy to follow.

He thought a lot about Sunny Wells, too, although he tried his best not to. When *she* entered his mind, she brought emotional turmoil with her, and he couldn't make himself think rationally. Warnings kept firing off like rockets inside his head: *It's the first time since Heather...you barely know this woman...she's another city girl...she's not for you...when will you learn?* And were swallowed up in the general tumult, like so many fireworks in a vast thunderstorm.

There were no words for the way she made him feel when he was with her, when he thought about her. There was lust, sure. He wanted her—what man wouldn't? But what about the other ways she came into his mind? The look on her face the first time she petted a cow. The sound of her laughter when she galloped her horse in the meadow. The gentleness of her hands as they stroked a calf's head. The vulnerable look of her nape as she was milking. The way she closed her eyes tightly as if in ecstasy when she hugged his dog. The way she made him smile, and at the same time made his throat ache. How could he explain that away as something as simple as sex?

A line from a song popped into his head. "Who can explain it, who can tell you why?" He thought it was from a Broadway musical but he couldn't be sure. Sunny would know.

Hopeless—that's what he was. Knowing it was futile, he tried again to crowd thoughts of the woman out of his head by concentrating on the trail, the terrain and the weather.

Abby found the trail without any trouble. She was pretty sure it was the right one, because she could see the tracks of a horse's hooves here and there where they'd torn up the grass newly sprouting from the soft, moist earth. *Look at me,* she thought, feeling most pleased with herself. *New York City girl, tracking a man through the wilderness. Who knew?*

After leaving the meadow, the trail climbed steadily, sometimes following the creek through rocky canyons, sometimes angling across steep mountainsides with granite walls on one side and bottomless chasms on the other, over saddleback ridges and through fragrant pine forests. She could feel the air growing colder, and snow lay in thick blankets on protected north-facing slopes. The wind blew in fitful gusts, and the sun came and went behind clumps of ominous-looking clouds.

The first time Morning Glory whinnied, it startled Abby so that she nearly toppled out of the saddle. What a sound it was, so unbelievably loud, from so close up, and it shook the horse's whole body. To Abby it felt like sitting on top of an earthquake.

"Whoa, what was *that?*" she said aloud, thinking it was okay to clutch the saddle horn, since Sage wasn't there to see.

As if in reply, Morning Glory whinnied again. And this time in the following silence, carried, perhaps, by a gust of wind, she heard, from far, far away, an answering whinny.

A smile burst across her face, and her heartbeat quickened. It was Diamond—it had to be. Sage was out there, somewhere up ahead. The thought filled her with warmth, but also with twinges of fear. *Does he know I'm here? Can he hear Morning Glory, the way I hear Diamond? What will he do when*

I catch up with him? Will he be angry? He won't—he can't make me go back!

He wouldn't make her go back, would he, when she had already come so far? Especially with the storm coming. If he was concerned about her safety, she reasoned, it would make more sense to keep her with him than to send her back down the mountain alone. Wouldn't it?

She was pretty sure she was right, but just to be safe, decided she wouldn't catch up with Sage until she absolutely had to. Preferably after they'd arrived at their destination.

To that end she began to dawdle a little, even getting off the horse to walk around and stretch a couple of times, eat a granola bar, drink some water…yes, and to relieve herself behind a friendly looking pine tree. It was during the latter process that she discovered some angry-looking patches on the inner sides of her knees, where the friction from the saddle and her jeans seemed to have rubbed off most of the skin. The sores *hurt,* too, but not having a first-aid kit on hand, there wasn't much she could do besides ignore them. It wouldn't be the first time she'd soldiered on through excruciating pain; she'd once danced an entire Saturday matinee with bleeding blisters.

The trail grew steeper, the clouds thicker, the wind colder. The woods were dense, the trail thick with pine needles and hard to see in some places. Abby untied the poncho from the saddle and put it on, and although it did itch and smelled strongly of animals, at least it helped to cut the wind. The moan of the wind in the pines seemed the loneliest sound in the world.

The truth was, Abby was tired and sore and cold, and as much as she hated to admit it, was beginning to wish she'd listened to Sage when he'd told her the trip was too much for her.

Too bad Sage hadn't known the surest way to get Abby to do something was to tell her she couldn't.

Just when she was beginning to feel like Hansel and Gretel

in the witch's forest, the trees began to thin, and she could see light—a clearing up ahead. Her heart gave a leap when she emerged onto a plateau and a lovely green meadow patchy with snow and lush with wildflowers that stretched away toward a dark bank of pines on the far side. Yet any hope that she might have reached her destination faded as she shaded her eyes and squinted into the distance, searching the meadow and the pine-clad slopes that surrounded it for any signs of human habitation.

But there was nothing here—no cabin or corrals, and no red-brown horse and dark-haired rider. Nothing but wind-rippled grass and overhead a sky full of boiling blue-black clouds. She seemed to be utterly alone in that vast wilderness.

She remembered Sage telling her that Sam Malone had a cabin in *one of the high meadows.* All she could do now was push on and hope she found the right meadow before the sky opened up. When it did, she had a feeling it wasn't going to be rain that fell out of it. She was from places where it snowed *a lot.* She knew about snow. And right now, the air looked like, felt like, smelled like *snow.*

Oh, God, she thought, *what have I done? Sage is going to kill me. And Sam...*

She didn't want to think about Sam Malone. The man had already lost his real granddaughter, and now it looked like he might lose the fake one, too. Which was almost ironic enough to be funny, in a twisted sort of way.

She clicked her tongue and urged Morning Glory into the meadow. When they were out in the open, the mare quickened her gait without instruction from Abby. Her ears were pointed straight ahead, and her body quaked and shuddered as she gave a gusty whinny.

Abby leaned over and patted the mare's neck. "What is it, girl? What do you hear...or smell? Are they out there?" *Or is it something else—like...a bear or a mountain lion, for instance?*

The mare broke into a lope, and Abby didn't stop her

though even that gentle motion made her sore places burn like fire. They were halfway across the meadow when she heard the first boom of thunder.

Abby was from places where it thunderstormed a lot, too. She knew about thunder. And lightning. And she knew the last place anyone would want to be when there was thunder and lightning about was on a boat in the middle of a lake.

Or on a horse in the middle of a meadow.

She leaned low over Morning Glory's neck and kicked her heels against the mare's sides, then hung on for dear life as they raced at full gallop, making for the shelter of the trees.

The snow didn't surprise Sage, or particularly trouble him, either. It wasn't unusual for it to snow at this altitude, even this late in the spring, and these spring storms didn't usually last long—just blew in and out pretty quickly and didn't drop a whole lot of moisture. Sam's cabin was snug and warm, and he had supplies brought in regularly by chopper, so he'd be okay overnight. Tomorrow the storm would have cleared out and headed on east. He shouldn't have any problem getting down the mountain.

He was beginning to be a little bit concerned about Diamond, though. The crazy horse had started acting up again, shaking his head and dancing around and whinnying. It seemed pretty early for him to be saying hello to Sam's paint horse, clear over the hill in the next meadow, although he supposed it was possible. Horses had keener senses than humans did. Still…he couldn't help but wonder if it might be something else bothering Diamond. This time of year a bear could be a real threat, just coming out of hibernation, particularly if she had a couple of cubs with her, born in her den over the winter. Then there was the possibility of a mountain lion. *Tuugakut.* The word made him smile, thinking of Sunny's crazy, wild kitty cat.

Thoughts of Sunny warmed him as he and Diamond plodded on through the thickening snowfall. He turned up the collar of his sheepskin-lined coat, enjoying the beauty of the snow as it sifted through the pines and settled like lace onto the carpet of needles. The snow and thickness of the cloud cover had brought an early twilight. The wind had dropped and the stillness was profound, making him think of churches...

And then it wasn't still. He could hear something moving through the trees, something big, by the sound of it. It was behind him somewhere, following him. Coming fast.

Diamond whickered softly as Sage guided him off the trail, into a copse of young trees. "Easy, boy...that's it. Quiet, now." He patted the horse's neck, then settled down to watch...and wait.

Chapter 10

Abby wasn't sure exactly when the realization came to her that she was no longer in control of her horse—if she ever had been. They reached the trees, but Morning Glory's speed didn't slacken, not even when Abby pulled on the reins the way Sage had taught her. When she tried that, it felt a little like trying to stop a moving car by hanging on to a rope and digging her heels into the ground.

Her wild ride through the forest continued without slackening, and her only hope of keeping herself from being swept out of the saddle or decapitated by a tree branch, or left behind in a snowdrift during one of the horse's lightning-quick zigzags, was to crouch down in the saddle and hold on for dear life.

It was one of the most terrifying experiences of her life, and she was pretty sure it wasn't going to end well for her.

But then, miraculously, she felt the presence of something huge and powerful moving alongside her, matching her horse stride for stride. She heard the thunder of hoof beats, the creak of saddle leather, the heavy breathing of another hard-working animal. And she heard a voice—Sage's voice—speaking in a deep, low croon.

"Whoa, girl…easy, girl…whoa, now…"

Morning Glory's headlong charge slowed, then bumped to a prancing, panting stop, with Sage's hand firmly holding her bridle.

Abby lifted her head and slowly straightened up in the saddle. She was shaking violently, from cold, from shock, from fear. She turned her head to look at Sage, dreading his anger. But he was silent, the expression on his face lost in shadows. He seemed very big and imposing on his tall red horse, with his sheepskin collar turned up and snow sifting over his dark hair and broad shoulders. He seemed…not dangerous, but like a rock, a haven, like safety and shelter.

"I'm…s-s-sorry—" she croaked, but her words came stuttered and broken.

Sage leaned over and took the reins from her stiff fingers. "Hold on," was all he said.

Abby was much too cold and contrite to do anything but obey. Morning Glory, too, seemed relieved to have someone take charge, and trotted docilely at Diamond's side as Sage led her back to the trail.

The trail climbed steadily through thick pine forest. Wind whistled in the high branches, and the snow came in fitful bursts, sometimes sifting down in picture-book flakes, sometimes swirling so thick it was hard to see even a few feet ahead. Crouched miserably under her stiff, scratchy poncho, Abby wondered how long it would be before she got too cold to feel her grip on the saddle horn. How long before hypothermia took over, and she simply toppled out of the saddle?

Just when she thought she couldn't possibly stand much more, she noticed the trail was no longer climbing, that they were moving rapidly down a slope, and the trees were fewer and farther apart. Then…the snow lifted and she saw the dark shapes of buildings up ahead, on the far side of a clearing that

sloped sharply down to a wide-open meadow. She uttered a
joyful little cry and brushed tears of relief and thanksgiving
from her numb cheeks. At almost the same moment, both
horses sent up whinnies of greeting, and from somewhere up
ahead the reply came back, shrill and clear as a bugle call.

Abby straightened in the saddle and said, "Is that—"

Sage nodded. "Sam's place. That'll be Sam's horse, Paint,"
he added as the not-so-distant whinny came again. "You can
go on ahead to the cabin."

Go to the cabin....Sam's cabin...meet Sam...all alone?

Abby's heart was pounding, and she no longer felt the cold.
She sniffed and brushed her nose with the back of her hand.
"What are you going to do?"

"I'll see to the horses. You need to go in and get warm."

She shook her head. "So do you. I'll help you." Her chat-
tering teeth made it hard to get the words out.

Sage looked at her but didn't say anything.

A high fence made of logs loomed ahead. He dismounted
and opened a gate, then led both horses through and closed
and chained the gate behind them. A pinto horse came trotting
out to meet them, head high, whickering excited greetings.
Sage took a moment to stroke the pinto's neck and scratch
under his jaw, then, while the pinto trotted happy circles
around them, he led Diamond and Morning Glory across the
corral to a large three-sided shelter, also made of logs. Inside
the shelter was a hay-filled manger, and behind that, accessible through a wide wooden gate, Abby saw what appeared
to be a storage area, with several bales of hay, sacks of some
kind of feed, and log racks for saddles. An assortment of tools,
ropes and bridles hung on the wall.

Sage looped Diamond's reins over the manger and unbuck-
led his cinch. He pulled the saddle off, hefted it once and
started through the gate with it. Then he paused, looked at
Abby and said, "You can get off, now."

She nodded. And didn't move. "I don't know if I can."

For a long moment he looked at her, his eyes dark, his

expression unreadable. Then he nodded, said, "Hang on a minute," and pushed through the gate with the heavy saddle in his arms.

Abby closed her eyes, feeling on the verge of tears. The thought of being lifted off her horse like a baby was beyond humiliating. *I did this to myself. I can't—I won't—let it defeat me. I will carry my own weight if it kills me.*

Clenching her teeth tightly together and summoning all her willpower, she gripped the saddle horn, lifted her leg over the back of the seat and slid down the side of the horse until her feet touched the ground. She paused there for a few moments, leaning against Morning Glory's neck, trying not to make a sound.

Oh, God, I hurt. She hurt in so many places and in so many ways, she couldn't tell where one sore place left off and another began.

Move, damn it. You can do this. Breathing through her nose, lips pressed together, she took a step back, lifted the stirrup and folded it back over the saddle. Then, though her fingers were stiff and cold and didn't seem to do what they were told, she began clumsily to unbuckle the cinch.

"Here," Sage said. "Let me get that."

"I can do it. I can do this, damn it."

His hands covered hers, gently moved them aside. His breath was warm on her cheek, and his body strong and solid against her back. She turned blindly, tipped forward, lifted her arms around his neck and buried her face in the damp sheepskin collar of his jacket. It felt like razor blades on her icy cheeks.

"I'm sorry," she mumbled. "I'm so sorry. You were right. I'm an id…id…idiot."

"You're not an idiot," he said with gravel in his voice. He thought about it while he stroked her hair. "Probably just ignorant. And too damn brave for your own good."

She gave a tiny sobbing squeak of a laugh and lifted her head from his shoulder, though her eyes crossed when they tried to meet his. He took hold of her chin and tipped it so that he could look at her. Her eyes were misty and soft, and her cheeks and the tip of her nose were rosy pink. Tiny drops of moisture clung to her lashes and glistened like diamond dust.

He sucked in a breath and whispered, "What am I gonna do with you?"

The thing was, he didn't know how to *feel*. It seemed to him he ought to feel angry with her for scaring him half to death, at least. That he ought to think less of her for doing something so dumb, stupid, foolhardy, yes, and *idiotic,* that could very well have gotten her killed, and brought the wrath of Sam Malone down on *his* head. He thought he might be forgiven for feeling profound relief and gladness that she was okay, even for feeling shaken to his toes with fear of what might have, could have happened to her. But what was this soft, mushy, aching goofy *tenderness* that seemed to have overtaken all those other feelings and wiped them out of his mind? What was it making him feel like he wanted to wrap her up and protect her and take care of her and make sure she never got hurt or in danger or wanted for anything, ever again? What was he supposed to do with feelings like that?

He didn't know. So he did what seemed to him then the only thing he could do. He kissed her.

Her lips were cold, but they warmed quickly under his, a moist and heady mixture of cold and warm more potent than wine. He couldn't get enough of it.

Except…it occurred to him then, that, although she was definitely kissing him back, that was about the only thing her body was doing on its own. Her weight sagged against him and her head had fallen back on his arm as if her neck had lost the ability to support it. Her hands lay limp on his chest, her fingers curled like wilting flower petals. He drew back and looked down at her. Her eyes gazed back at him, sleepy and unfocused.

Damn, he thought. *Hypothermia. And here I am, kissing her. Probably the last thing she needs.*

He stroked her wet hair back from her forehead. "Sunny—wake up. Look at me."

Her eyes slowly uncrossed as they struggled to focus beyond the tip of her nose. "I'm awake...don't be silly. You were kissing me." Her lips widened in a sleepy smile. "Nice. Do it some 'ore..."

"I'd like to," he said grimly. "Believe me." Damn. He didn't know what to do first. She needed warming up, and quickly. But there were the horses. He couldn't turn them out in the cold, hot and sweaty like they were. "Right now I've got to get you warm. And the horses—"

"I'm helping." Her face took on a stubborn look. She tried to turn back to the horse and swayed. He steadied her, and she said, "Oops," and giggled. "I feel a little dizzy."

"Yeah. You probably have hypothermia. You need to get out of your wet clothes. What's this thing you're wearing?"

"I don't know..." She looked down at her shoulder and plucked at the wool poncho. She sniffed and made a face. "It smells funny."

"Um, hmm—wet wool. Or wet dog—it's possible Freckles has used that thing for a blanket. Here—arms up." She obeyed, more or less, and he managed to get the sodden poncho over her head. She gave a little gasp when the cold air hit her, and shivered violently.

Moving as quickly as he could, he took off his jacket and wrapped her in it, then walked her into the back of the shed and sat her down on a hay bale. Leaving her there looking hunched and miserable as a lost sparrow, he went back and finished unsaddling Morning Glory. He used the poncho to rub down the two horses as best he could, threw a couple of flakes of oat hay into the manger, and went back to get Sunny. She'd gotten her arms into the sleeves of his jacket but was still shivering in waves. Which he thought might actually be a good thing—her body's way of warming itself. At least when she looked at him now, her eyes seemed to focus.

"I'm sorry," she mumbled between those violent shudders. "Really. It was really stupid."

"Forget it," he growled. He took hold of her arm and lifted it, lowered his shoulder under it and hoisted her to her feet. "Can you walk?"

She threw him a look of pure misery, but sniffed and then nodded. He put his arm around her waist and snugged her close to him, and they slipped past the horses, now contentedly chomping on hay as wisps of steam rose from their backs.

The snow had stopped, but the wind had picked up. It punched through Sage's shirt like daggers, making the gentle uphill climb across open ground to Sam's cabin seem more like half a mile than the hundred yards or so he knew it was.

Later, he thought it might have been because he was so damn cold—or worried about getting Sunny to a warm place, maybe?—that he didn't notice there wasn't any smoke coming from the chimney, or light showing in the windows. It didn't occur to him until he was stomping his way across the porch, making enough noise to raise the dead, to wonder where Sam was and why he hadn't come to see what all the ruckus was.

Cold settled into his belly that had nothing to do with the weather.

It was his worst fear. Sam Malone was an old man— nobody, probably not even Sam, knew exactly how old, but most likely getting pretty near a hundred. One of these days, Sage had always figured, he'd come up here and find nothing but Sam's dead body. This looked like it might be that day.

He turned the knob on the heavy plank door—which Sam naturally would never bother to lock—and kicked it open. Inside, the cabin was all shadows, and not much warmer than it was outside. And there was something else: a peculiar metallic smell that made Sage's belly clench with dread. He knew what blood smelled like.

"There's no one here," Abby said. Disappointment drained

her of her last ounce of strength, and she sank heavily onto a wooden chair beside a small table made of pine planks.

Sage didn't answer. In the half-dark cabin, he moved like a shadow himself, closing the door, first, shutting out that cold, howling wind, then turning on the battery-powered lantern that sat on the table near Abby's elbow. He picked it up and held it high, splashing weird shadows across the pine walls as he slowly turned, lighting up every corner of that single room. Illuminating first the old-fashioned iron bed against the wall to the left, neatly made and topped with what looked like a down comforter, and next to it a small dresser with a smoky mirror hanging above it; the stone fireplace—dark and cold, now—opposite the door, and the chair made of lashed-together logs and thick canvas cushions that sat in front of it; the ornate cast-iron cookstove against the wall to the right, and next to it a porcelain sink with an old-fashioned hand pump. There were only two windows in the cabin, one on each side of the door, looking out over the meadow. Under the one nearest the bed was a small writing desk and chair. Under the other one was the table where Abby sat, occupying one of two small chairs. There were two large Navajo rugs on the floor, and some old black-and-white photographs in frames on the walls. A couple of hooks beside the door held a long black Western-style overcoat and a black cowboy hat. Everything seemed very neat and clean, although it was hard to tell for sure in the dim and wavering light.

Having evidently satisfied himself that the cabin was indeed—except for themselves—unoccupied, Sage let out a gusty breath and carried the lantern over to the sink. Holding the lantern in one hand, he squatted on his heels and seemed to study the floor for a moment. Then he picked up something from the floor and rose with it in his hand.

Abby gave a sharp gasp. Sage glanced at her as he dropped the large hunting knife into the sink. And she saw then that the sink and the floor in front of it were stained with some-thing dark, something that still glinted red when the lantern light moved across it. "Is that...*blood?*" she asked in a horrified whisper.

Sage nodded. "Yeah," he said absently, drawing the word out as he continued to move the lantern around, obviously looking for something. He let out a breath that wasn't quite steady and threw her a troubled look as he set the lantern back on the table.

"Is it—" she whispered, and stopped for lack of breath. Her chest felt tight, and there was a cold knot in her stomach.

"Don't," he said quietly, holding up a hand. "I know what you're thinking, and for a minute I..." He took another deep breath. "Let's just think this through. First, there's quite a bit of blood, but not a *huge* amount. Okay? And it's just here— no blood trail leading outside, no arterial spray—"

She laughed a little. "You sound like a cop."

His smile was brief and crooked. "Watched too many television police procedurals, I guess. So anyway, what I'm thinking is, Sam must have cut himself pretty badly, not badly enough to bleed out, but badly enough that he called for his chopper to pick him up and take him to get medical treatment."

"How could he do that?"

"Sam has a satellite phone. Which I don't see around here anywhere. Which means he must have taken it with him. And that's too bad, because it means we can't call out to find out where he is and how badly he's injured. Or, to let anybody know where you are, either."

Abby clamped a hand over her mouth and closed her eyes. *Oh, God.* "I didn't tell anyone I was leaving. What must your mother be thinking?"

"She'll be thinking you're with me. Although," Sage added dryly, remembering the worried look Josie had given him at breakfast that morning, "I'm not sure she'd find that thought reassuring." He dredged up a smile to give her and touched a lock of wet hair away from her cheek. "There's nothing we can do but wait for morning, so we might as well get comfortable. Okay?"

He hoped for a smile back, but had to settle for a nod. She looked cold and miserable and scared.

He was pleased to discover the wood box full, and a bucket of kindling set close by the hearth along with a cast-iron pot filled with wooden matches. He got a fire going, then went to rummage through Sam's chest of drawers to find some dry clothes. The best he could come up with was a couple of sets of thermal-knit long johns—men's, naturally—and a couple of flannel shirts and some heavy work socks.

When he laid the pile of folded clothes on the table beside Sunny, she lifted her drooping head and gazed at him with tear-shimmered eyes.

"They're not pretty, but they're warm," he said gently, knowing the tears were just general exhaustion and misery.

She sniffed, and nodded, and if possible, looked even more miserable.

"What—" he began, but she closed her eyes, drew a shuddering breath and whispered, "Is there...um...someplace I can go to the bathroom?"

Oh, Lord. He scrubbed a hand over his hair and swore under his breath. "Uh...yeah. There's an outhouse. It's, uh... outside."

The last thing she needed was to go back into that cold wind, but he didn't see how it could be avoided. She didn't, either, evidently, because she set her lips in a determined line and pushed herself to her feet.

"Point me in the right direction," she said staunchly, swaying a little.

"Uh-uh," he said, and reached for Sam's big old overcoat, the one he'd saved from his days in the Western movie business. "I'll take you."

She looked like she might argue with him but thought better of it. He walked her through the howling wind to the outhouse and waited while she took care of business, then sent her on back to the cabin while he made use of the facilities, such as they were. When he got back to the cabin he found her shivering in front of the fireplace, rubbing her hands and muttering to herself.

He went to her and put his hands on her shoulders and said, "What?" softly in her ear.

"I said, I can't believe he lives like this. Sam Malone. He's a billionaire, right?"

"Hmm…*eccentric* billionaire—don't forget that part. He doesn't always live like this—just when he wants to escape from the world."

"From us. Me. His family."

He didn't answer, but reached his arms around her and unbuttoned his jacket and slipped it off her shoulders. He tossed it onto Sam's homemade easy chair, then opened up both sides of the big old overcoat and drew her inside, snug up against him. She gave a happy little chuckle when he wrapped the overcoat and his arms around her.

"I don't know if I'll ever be warm again," she whispered unevenly.

"You will be," he said with gravel in his voice, then cleared his throat and growled, "I'll personally guarantee it."

She turned her head against his shoulder, and he kissed her temple. Her skin was damp and chilled, but he could feel her pulse beating, steady and strong, and inside the overcoat, her body's heat blended with his. He imagined the flesh beneath the damp clothing growing warm and pink with desire….

"You need something warm in your stomach," he said, murmuring the words against the racing pulse in her neck. "I'm going to fix us something. And while I'm doing that… you're going to go over there and change into those dry clothes. Okay?" He waited for her nod, then released her. With great reluctance. His body felt cold and raw wherever she'd touched him.

"I'm going to keep my back turned," he said as he returned

Sam's overcoat to its nail, striving for a light touch. "And I promise not to look."

I wouldn't mind if you did, Abby thought, but didn't say. And the realization, the truth of it, surprised her. Like most show business people, she wasn't terribly modest—costume changes in close and crowded quarters cured that in a hurry—but she wasn't an exhibitionist, either, especially in intimate circumstances. And yet she somehow knew she would have no hesitation or reservation about showing herself to Sage. How she knew was a mystery to her, but she had absolutely no doubt that she would always be safe with him.

Safe. It was that thought rather than the act of stripping naked in the cold cabin that made her feel joyously shivery all through her body, even deep, deep inside.

Sage smiled to himself as he got the cookstove fired up and searched Sam's cupboards to find a can of hearty beef stew to warm for their supper. He smiled, thinking of the woman dressing in the room behind him, close enough he could hear her breathing. It was a revelation to him that he could think of her, even imagine her body naked and vulnerable, and not be tempted to violate her privacy, not with the smallest, quickest of glances.

He smiled, because it was tenderness, not lust, that filled his heart when he imagined her peeling off her wet shirt and bra, imagined her breasts rising and falling with her breathing...her breasts round and hard, nipples budded with cold. Oh, he wanted her, too, and his body ached with that wanting. And that she was his for the taking he knew in the depths of his being. That knowledge made him smile, too, with pride because he was capable of restraint, of tenderness, of waiting. And because he was learning that this was the difference between getting hot and sweaty with someone in the darkness in the backseat of a car, and something that would stir his very soul, even in the quiet light of morning, and through all the years of babies crying and illnesses and heartaches and growing old.

He smiled because this was love, and because he was proud and humbled that he knew the difference.

"Your turn," she said, coming silently behind him in her stocking feet. He turned to smile at her. She was rolling the sleeves of Sam's flannel shirt to her elbows, and her unbraided hair hung past her shoulders and down her back in a wavy tangle. She looked impossibly young and incredibly alluring, and for an instant he thought he saw her through a haze of memories…memories of things that hadn't happened yet. Memories of countless moments just like this one, in which the passing years had somehow left both her allure and his feelings for her forever untouched…forever unchanged.

"It's okay," he said, "I'll change later. I didn't get as wet as you did. And…I think this is hot…"

She'd wanted to come quietly behind him and slip her arms around his waist…lay her cheek on his shoulder. It had seemed a natural and easy thing to do. Now, though, facing him and his incredible beauty, his quiet dignity and supreme self-assurance, she felt just a little intimidated—enough, anyway, that she couldn't bring herself to simply walk uninvited into his arms. Plus, his hands were full. He held a large tin cup in each hand, and the cups were filled with something that gave off steam and a delicious aroma.

Her stomach rumbled, and he heard it. He was smiling as he set the cups on the table and pulled out one of the chairs and held it for her.

"Oh, my God, that smells amazing," she said, sliding into the chair and leaning forward to inhale the rich, fragrant steam. She picked up the spoon lying on the table and peered into the cup. "What is it?" In the dim light of the single lantern and the flickering fire it was impossible to identify the cup's contents.

"Stew," said Sage. He had taken the chair across from her and was blowing on a large spoonful to cool it before popping it into his mouth.

Abby sighed, closed her eyes and took a bite. She made happy little humming noises, then laughed.

"What's funny?" Sage asked.

"Sun—uh, my roommate used to say…" Tears sprang into her eyes, but she smiled through them and took another bite. "You know the food's good when you have to sing to it."

"That's true." His eyes gazed into hers, and—it might have been the reflection of the lantern, or the firelight—she thought it was the first time she'd seen them smile.

She ate every bite of the stew. Although his own hunger had been well satisfied, Sage's mouth watered as he watched her run her finger around the inside of the tin cup then pop it in her mouth and lick off the gravy. Then she sat back and gazed sorrowfully at the empty cup and sighed.

"I've just eaten meat, haven't I?"

He quelled an impulse to laugh and said gently, "Yup. But you needed it."

She heaved another sigh. "I keep seeing those beautiful baby calves…"

Her sadness made his own heart ache. He pushed aside the empty cups and reached across the table to take her hands. "I can't speak for them all, but I know many of my people— the Native American tribes—have a special prayer they say when they have to kill an animal for food. We say thank you to our brother for giving his life so that we can live. It is the natural way of things, you know. We can't live on grass, so we honor our brothers, the deer and the cattle and sheep and so on, for turning the grass into meat for our sake. Does that help you to not feel so bad?"

She nodded…then yawned. Her eyes popped open and she belatedly put her hand over her mouth and murmured, "Oh, my goodness—I'm sorry."

"Don't be. Perfectly natural, under the circumstances." He shoved back his chair and gathered up the cups and spoons and put them in the sink. "Survival instincts, Sunshine. You're warm, you're dry, and your belly's full. Next comes rest. You take the bed. The chair cushions will do for me."

Trying not to wince, Abby rose stiffly to her feet. Bracing herself with one hand on the table top—she hadn't realized how exhausted she was, so exhausted everything felt weak and shaky—she faced Sage and said, "I think there's only one comforter."

"I'll keep the fire going."

"That's just ridiculous." They were speaking softly across a narrow chasm of golden light and dancing shadows. Tiredness sang in her head like the whine of hungry insects. "It's ridiculous," she repeated. "We share the bed, or I'm not taking it, either."

"Now who's being ridiculous?" He looked mildly amused. She planted one hand on her hip, raised her eyebrows and waited. The moment stretched…the air between them grew dense and viscous. Sage laughed softly. "Okay, you're right. We can share the bed." He reached for her, held her gently by the arms and leaned to brush her temple with his lips. It felt so incredibly sweet her breath caught and held; she went utterly still, in awe of him. "You go get in…I'm going to change my clothes. Okay?"

She shook herself, breathing again, and said grudgingly, "Okay…" She took a few hobbling steps before turning back to add, "You'd better come to bed, too, because if you don't, I'm coming to get you. Don't think I won't."

His laughter followed her as she limped to the iron bedstead, and warmed her long after she'd moved beyond reach of the fire's heat.

Shivering now not with cold but a strange low-voltage excitement, Abby lifted the comforter and laid her aching body on the bed. The deep feather mattress instantly enveloped her in softness and warmth, but she was incapable of relaxing. Stiff and shaky, she propped herself on her elbows and watched through half-closed eyes as Sage undressed before the fire.

Well, he hadn't told her not to, had he?

Men's bodies held no mystery for her; she'd seen dozens, if not hundreds of dancers in costumes that left little or nothing to the imagination. But this was different. This was Sage. Even fully clothed he'd captivated and fascinated her. She'd seen him shirtless before, that day in the meadow, but that, too, was different. A man working bare-chested in the sun was one thing; a man undressing by firelight in the intimacy of a one-room cabin was...another.

Even silhouetted by the firelight, she could see the lower half of his body was several shades lighter in color than the top half. And though he kept his back modestly turned to her, the shape of his body was clearly defined—hips narrow, buttocks small, the muscles taut and concave on the sides.

She realized suddenly that it had been a long time since she'd drawn a breath. She lay back on the pillows with a barely audible groan and put an arm across her eyes. Her mouth was dry, and the sizzling beneath her skin was like an intense all-over itch that was impossible to scratch. She knew it was only desire. Except she'd never felt anything quite like it before.

"That bad, huh?"

Abby removed the arm from her eyes and focused them on Sage. He was standing beside the bed, looking down at her, and though his face was in shadow, his voice was soft and she could hear a smile in it. He was dressed, now, almost exactly as she was, in thermal long johns, warm socks and a flannel shirt, which he was in the process of buttoning.

"What?" she demanded, hiding her awareness of him behind false belligerence.

"The sight of my naked body. So bad you had to cover your eyes?" There was laughter in his voice, now, and the kind of confidence she could only wish for.

"Hah," she retorted, "what makes you think I watched?"

"I just know you." The way he said it was more tender than arrogant.

Her chest tightened. "You *don't*. You might think you do, but you don't know me at all."

There was a pause, and then, "I don't know you as well as I'd like to, that's true."

While she tried to think of a reply, he crossed to the other side of the bed. She felt a rush of air as he lifted the comforter, and the mattress sagged with his weight.

"Come 'ere, Sunshine." He put his arm across the pillows and got her lifted and nestled into its curve, snuggled against him. Inexplicably, now that she had his body heat to warm her, she'd begun to shiver again. She felt his lips touch her hair and his words formed against it, warmed with his breath. "We're both fully clothed. I'm going to hold you, if that's okay. Okay?"

She managed to nod. After a moment she sighed, and her fist, clenched on his chest, slowly unfurled.

Beneath her head, she felt his body relax with a deep exhalation. "That's all I'm going to do…tonight. Even though I want you so bad it hurts. Do you understand?"

Brokenly, she whispered, "No, I don't think I do."

"Two reasons. For one, you're exhausted and wounded. And I want you strong and whole when we make love." She couldn't have spoken if she'd tried; she simply had no breath to spare.

He drew another deep breath, and slowly let it out. "For another, Sam Malone raised me. He's the only father I've ever known. And you're his granddaughter. I don't feel right, letting this go any further, without—"

"You need his *permission?*" Her voice was thin; she still felt desperately short of air.

"No…" Sage answered slowly, "not his permission. His blessing, maybe."

She tried to laugh. "You want my grandfather's blessing in order to *sleep* with me?"

He laughed softly. "Well…that's the problem." His voice

was gruff. She could feel his muscles tense and his head lift as he looked down at her. "You see, Sunshine, the problem is I don't just want to sleep with you."

Chapter 11

He wasn't prepared to feel her body jerk, as if he'd struck her. Or for the small cry she uttered, like a hurt animal, as she turned her face against his chest. His shirt grew warm with her breath, and he wondered if maybe there were some tears, too.

Something quivered inside his chest. He cleared his throat. "Well, that's not quite the reaction I was hoping for."

He waited in stealthy silence, barely breathing, feeling as though she were a wild animal he was trying to get close to. *Patience,* he reminded himself. *She's wary...she's shy...you don't know what she's had to deal with.*

Moments...minutes ticked by. He felt her hand move secretively...wiping away tears? There was no trace of them in her voice when she finally spoke.

"How can you know that? You've known me...what? A couple of days?"

"True."

She lifted herself on one elbow and looked down at him.

Her hair tumbled forward across one shoulder and onto his chest.

He touched a lock of her hair...twisted it around his finger. It felt like cool damp silk. "I know all I need—"

"You don't," she interrupted, shaking her head earnestly. "What do you know? Okay, say you know my name—and it's a pretty weird one, right? I mean, who has a name like Sunny Blue? And say I'm Sam Malone's granddaughter, and I live in New York, but that's not *who I am*. Don't you get it? That's not *me*. You don't know *me*."

Even in the dim light he could see her face looked bunched and tense, like a little girl trying not to cry. Watching her struggle made him feel as though his heart was too big for his chest. He tugged gently on the lock of her hair.

"You're right about one thing...*Sunshine*. A person's name isn't who they are. But, when I call *you* that, it's because to me, it *is* who you are. Understand?" He waited, and she shook her head almost imperceptibly. She closed her eyes, and he watched a tear trace a red-gold track on her cheek, reflecting the dying firelight.

"Shall I tell you what I know about you?" he murmured, as his thumb stroked the tendril of her hair coiled around his finger. "I know you're kind. I know you're gentle and that you have respect for all living things." A smile warmed his chest and blossomed over his face as he remembered her look of profound sadness when she'd realized she'd just eaten meat. He took a careful breath. "I know you're funny and smart... but sometimes you're not very sure of yourself."

She opened her eyes and sniffed, and lifted a hand to her face, obliterating the tear track. "What do you mean? Just because I said I can't sing—"

"No." He silenced her with that word and a tug on her hair, but then fell silent himself while he searched for the right words. "Sometimes," he said slowly, softly, "I see...fear in your eyes. And I think...it's because sometimes you're not sure you're going to be accepted. As you are, who you are.

And I think you desperately want to be that. Maybe more than anything." He paused, giving her the chance to refute him. But she remained silent. After a moment he tried what was meant to be a smile but felt strangely like a spasm of pain. "Kind of makes me wonder what kind of childhood you must have had."

She suddenly squinched her eyes shut and drew a shuddering breath. He whispered an apology as he hooked his arm around her neck and drew her head down onto his shoulder.

"In some ways," he said in a voice that rumbled deep in his chest, "it wasn't easy for me, either, growing up half Indian, half white, not knowing who my father was. But one thing I always knew, was that I was loved. That's a precious gift, and it's one every child born on this earth is entitled to. I had that, but..." He looked down at her head, tucked under his jaw, and tenderly touched it with his lips, then laid his head back with a sigh. "Somehow, I don't think you did."

Once again, she had no answer, except to turn her face into the curve of his neck and shoulder. He held her and stroked her hair while her tears soaked the collar of Sam's soft old flannel shirt.

They woke the next morning to bright sunshine and the sound of water dripping as the last night's snow melted off the cabin's tin roof.

The first thing Abby discovered when she tried to get out of bed was that she was so stiff she could hardly move. The second, that the sores on the insides of her knees had oozed in the night and were now stuck to her borrowed thermal long johns.

Beyond that, she didn't want to think. Memories of the night just past hovered, scary and formless, just beyond the boundaries of conscious thought.

Sage was already up and fully dressed, and had fires going in both the fireplace and the cookstove. The tiny cabin was warm and filled with the scents of wood smoke and fresh coffee.

When he heard her stirring around, he called, "Morning, Sunshine," and came with a smile and a cup of coffee in his hand. The smile disappeared when he saw the dark patches on her thermals.

"Why didn't you tell me?" He set the coffee cup on top of the dresser and ignoring her protests that she didn't need to be babied, put his arm under her and half lifted her out of bed.

"I had other things on my mind," she muttered as he walked her slowly to the chair in front of the fireplace and gently lowered her into it.

He put his hands on the chair arms and leaned on them, looking into her eyes. "I think I know why you didn't tell me you were hurting. You didn't want to complain, right? You figured, 'Okay, I disobeyed orders, I got what I deserved.' And besides..." His eyes were dark and soft as mink, and the compassion in them made her throat ache. "I think you learned a long time ago your best chance to be accepted was to lay low, follow the rules, and most of all, *never complain*. Right?"

She couldn't answer; the ache in her throat had spread to her jaws, her chest, her head. She wanted to scream at him. *You think you know me, but you don't. You don't!* But even if she could have spoken, how could she explain to him that all his understanding and caring only made her feel more wretched. That every kind word was like a knife digging into an open wound.

He made her take off the thermals, then rubbed some evil-smelling salve on the sores and wrapped them with a clean dish towel, all the while seeming as dispassionate as a nurse. When he'd finished doctoring her, he left her to dress while he heated another can of stew for himself.

For *her* breakfast, she discovered, he'd arranged a plastic container of applesauce, a spoon, a handful of nuts and a stick of string cheese on a tin plate. She smiled and said, "Well, look at you, Martha Stewart!" while the ache inside her grew vast and all but unbearable.

I have to tell him. I can't wait for Sam Malone. I have to tell him. *I have to tell him* now.

But when she thought about telling him…imagined the softness and warmth in his eyes turning black and cold as flint…imagined his lips, curved not in a smile of heart-stopping beauty but with contempt…the words stuck in her throat like shards of glass.

I have to leave.

Yes, that's what I'll do. I'll just quietly run away, forget I ever dreamed up this crazy scheme.

Yes, that's what she'd do. She still had the credit card the lawyer had sent for Sunny to use. She would use it to take a bus to L.A. Maybe find a place to live…get a job. She'd write to Sam and tell him about Sunny…tell him how sorry she was. She'd send back the credit card and tell him she would pay back every cent.

It made her feel better, having a plan. And somehow, some-day, assuming she stayed out of jail, maybe she would find a way to forget a dark-haired, dark-eyed man named Sage.…

Over the thoughtfully prepared breakfast and a cup of strong coffee, she asked Sage about the animals he'd left behind. Who would feed them? And what about Freckles?

He assured her he'd called one of his ranch hands before he'd ridden out of cell phone range the day before, and asked him to send someone up to take care of everything, including Freckles.

He asked her about Pia, and Abby explained the cat was used to being left alone in a tiny apartment, sometimes until the wee hours of morning, when she was working.

"She'll be fine," she said, staring down at her plate, while the food she'd just eaten formed a lump in her stomach. "I'm not worried about *her*." She lifted her eyes miserably to Sage. "What must they think of me? Your mother…"

"Yeah," he drawled as he indulged in a massive stretch, "I

don't think I'd want to face Josie, either, if I were you." Then he grinned and pushed back from the table. "Don't worry, I'll come with you…help deflect the fury. She's more bark than bite. So…ready to head down the mountain? Think you can sit a horse?"

"I pretty much have to, don't I?" she said darkly, and quickly added with a wry smile, "I'm not complaining."

The ride down the mountain seemed a lot shorter than it had going up. And not nearly as scary with Sage up ahead, leading Sam's horse, Paint. As they come down through the meadow above the ranch, they could hear the horses in the pasture below the barns whinny a welcome home, and Freckles came bounding out to meet them, yipping and dancing in circles, a black-and-white bundle of pure joy.

"Looks like he's forgiven you for tying him to a post," Abby said to Sage, after he'd dismounted to give his dog a roughhousing hug and they were on their way again.

"Yeah, that's the thing about dogs," he replied. "If they love you, they'll forgive you just about anything."

And Abby thought: *If only people could be like that.*

While Sage took care of unsaddling, rubbing down and feeding the horses, Abby checked her cell phone for messages. There were three more calls from Pauly. As she stood with the phone in her hand, staring at the familiar name and phone number, she felt a strange little chill.

What was with Pauly, anyway? Had he actually suggested that Abby go on pretending to be Sunny? Had he really said— had it meant what it had sounded like—that she should defraud Sunny's grandfather and claim her share of the old man's riches?

Standing in the lane in the warm California sunshine, Abby shivered. He *had* said that. And he'd meant it, too. And what was worse, he'd said he'd told Sunny to take Sam Malone for his money, and Sunny had gone along with it.

Sunny? You were my friend, my roommate, almost like my

*sister. Would you have done such a heartless thing? Could
you? I can't believe it. I won't believe it. You would have
changed your mind, once you—*

"Sunshine? Ready to go face the music?"

Abby tucked the phone in her pocket. Voice mail could
wait.

In spite of her saddle sores, Sunny wanted to walk to the
hacienda, probably, Sage thought, because she wasn't in any
great hurry to face his mother. He couldn't say he blamed her.

As they emerged from the trees onto the wide flagstone
drive, the heavy front door banged open and Josie came running down the flagstone steps to meet them. Unlike the day
of Sunny's arrival, this time she wasn't smiling, and he heard
Sunny mutter, "Uh-oh," under her breath.

He put his hand on the back of her neck and gave it a reassuring squeeze.

Rachel and J.J. were there, too, right behind his mother.
When Josie halted at the bottom of the steps and pressed both
fists to her mouth, the others flowed on around her like a
flood around a rock, babbling questions faster than he could
answer.

"Where is Sam? Did you find him? Did he come back with
you?" That was Rachel, eager as a little girl asking, "Daddy,
what did you bring me?"

Sage got his arm around his mother's shoulders, but she
slapped at him furiously, then socked him in the arm—the
one with the still-healing bullet wound in it. He said, "Ow!"
and she was instantly contrite, but somehow to him her quiet
tears were harder to take than her anger.

"I'll tell you all about it." He ushered the two women ahead
of him up the steps, then fell back to talk to J.J., who was
hitching along on his crutches. Rachel moved up to slip an
arm around Sunny's waist.

"We may have a problem," Sage said to J.J. in an undertone when he thought the women were out of earshot. "Sam

didn't come back with us. When we got there his horse was in the corral, but the cabin was empty. Except…" He drew in a breath…let it out. "There was blood. A lot of it. And Sam's hunting knife. So, I'm thinking he cut himself and called his chopper to come get him."

He paused, and so did J.J., leaning on his crutches. He had an impassive look—a cop look—on his face, and listened intently.

"Should be easy to find out," J.J. said.

Sage nodded. "Yeah, except I don't have the chopper pilot's number. His lawyer probably does. Would you mind giving Alex Branson a call? His number's in the Rolodex on the desk in the den. Meanwhile—" he grinned and rubbed his sore shoulder "—I'll go try and put out the fire in Josie's bonnet."

"Yeah," J.J. said, "she's been pretty worried. Don't think I've seen her that upset since the day we both got shot."

They parted company in the entry, J.J. heading left to the den, while Sage followed the women to the kitchen. When he joined them, Sunny was explaining about the storm coming in, and the snow, apologizing for causing them to worry and pleading for forgiveness with every other word. Rachel was assuring her it was *okay,* they just *cared* about her, and she'd checked on Pia and made sure she had plenty of food and water, but the cat had hidden under the bed when Rachel tried to pet her and wouldn't come out. Josie was bustling around getting out food, intermittently sniffling and wiping her nose on her apron. When Sage walked in, she threw him a tragic look worthy of a stage drama queen.

Rachel and Sunny left to tend to their respective babies. Sage went over to his mother and put his arms around her and pressed his chin against her temple. "Hey, Ma," he said huskily.

The only reply he got was a prolonged sniff, as she went on laying bread slices on the counter for sandwiches.

"Look, I'm sorry—we both are. It was a lousy thing to do, making you worry like that. But it's okay…we're okay. You knew where I was, right? Because I called Ramon. And by the time I knew she'd followed me, I was out of cell phone range. Look, it won't happen again, I—"

She turned suddenly in his arms, and her eyes were swimming with tears.

"Ma, what—"

"You spent the night together. Up there. In the cabin."

He burst out laughing. "Is *that* what's got you so riled? Jeez, Ma." She went on gazing at him, not angry, but more as if her heart was breaking. He heaved a sigh. "Okay, first of all, nothing happened. Okay? I wouldn't do that—go behind Sam's back like that. And second—"

"Nothing happened?"

"No, Ma."

She closed her eyes, and a tear spilled over and ran down her cheek. When she opened them again, she still looked at him as if the world was about to end. "But you want her." He didn't answer, and she took a step back, pushing away from him. "I know you do. By the way you look at her." It was an accusation.

He began to feel stirrings of anger. "Yeah, Ma, so what if I do? I like her. More than like her. What's wrong with that?"

"You *can't.*"

His mother's voice was like tearing cloth. He didn't know what to make of such grief. It didn't make sense.

"Why? You think I'm not good enough for Sam's granddaughter? You think Sam would think that? Why would he? He's never—"

She lifted her hands in despair and let them fall. *"You just can't."*

She turned, shaking her head. The ember of his anger blossomed into flame, became an inferno raging inside him, fed by all the slights, big and small, that had plagued him throughout his life because of his ethnicity. But this—from his own mother…

"I can't…I can't…tell you," she said in a rasping voice,

drawing quick shallow breaths as if she couldn't get enough air. She walked rapidly away from him, and at the door to the dining room she paused and motioned with a jerky wave of her hand.

He was so angry he could barely see, but she was his mother. So he followed her.

Marching with head down, like someone on a mission, Josie led him through the dining room and living room and into the entry. Through the open door to the den, he could hear J.J. talking on the phone in a low voice. Josie turned and pushed open the double French doors that led to the courtyard, then resumed her headlong march, across the courtyard to the wing opposite the one where Sunny, J.J. and Rachel had their quarters. Down the veranda she went, with Sage keeping pace a few steps behind. He knew, now, where she was going.

At the far end of the courtyard, the white stucco wall of the chapel rose a full story higher than the rest of the hacienda, broken by three narrow-arched stained-glass windows, and an arched carved wooden door. Jutting another story higher than the red tile roof of the chapel was the bell tower. It was square, with a red tile roof and arched windows on three sides that Sam had had installed when he took the bell out of the tower and converted it to a room, and mounted the bell on the patio overlooking the valley. The tower was his hideaway, his private place, and when he came to the hacienda it was where he stayed.

The door to the chapel wasn't locked. Josie opened it and went through without looking to see if Sage followed. As his mother marched the length of the narrow chapel, lit only by the light from the stained-glass windows, he hung back, his footsteps slowed partly by anger, and also by nameless dread. His heart pounded now, not from anger, but from fear.

What the hell's going on?

Up ahead, Josie was mounting the steps to the altar. She reached up to turn the candle sconce on the right, and the altar moved slowly outward to reveal the low door behind. She opened the door and went through. After a moment's hesitation, Sage went after her. He'd been to the tower room many times before, of course; he couldn't explain why this time felt so different. As if he was about trespass in a different world. A different and unfamiliar reality. One he was beginning to realize he probably wasn't going to like.

When he reached the tower room, he found his mother searching through Sam's desk, opening and closing drawers and muttering to herself. In one of the deep bottom drawers, she seemed to find what she was looking for. She hesitated, gazed down at it for a moment before picking it up and placing it on the desktop.

It was a stack of paper, what appeared to be handwritten manuscript pages. She sniffed, wiped both cheeks with her hands, rubbed her hands on her thighs, drying them. Then, never once looking at Sage, she began to lift pages, turn them over and set them aside. He waited in stifling silence broken only by the whisper of those pages as she searched through them for the one she wanted. At last, she let out a hissing breath, placed a hand palm-down on the page, and looked up at him. Her face was blotched, her eyes liquid and full of so many things—sorrow, compassion and even fear—none of which made any sense to him but somehow made the dread that weighed on him all the more oppressive.

"Read this," she said, and quietly left him.

Sage stared after her with burning eyes, then pulled the pages toward him. His hands felt stiff, and his movements were jerky, with anger, resentment…fear. Almost against his will, he looked down at the pages and began to read.

After a moment, he inhaled sharply and sank into the chair behind him.

From the memoirs of Sierra Sam Malone:

> *She was walking down the road when I first saw her. Her hair was black as a crow's wing, and she wore it*

pulled back in a ponytail, straight as string and hanging down her back. She had a pink diaper bag slung over one shoulder, and she was holding the hand of a little bitty child—a girl-child with hair as black and straight as her mother's, tied up in two little tufts, like ears. The woman was walking slowly, but even so, that little girl's short chubby legs were having to work pretty hard to keep up.

I pulled up alongside in my pickup truck and rolled down the window. Told her to get in, I'd give her a ride. She threw me a look, quick and kind of scared, but it was enough for me to see the bruises on her face, the cut lip and tears in her eyes.

"Honey," I said, "you come on now and get in here. I'm not gonna hurt you, but if you tell me where I can find the sonuvabitch who did that to you, I'll see to it he never hurts anybody ever again."

Well, she sort of smiled, but that must have reminded her about her cut lip, because she touched it with her fingers as if it shamed her. She got into my truck, and I asked her what her name was. She told me it was Josephine, and her little girl's name was Cheyenne. I asked her where she was going, and she said she didn't know, so I took them both home with me.

She was a good cook, Josie was, and she fixed my meals and kept house for me. I never asked more of her, but the night she came to me, I didn't turn her away.

She was young and warm and good, and I was an old man who'd given up on finding anything good in this world. She brought laughter and light and love into my life, and in the last years before I met her I'd known precious little of those. And in time, she bore me a son, when I'd lost all hope of having another child.

We named him Sage, his mother and I, though my name's not on his birth certificate. And I made Josie promise me she'd never tell him who his father was,

*not until after I'm gone. I did that for the same reason
I never married her, and she said she understood.*

*The truth is, I only ever failed at two things in my
life. One was being a husband.*

The other was being a father.

*He's a good boy, my son. And the finest man I've ever
known. I think he loves me. I know he respects me. And
if he never learns the truth, I figure I might have a shot
at keeping it that way.*

She was watching for Sage. Waiting for a glimpse of him.
Wondering where he was. *This is terrible,* she thought. *When
did I start needing him like I need food and water...air to
breathe?*

She and Rachel and Sean were in the living room. Rachel
had changed Sean's diaper and nursed him while Abby show-
ered and changed her clothes and checked on Pia, who was
still sulking, naturally, and bit Abby's hand when she tried
to pet her. Josie was in the kitchen getting dinner, and had
chased Rachel and Abby away when they'd offered to help.
Now, Sean was on his tummy on a blanket on the floor being
cute, while Rachel sat cross-legged on the blanket with Sean
and peppered Abby with questions about the cabin and the
ride up there and back, which, she said, she would have given
anything to see and do. Abby sat on the couch and tried her
best to describe everything while her mind kept wandering
off, wondering about Sage.

J.J. came in from the den, and Rachel's face lit up like a
child's on Christmas morning. And Abby thought, *I wonder
if my face does that now when I look at Sage.*

J.J. leaned down to touch Rachel's hair and tickle Sean's
tummy, then asked where Sage was. Abby told him she didn't
know. J.J. shifted direction and was heading for the kitchen
to ask Josie when Sage walked in.

He came in slowly, hesitantly, as if he wasn't quite sure
where he was. Abby felt her stomach drop in a sickening

way—something like being on a fast-moving elevator. His face was gaunt. His skin, normally a warm brown color that seemed to glow from inside with health and vitality, now looked like old parchment. Oh, God, Abby thought. *Something's wrong. It must be Sam. Something's happened to Sam.*

She half rose to go to him, but he bypassed her and went directly to J.J., not even glancing at her.

J.J. pivoted awkwardly on his crutches to face him. "I was just looking for you. Couldn't get hold of Alex Branson. Left him a message. Found the chopper pilot's number, but he's not answering his phone, either." Sage nodded, in the vague sort of way of someone who isn't really listening. "Anyway," J.J. went on, speaking in an undertone, "in the meantime, I called a friend of mine with the Kern County Sheriff's department. They're sending a forensics team up to the cabin." Sage let out a breath. J.J. added with a shrug, "Just in case."

Sage nodded, and a grim silence fell. Just as J.J. was clearing his throat, about to say something more, Josie appeared in the doorway to tell them dinner was ready. Her face was a softer, rounder version of Sage's, and her eyes looked swollen and red, as if she'd been crying.

Sage turned abruptly away without looking at her, and gave a brief, awkward wave of his hand. "Uh...think I'm gonna pass. I'm not really hungry, and anyway...got things to see to down at the ranch. So...guess I'll see you. J.J., call me..." His voice sounded like something being ground up.

He must be sick, Abby thought. But if her son was sick, why wasn't Josie showing any signs of motherly concern? She didn't protest, or ask any questions—didn't act as though her son was even in the room. As Sage made his exit, Josie just smiled in a desperate sort of way and cooed at Sean, then directed everyone to the dining room, explaining the wind was still blowing too hard to sit on the patio.

Something's wrong.

Hoping not to look too obvious, Abby made muttered excuses about needing to use the bathroom and went after Sage.

She caught up with him halfway down the front steps. He glanced at her and she had only a glimpse of a face impassive as a mask before he looked away, off across the meadow to the blue-shadowed mountains. He didn't speak. She fell into step with him and they walked together down the lane, into the shade of the tall pine and poplar trees, past beds of rose bushes heavy with blooms and fragrance.

Finally, unable to stand it any longer, she said flatly, "Sage, what's wrong?"

He looked at her, then, but with such anguish, she caught back a little cry and moved instinctively toward him. His face contorted as though with intense pain, and he gripped her arms and held her away from him as if her touch was poison. She felt as if he'd struck her.

"Something's wrong. *Tell me, damn it.*" She didn't shout. Her voice was low, and she could hear it tremble with fear.

He couldn't look at her, at first. When he finally brought his eyes back to her face, it was as if he had to struggle against a powerful force. The cords in his neck stood out, and she was sure his grip on her arms would leave bruises. That realization seemed to come to him, too, because he let go of her, suddenly, and put both hands to his head as if to smooth back windblown wisps of hair. He exhaled, then spoke in a voice she could barely hear.

"I can't— We can't…be together, Sunny. Ever."

She shook her head; the words made no sense to her, like something spoken in a foreign language.

But she must have understood, because she answered him. "Why? I don't understand." Her voice trembled, and she fought to control it. "Is it Sam? Did you talk to him? Does he object because…I'm his granddaughter?"

His lips stretched, showing his teeth in a travesty of a smile. He began to laugh, silently, wrenchingly. She'd never seen such pain in the face of a man who hadn't shed a tear.

"No," he said, "because I am his son."

Chapter 12

This is a joke, Abby thought. *It has to be. Some gigantic cosmic joke.*

Voices were screaming inside her head: *Tell him. Tell him now. Tell him it doesn't matter that he's Sam Malone's son, because you're no relation to him at all. You can fix this.*

But the shouts were silenced by another voice, this one sadly whispering, *No, you can't. Right now, he thinks he's your uncle. If you tell him the truth, he'll know you for a liar and a fraud.*

"Wow," she whispered into the silence, and Sage gave a sharp, bitter laugh.

"Yeah, hell of an irony, huh? I find out Sam's my father, and I don't even know if the man is still alive."

With flawless theatrical timing, at that moment a helicopter swooped over them at treetop level and dropped into the meadow.

"That's Sam's chopper," Sage said.

Once again, Abby felt the bottom drop out of her stomach.

Freckles came racing past them, heading for the meadow. Sage took off after him, breaking into a jog a few yards down the lane. After a moment, dimly aware that Josie, Rachel and J.J. had come out onto the hacienda's front steps, Abby followed.

When she reached the place where the trees ended and the lane straightened out to run parallel to the meadow, she halted. Up ahead, she could see Sage and another man helping a third man through the barbed-wire fence. She was pretty sure the other man helping Sage must be Alex Branson, Sam's attorney. He was tall and slim, with a natural elegance that said *city* even dressed in casual clothes. The other man wore jeans and cowboy boots, and a faded blue flannel shirt that was the twin of the one Abby had slept in the night before. His hair and beard were white, and one hand was heavily bandaged. Out in the meadow, the chopper's blades still turned slowly.

She heard Sage say, "It's about time you showed up. We were beginning to think you might be dead."

The white-haired man straightened up, brushed himself off and gave a belligerent wave with his good hand. "Yeah, I knew you'd sic that sheriff on me—the one who's about to become my grandson-in-law." He cackled with laughter, and his voice was cracked and hoarse with age. "Figured I'd better come and convince you all I'm still alive before a bunch of those damn lab rats start crawling all over my personal property."

The men had begun walking toward the house. As they strolled along the lane, Sage said something Abby couldn't hear. Then all three men evidently noticed at the same time that someone was standing in the middle of the road.

This is ridiculous, Abby thought.

Here he was, the man himself, the legendary Sam Malone. The man she'd come so far—under questionable circumstances, to say the least—and wanted so badly and waited so long to meet. And she seemed to have taken root in the hardbaked dirt of the lane. She was trembling, one shallow breath away from bursting into tears. This was it—the moment she'd been waiting for. She could tell him, now, and it would all be over. Over…

Sam Malone turned his keen blue eyes on her, and she flinched.

Sage made a gesture with his hand. His face was impassive. "Sam, meet your granddaughter, Sunshine."

Abby felt her hand being swallowed up in one that was big and rough, dry and gnarled as an old tree root. Sam Malone didn't speak, but his eyes held a gleam that seemed to see right through her skin, flesh and bone, down to where she kept her secrets.

Through a humming in her ears, she heard Sage's voice. "Sunny's been crazy to meet you. So crazy she followed me up to the cabin—in a storm, no less."

Sam was still holding her hand, still looking deep into her eyes. She opened her mouth, but words wouldn't come, and instead she swallowed paper.

At that moment, the rest of the family came hurrying up to join them, and Abby slipped away to the edge of the crowd now gathered around the prodigal Sam Malone.

The old hound dog, Moonshine, reached them first. Sam stooped down and gently grasped one of the dog's long ears in his one good hand. "Well, howdy there, ol' fella, I think you and me have met before." He gave the dog's head a good rub, then turned to Rachel, who was hugging herself, shivering with excitement. "And you, too, little lady." It was an exaggerated imitation of John Wayne, and Rachel burst out with a laugh that was half a sob. "How's that great-grandson of mine?" Sam asked.

"Good…he's great—I can't wait for you to meet him," Rachel said, still half in tears but laughing, too.

"Looking forward to that." Sam turned to J.J. and shook his hand. "And this is the sheriff that saved my granddaughter's life. How's that leg coming along, son?"

Abby didn't hear J.J.'s reply. She watched the little group as if from a great distance, as if it was all happening on a stage, and she was the only audience.

They're a family. And not yours. They were never yours. You were only pretending.

They are Sunny's family. It should have been Sunny standing here, not you.

She tried to imagine Sunny standing in her place, and could not. According to Pauly, Sunny had only wanted the old man's money.

Sunny didn't deserve this. She didn't care about these people. But I do. I do!

She was suddenly overwhelmed with emotion—anger, envy, longing—once more the little girl desperately wanting to be part of a family but always left on the outside, looking in through locked windows.

Sam was petting and talking to Freckles. Then he turned to Sage and said, "How've you been, son?"

And Sage replied in an even tone, "I'm just great…Dad."

Sam's mask of charm slipped, and he seemed to sag, suddenly and for the first time looking close to the age he must have been. He looked past Sage to where Josie was standing by herself, silent and stoic. "Aw, Josie…" he said in a cracking voice, "you told him?"

"Don't blame her, Pop. I didn't leave her much choice." Sage's face was impassive, but his voice held all the rage, disappointment and grief he kept locked inside.

For a long moment, Sam looked at him. Then he looked at Abby, and she realized she was quietly crying. He nodded, and said, "Ah…I see."

For Abby, it was as if the house lights had come on, and she was once more part of the drama. This wasn't a play, it was happening to *her.* This was her story, her part to play. This was her cue; all she had to do was speak her lines.

She wiped her cheeks, lifted her head and stepped forward. She cleared her throat and spoke for the balcony seats…and an audience of one. "Mr. Malone, there's something I need to tell you."

Piercing her with his daggerlike gaze, he nodded. "I'm listening."

She hauled in a deep breath. "I'm not your granddaughter. My name is Abigail Lindgren. Sunny was my roommate." She heard a gasp—from Rachel? From Josie? She blocked it out and went on. "I'm sorry to have to tell you this, but she's dead. She was murdered—they don't know who did it, or why. That's what I came here to tell you. I thought you'd be— I never meant to—" *Oh, my God, what comes next? I've forgotten my line.*

In a panic, she looked around at the five people gathered there in the dusty lane. At Josie's face, and Rachel's, both stricken...shocked. At J.J., who was frowning, at Alex Branson, the lawyer, whose face held no expression at all. Her eyes glanced fearfully off Sage, who looked as if he'd been hit with a club. Finally, she brought them back to Sam. "I'm sorry," she whispered. "I'm so, so sorry."

Sam merely nodded. "So am I, young lady. So am I." Oddly, he seemed...not angry, but sad.

Abby looked at Alex Branson. A strange, cocooning calm had settled over her. "I'm going now, but I want you to know I'll pay you back—as soon as I can—when I get a job. For the plane ticket, and what I spent on the credit card."

She paused and glanced once more at Sage, who still hadn't spoken. He was gazing off toward the mountains, and she could see a muscle working in the hinge of his jaw. For a moment longer she hesitated, then, with her head down and her arms folded across her waist, she began walking back up the lane toward the hacienda.

"Hey—hold on." That was J.J. Abby stopped and looked back. Trembling all over. Trying desperately to hold herself together, until she could make a dignified exit.

J.J. turned to Sam. "You're not going to just let her walk away, are you? She's committed fraud, at the very least. Not to mention there's a pretty strong motive suggesting she could be guilty of murder."

Abby caught her breath, then went cold and clammy. This possibility had never occurred to her. But then, through the rushing sound in her ears she heard Sam Malone's voice, cracked but strong.

"Ah, hell, this little gal didn't murder anybody—when my granddaughter was killed she was working at a club in front of a few dozen witnesses."

The earth seemed to tilt beneath her feet. For a moment she couldn't utter a sound. Finally, she whispered, "You knew?"

"And," Sam continued, still speaking to J.J., "I don't believe she's guilty of fraud, either, since I'm the person she's supposed to have defrauded, and I was in on it the whole time—at least that's what my lawyer tells me. Isn't that right, Alex?"

Branson exhaled in a put-upon way. "Well, pretty much, yeah." He then turned to Abby and said kindly, "Sam tells me there's no need for you to leave, Miss Lindgren. As far as he's concerned, you're welcome to stay here as long as you want to."

She glanced at Sage, who shook his head almost imperceptibly and looked away. Pain sliced through her, but she was expecting it and didn't wince. "Thank you. That's very kind of you," she said to Sam. "But...I don't think I can."

She began walking again, and this time no one stopped her.

For a moment, no one spoke. Everyone just looked at each other. Then, Rachel sniffed, wiped away a tear and said in a small voice, "Well, I liked her."

J.J. didn't say anything, just gathered her into his arms, crutches and all, and held her, stroking her hair.

Sage had had all he could take. The emotions bottled up inside him were close to exploding, and he desperately needed to get to a quiet place where nobody could see him before they did. He turned away and started walking, heading down the lane toward the ranch...his house. Behind him, he could hear Josie talking in an artificially bright voice, inviting everyone, including the chopper pilot—who had been tying down the chopper and was only now climbing through the fence and coming to join the party—up to the hacienda for supper. Someone called Sage's name, but he gave the pilot a wave and kept on going.

"Hold up, there, son. Wait for an old man." Sam's voice sounded out-of-breath and feeble.

What could he do? As bad as he felt, he couldn't ignore Sam Malone...just ignore him and keep walking. For so many reasons. He halted and waited without turning around. He could hear Sam's wheezing breath, and his footsteps scraping unevenly in the dirt road.

"You just going to let her go? Just like that?"

Sage shrugged and stared fixedly at the distant mountains. "What else can I do?"

"Well, hell, you could at least talk to her."

He didn't know whether to laugh or swear. Softly, patiently, he said, "What's the point? She's a thief and a liar. She lied to you, to me, to all of us."

Sam dismissed that with a rude noise and a wave of his hand. "She never stole a thing, I gave it to her. And shoot fire, son, everybody lies, sometimes. You, me, everybody. Lying doesn't make for a bad person."

Because he was hurting so badly, Sage laughed. "This isn't a little white lie, Sam. This is a great big ol' lie." His face hurt. He scrubbed at it with both hands. Tried to laugh again and felt the muscles in his face rebel. He walked a few paces while he struggled for control, knowing the one thing he could not let himself do was fall apart in front of Sam Malone. *My father.*

He filled himself full of breath and turned back to the old man. "Even if I talk to her...even if she can explain this... The point is, she lied to me once. And she's an actress, she lies for a living. How am I supposed to ever trust her?"

Sam just looked at him, with his beard working and his eyes swimming with sadness. Then he shook his head and poked Sage in the chest with a finger that was gnarled as an old root. "Son, everything you just said is true—and it ain't worth a damn. You can rationalize all you want to, but what it boils down to is you bein' a chip off this worthless old block after all. Because you're fixing to ruin the best thing that ever happened to you, and too damn blind and proud to see it."

That was about it for Sage. Anger boiled within him, and he brushed aside Sam's hand. "Is that right? Talking about lies, that's a pretty big one you and Mom have been telling me all these years. How could you not tell me you're my father?" He clawed furiously at the band that held his hair clubbed to the back of his head until it broke and his hair tumbled free into the wind. For the first time in his life he felt kinship with his ancestors—or their cousins—who smeared their faces with color and went off to slay their enemies. "Do you know," he shouted, "what kind of difference that might have made in my life?"

Sam shrugged. "Well, son, looks to me like you turned out pretty well."

All Sage could do was shake his head.

All he could think of was the fact that the three people he should have been able to trust the most—his parents and the woman he loved—had all lied to him. Who in this world, then, could he trust?

"Don't judge me, son," Sam said quietly. "Not until you're an old man looking at the emptiness of your life, thinking about everything you lost because of the stupid choices you made. Then you can tell me whether or not I did the best I could."

Sage didn't answer. With his eyes closed, he listened to the sound of an old man's footsteps, slowly fading into the distance.

He tried to make his own footsteps continue down the road to his place. He didn't want to talk to anybody. He didn't want to see anybody. Especially not Sun—no, what was her name? *Abigail.* Especially not her. So why did his feet keep slowing down?

Finally, they stopped...and turned around.

Abby was packing, and trying to ignore how hungry she was. Because she couldn't possibly join the people she'd deceived so grievously around the family dinner table, could she? No way, she told herself, swiping a hand across her streaming nose. She'd starve first.

Pia was lying on the pile of clothes Abby had laid out on the bed, switching her tail and glaring, as if daring anyone to make her move. The first clue Abby had that she was about to have company was when the cat jumped off the clothes and vanished under the bed.

A moment later, a shadow fell across the open suitcase. She glanced up, and the bottom fell out of her stomach. The man standing on the other side of the French door could have come straight out of a Western movie, the Indians-versus-Settlers kind. His hair streamed freely down past his shoulders, and his face was dark and menacing.

Sage lifted a hand to rap with a knuckle on one of the glass panes, then opened it and came in without waiting for an invitation. After that first glance, Abby kept her eyes focused on her hands as she went on methodically—if not neatly—folding her clothes and placing them in the suitcase.

The silence lengthened. Her chest began to ache from the relentless pounding of her heart.

"So, you're leaving?" His voice sounded like ground-up rock.

"Why not?" She threw that at him almost in defiance. Then exhaled and said haltingly, without looking up. "I always meant to, you know. I never intended to stay. I want you to know that. I thought—" she hitched in a breath "—I expected he'd be here. Sam, I mean. Or at least, his lawyer. I thought... I'd tell them about Sunny, and that would be that. I thought..."

she lifted a shoulder "…I don't know, maybe they could give me a job. So I could pay back the money I'd used to come out here. I just… I wanted to get out of New York…so badly." She stared down at her hands, which were still, now, and whispered, "I never meant to lie."

"And yet," said Sage, "you did."

She flinched, then laughed a little. She shook her head, then lifted it and faced him. *I won't cry. I must not cry.* "Okay, yes, I did. So I'm a liar, and you can't trust me. I get it." Pride came riding in like the cavalry, reinforcing her courage. "I really wish I could have figured out a way to do it differently. You know? Probably, I was stupid. I'm definitely not perfect—can't even imagine what that would feel like. But—" she swiped her hand across her nose; she was *not* crying! "—I always intended to tell the truth, even after—" She stopped in the nick of time and jerked herself around. Turning her back to him was the only defense she had.

"After?" he prompted, in a voice without sympathy.

After falling in love with you. Even knowing I'd lose everything…including you.

She only shook her head.

When she didn't answer, Sage said in an emotionless, conversational tone, "Why don't you stay? Seems to be okay with Sam if you do."

She wiped her cheeks, and as she turned again to face him, a strange calm settled over her. "I used to think," she said softly, "that the worst possible thing I could imagine was being homeless in New York City. Now…I know there are lots worse things."

His face was impassive, his eyes the flinty black she'd imagined. And dreaded. "Such as?"

"To go on living here, close to you. And you—" her voice broke "—hating me."

Tiny muscles near his eyes twitched—the only sign of emotion he'd betrayed so far. His lips parted as if there was something he wanted to say.

At that moment, Pia, who had crept unnoticed from her hiding place under the bed, in one of her patented surprise attacks, launched herself into the air to land squarely on Sage's shoulders. There she stood proudly, like a leopard on a tree limb, chirping her usual question.

Abby had gasped at the initial assault, then pressed her fingers to her lips. Sage didn't even seem surprised, but merely reached up and drew the cat down from her perch, into his arms. To Abby's shock, she came without resisting—although she did open her mouth and twist her head around, trying to bite Sage's fingers as he tried to pet her.

He didn't seem to notice, but spoke softly to the cat in his special language. Abby watched his strong brown hands stroke the speckled gray-striped fur, and felt a sob building like a tsunami inside her. Before it could break, Sage gently placed the now-purring cat in her arms.

"I don't hate you," he said, and left her.

After all the emotional drama, it was the practical aspects of leaving—and doing so with her pride intact—that nearly defeated her. It was one thing to *say* "I'm leaving." But how to do that, when she had no transportation, no workable cell phone, no money—except for the lawyer's credit card, which she supposed she would have to use for a little while longer. Considering how much she already owed Sam Malone, she thought a few hundred dollars more would hardly matter.

Beyond the matter of money, there was the transportation issue—which wouldn't have been quite as big a problem if her cell phone had been working. She decided her best option, the one that didn't involve asking for help from any members of Sam Malone's household, would be to walk down to Sage's place and call from there. Her phone seemed to work okay once she got to his lane. From there she could simply call for a cab to come pick her up. She'd take her backpack and Pia's carrier, since Sunny's old suitcase had no wheels and would be a problem no matter where she wound up. She could always send for it later, once she found a place to live.

Then…there was Pia. How to get her into the carrier without getting clawed to pieces? She'd already learned from painful experience that it was virtually impossible to stuff a cat into a small opening headfirst. After giving the matter some thought, she decided to try turning the carrier up on its end and dropping the cat in backward.

No one was more surprised than Abby when this method worked on the first try. Whether that was because Pia was still under Sage's spell, or simply blindsided by the unexpected maneuver, she didn't know. Whatever the reason, before the cat had recovered enough to take evasive or punitive action, Abby had the steel door shut and the locking mechanism snapped into place.

That's it, then. Time to go.

Refusing to allow herself to think, knowing she would cry again if she did, Abby closed and zipped the suitcase and left it on the bed. She slipped the backpack over her shoulders, picked up the cat carrier—with Pia growling menacingly and clawing at the gate—opened the French doors and stepped out onto the veranda.

The courtyard was utterly still and already in shadow, the sun having made its early exit behind the mountains. Abby moved quickly and quietly across to the doors that opened into the entry, bypassing the kitchen, dining room and living room, where, she was certain, the family would still be gathered, enjoying Josie's food and celebrating the return of Sam Malone. She tiptoed across the tiled entry floor, opened the front doors and peered outside. Not a soul was in sight, not even the dogs. Shaky with relief, she went out and closed the doors behind her.

Hurrying now, she went down the steps and across the flagstone driveway, knowing anyone who happened to look out toward the meadow would see her. She had her hands full trying to balance the weight as the cat shifted furiously inside the carrier, but made it to the shelter of the trees without being observed. When she got to the part of the lane that ran parallel to the meadow, she took out her cell phone and checked for bars.

Nothing. Still no service.

She was walking rapidly, head down, staring at the cell phone's lighted pad, waiting for some bars to show up, and the carrier was tipping and tilting back and forth with the shifting weight of the angry cat inside. Pia was complaining in earnest, now, growling and yowling and clawing at the steel bars of her prison. Which was probably why Abby didn't see or hear the car until it pulled up beside her.

She stared at the nondescript light blue sedan, partly because it seemed so out of place, but partly because it seemed unreal, as if she'd made a wish and the very thing she'd asked for had dropped out of the sky.

The window rolled down, and a familiar voice with a strong New York accent called out, "Hey, Abby—where you going?"

Pauly? It truly was a miracle. "Oh, my God, Pauly," she said with a stunned gasp, "what are you doing here?"

Without waiting for a reply, she opened the back door, set the carrier on the seat, slammed the door and climbed into the front passenger seat. Then she and Pauly were both talking at the once, peppering each other with questions.

"What are you *doing* here?"

"What is this? Are you *leaving?*"

"How did you find me?"

"The internet, what did you think?"

"How did you get here?"

"GPS—came with the car. Works great."

"You came all the way to California? *Why,* Pauly? Why would you do that?"

"What the hell was I supposed to do? You didn't answer my phone calls."

"There's no service—I told you. I couldn't even call for a cab."

"Are you crazy? There's no cabs out here. Anyway, why are you leaving? You can't leave."

She tried to laugh, but her voice broke and released a sob instead. "I've, um…kind of got no choice, Pauly."

He hit the steering wheel with the heel of his hand, and his face contorted. "Aw, jeez, don't tell me you told him already."

Pauly had turned the car around and they were heading down the rocky, bumpy dirt road. Jouncing and bouncing, they dipped down into the creek bed, then growled their way up the other side. Dusk was falling. Even in her own distraught emotional state, Abby could see Pauly was driving too fast for the conditions and the road.

She wiped her eyes and tried to make her voice calm, reasonable. "I told them. I had to, Pauly. Sam—Mr. Malone showed up, and turns out he already knew—about Sunny being dead."

If she'd hoped to settle Pauly down, she was out of luck. Her words seemed to have the opposite effect. Pauly was gripping the wheel as if he wanted to pull it loose and hit something with it. His voice started at a mutter and rose quickly to a scream as he began to rant about Sunny ruining everything…they could've had it all…*she* wasn't going to do anything about the letter, *he* was the one who convinced her she should. Abby listened, staring at him, paralyzed with shock, growing colder and sicker with every word that came out of his mouth.

They'd had it all planned. Sunny would take her share of the old man's money, Pauly would get a cut—not a big one, he's not a greedy man, but he had these expenses…got into a little problem with a bookie—had a losing streak—it happens sometimes. He was in real bad trouble. But Sunny was going to help him out, and in return, he'd use his connections, they'd open a club, maybe even finance a show— off-Broadway, to start with, then…who knows?

"But then… *Damn it, Sunny!* She had to go and change her *mind.*" His face contorted, became a stranger's face, a mask of grief and rage. His fingers let go of the wheel and curved as if he were gripping something…shaking it. He spoke now as if to himself. "And at the last minute. *The last minute.* When I was counting on her. *She had to go and ruin everything….*"

It dawned on Abby then, as she listened to the man who had been her friend, her agent…Sunny's friend…that she was trapped in a car, careening down a mountainside with Sunny's murderer.

Chapter 13

Sage was pacing in the space between the barn and his front yard. He couldn't make up his mind where he wanted to go, what he wanted to do. The places of his life, the places where he'd always felt safe and comforted...*happy*...seemed alien and unwelcoming to him now, as if doors had slammed shut in his face. Accusing voices rang in his ears.

You going to just let her go?... The best thing that ever happened to you, and too damn blind and proud to see it... Everything you lost...stupid choices you made... There's worse things...worse things... You...hating me....

He answered the voices with every argument he could think of, most of which he'd already used on Sam...and on *her*. They hadn't impressed Sam, much. And they weren't impressing him now.

To go on living here...without you...

Damn it, Sam was right. She *was* the best thing that ever happened to him. The one person he'd been searching for his whole adult life, a woman who seemed to love the place he called home as much as he did. A woman with music in her soul—whether she knew it or not. And kindness, and warmth. And love. Yes…love. A woman he would love and cherish until they both grew old. And who would love him, too.

He couldn't let it end this way. Couldn't let her leave. He was the only one who could stop her. The one who had to forgive.

He was walking down the lane toward Sam's hacienda, head down, twisting his hair back into its knot, when he heard the car. He looked up in time to see Abby open the door and get in, and stood rooted like an old tree while the car turned in a cloud of dust and headed back down the mountain.

Swearing, he turned and ran for his house, where he'd left his pickup. *It's not too late,* he told himself. *It can't be too late. If I have to chase her all the way back to New York…*

Don't panic. Don't let him know you know. Stay calm. Keep him calm…

"You know, maybe you're right," she said, trying desperately to keep her voice from trembling. "Maybe I shouldn't leave. It's not too late to change my mind. Why don't you… if you can find a place to turn around, you can just take me back…"

He looked at her. And she thought, *He knows.*

His face crumpled like a little child's. And to her added horror, he started to cry. "Aw, no, Abby, not you, too. Don't do this, Abby."

She put out her hand, reached toward him. Then, as suddenly as they had begun the tears stopped, and he became eerily calm. He began to explain, in the same voice he might have used to give her directions to an audition, that he never meant to hurt Sunny, that it was all just an accident, a misunderstanding, and then he just got so upset with her, and he was desperate, and what was he going to do now? And before he knew it…

Abby felt numb. Terror seemed to have frozen her…dulled

her wits. She couldn't think of a way out. There was no place to turn around. She was stuck in a car with a murderer, one who was now almost certainly going to feel he had no choice but to kill her, too. Should she open the car door and bail out? There was nothing out there but rocks. She'd probably be killed. Should she take a chance? It seemed better than meeting the same fate as Sunny…

She was gripping the door handle, sweat making the handle slippery. Her heart was pounding, her mind screaming. She took a huge breath—

There was an ear-splitting screech, and a yowl that seemed to come straight from hell. That was followed by a loud clank, then a thump, and a ball of spitting scratching clawing mayhem came shooting out of the backseat as if it had been launched by a catapult. It landed squarely on Pauly's shoulders. He gave out a scream and let go of the steering wheel as he tried desperately to rid himself of the demon clinging to the back of his neck.

After that, everything happened so fast Abby could never quite recall the exact sequence of events. It was the noise she would never forget. She would hear it in her nightmares, and in quiet moments, for years to come. The grinding, groaning and screaming of metal, as if some giant living being were dying in agony. The crunch of shattering glass…thumps and bangs and screeches like all the demons of hell in chorus.

And then…silence.

Sage was driving too fast. He knew it. It was dusk, and the headlights weren't much use, and he wasn't keeping his eyes on the road ahead of him, anyway, because he was trying to watch for the lights of the sedan farther down the mountain. They would slash across the rocks and brush, then disappear…and he would hold his breath while his mind played his mantra: *Not too late…not too late.*

He seemed to be gaining on the car. Now he could see its taillights, flashing red, not too far up ahead. Then…as he watched in frozen horror, the car lurched wildly, hit a boulder with a sickening crunch...then seemed to rise in slow motion into the air. Slowly, slowly, it toppled...and rolled.

His breath stopped. Only his heart thumped on, pounding out the rhythm: *Too late. Too late. Too late.*

Abby knew she was alive, and awake. Beyond that, nothing made sense. She couldn't seem to figure out where she was, or what had happened, or which end was up. She held herself very still, listening. After the terrible noises of a moment ago, the silence seemed absolute. Then...she began to hear sounds. The ticking of a cooling engine...her own ragged breathing... the distant scrape of tires on hard-packed earth.

Her other senses began to function. She could tell it was getting darker, but there was light coming through a window above her head. She could feel something under her—a body. *Pauly.* Her powers of reasoning came back to her and she was able to figure the car must be lying on its side—the driver's side. She could smell hot oil. What if it caught fire? Exploded? She had to get out of the car. The window above her head was broken. All she had to do was climb out...if she could only...get...her...seat belt...unfastened! Something— the airbag!—was in her way.

Headlights swept over her. She heard the crunch of tires on gravel, the slam of a car door. Running footsteps. Some-one called her name.

Sage? "Sage—"

She hadn't known she'd cried out his name, but suddenly he was there, his dark form blotting out the light from the window above her head. His hands were reaching for her... touching her. He was talking to her, asking if she was hurt, telling her it was going to be okay.

Then, somehow, she was out of the car and on the hard bare ground, cradled in Sage's arms. He kept stroking her hair and whispering to her that everything was all right. But she shook her head, sobbing, because she knew it wasn't.

"Where's Pia? I can't find Pia. She got out of her carrier somehow. She attacked him. She saved my life. Where is she? Oh, God…where is she?"

It was sometime after midnight when Sage brought Abby back to the June Canyon Ranch. The paramedics had arrived remarkably quickly, considering the remoteness of the area, followed soon after by fire trucks, since the danger of a brush fire starting from sparks or fuel from the accident was extreme. Then came the sheriff's department, and even the CHP, since the crash had happened just off of a state highway. Both Abby and Pauly were airlifted to a trauma center in Bakersfield, over Abby's protests that she was fine except for a bump on the head. After receiving numerous tests and a CT scan, doctors agreed there was no concussion, and she was released.

Pauly's condition was critical, but he was alive. He remained in the hospital, in police custody, and would eventually be returned to New York City, where, if he survived, he would stand trial for the murder of Sunshine Blue Wells.

Sam Malone's chopper flew them home. Because it was dark, Abby didn't realize until she stepped out of the chopper onto bare earth that the pilot had set them down in the open area in front of Sage's house, rather than the meadow. Sage guided her away from the rotors' wash, then waved to the pilot.

Abby waited until the growl of the chopper's motor had diminished as it disappeared behind the barn, while her heart thumped in time to its rhythms. Then she looked at Sage and said, "Why?"

"That was going to be my question." She couldn't see his face clearly, but his voice sounded wry.

"I mean, why did you bring me here?"

He shrugged as he guided her, with a light touch on her back, toward the front door, which was brown, not blue, of his little adobe house. "We need to talk, and there's more privacy here. And…I'd just feel better having you where I can keep an eye on you."

A shiver rippled through her. "The doctors said I'm fine. Or," she added in a dull, flat voice, "is it that you're afraid I might run off with the family silver?"

He gave a mirthless little laugh. "Oddly enough…I believe you when you said it wasn't about the money." He paused to open the door and gestured for her to go in ahead of him.

He turned on the lights, and she faced him, arms folded across her waist, because exhaustion, physical and emotional, had left her feeling weak and hollow inside. She wasn't sure how much more she could take, but summoned what remaining reserves of strength she had and lifted her head high. "How can you be sure, knowing what a liar I am?"

"Ah. Yes." A smile tugged at his lips. "That. You know, that's what I thought, too, until it hit me. Something I'd known all along, just hadn't realized it." He walked slowly toward her. She stared at him and in spite of all her efforts, began to shake. He lifted a hand and brushed gently at her cheek, as if wiping away a smudge. "You," he said softly, "may be a good actress—I don't know about that—but you are a terrible liar." She gave a tiny gasp, and he smiled and went on. "Yeah, you are. You have a tell." His thumb grazed her cheek, just below her eye. "It's in your eyes. You get this scared look… like a little rabbit looking for a place to hide. Which brings me back to my original question. If not for the money…then *why?* What made you do it?"

She closed her eyes, sniffed and said in a muffled voice, "I'm not sure you'll understand."

"Try me. And you're shaking," he said, taking her by the arms. "Come here and sit down."

She shook her head, resisting him and his inexplicable kindness, knowing how little it would take of that for her to completely fall apart. "It was…the family thing," she said tightly. When he didn't comment, she wiped a hand across her eyes and lifted them to his. "Because I didn't have one.

And Sunny didn't, either—I thought. We were a couple of orphans, all we had was each other. And the cat. That stupid, awful *cat.* That's why…" Her voice broke. She waited until she could talk again. "Then…Sunny was gone, and I found out she had this…family. This family who wanted her, and she'd never told me about, and she was going to go…but she died before she could. And the thought of phoning, or emailing, and telling them she was dead—I just couldn't. Then… when I got here, and everyone was so welcoming and kind… and Sam wasn't here, so I had to go on pretending. Pretending it was mine." She ended it in a whisper. "I really…*really* wished it could be mine."

Long before she finished, Sage had gathered her into his arms; there seemed to be no other remedy for the vast ache that filled him. He held her now, one hand cradling her head against his beating heart, and pressed his lips to her hair as he whispered meaningless comforting words. Then…the answer came to him. The words that would heal her heart, and his.

"It can be," he said, and the words came from deep in his chest. From his heart…his soul.

She went utterly still. Then…she raised her head and her shimmering eyes gazed into his. "What?" she whispered.

"This…can be your family. If you still want it." She pushed away from him, staring at him, and he let her go. He folded his own arms over the place she'd left cold and empty. "It's one of the reasons I brought you here, actually. I wanted you to see…my home. It's old, it's small, it's simple. I've thought of adding on to it, if…I needed to. It's not the hacienda. But it's mine. I wanted you to see it before I asked you if…" He hauled in as much air as he could. "If…you'd want to share it with me."

She just kept staring at him. Her face… He thought he'd never seen anything so heartbreaking. So beautiful. It was a child's face, full of hope. A woman's face, full of love.

Her lips moved, and he had to bend close to hear her. "You mean…forever?"

A laugh burst from him. He lifted his hands to her face and held it between them, stroking dampness from her cheeks into her hair as he gazed at her. "Yep," he said. "Forever."

She closed her eyes and drew in a long sniff. "I never expected...you," she whispered.

"You came as a pretty big surprise to me, too."

She laughed, with tears. He felt her trembling. Guilt and contrition filled him. "You're exhausted," he said huskily. "We can talk about it in the morning." He paused, tilted her face to his. "Will you share my bed, Abigail?"

She sniffed again and wiped her eyes. "Are you going to just hold me again?"

"Well, you've been in a pretty bad car wreck..."

"The doctors said I'm okay—no concussion."

"And, you're exhausted..."

"Not *that* exhausted. Hey, I'm a New Yorker, I'm—"

"Tough—I know. Yes, my love, you are..."

He kissed her. Gently at first. Then he unexpectedly deepened the kiss, and she moaned softly.

She wasn't tired, anymore, or sore or aching, except for the part of her that ached for *him*. She felt hungry, so hungry, and knew that only he could fill her. She didn't care if she hurt tomorrow, if her lips might be swollen from his kisses. She had forever to heal. *Forever*.

"Bedroom's this way," Sage growled, breaking the kiss. "I was going to show you around, but..."

"If I'm going to live here forever," she whispered, "we'll have plenty of time for that."

"Just so you know what you're getting."

"Oh, I know." She didn't have the words, yet, or the confidence in her miracle, to tell him she couldn't have cared less what his house looked like. That she'd live with him in Sam's cabin, if he asked her to.

"I'll be gentle," he said.

"I know that, too."

He undressed her, taking his time, then let her do the same

for him. When they were naked, facing each other in the moonlit darkness of his bedroom, she slowly reached up and took the fastenings from his hair. He did the same, then drew her close so that their hair flowed together over their bare skin. He smiled as he murmured, "Black and white..."

Then he laid her carefully down and showed her how gentle he could be, tenderly kissing each bruise and scrape and healing saddle sore, including the ones on her bottom she hadn't told him about.

He made love to her with his mouth and his hands, and with murmured words that were his own special language, only for her. As he kissed her body, his hair slithered over her skin, and she wove her fingers through it and lost herself completely in the beauty of it...the warm silk caress of it.

Until she could stand it no more, and tangled her hands in his hair and, whimpering and crying his name, drew him up to her, back to her famished mouth. Her body lay ready and open for him, and she wrapped her arms around him and drew him in as if she were the one welcoming him home.

He would have held his weight off of her, but she pulled him close and lifted herself to him, and the wonderfulness of the feel of his body in her arms, his weight on her, was almost more than she could bear. A sob shuddered through her from head to toe.

"Are you okay?" he asked, his voice strained and rough.

"Yes—just full of...you know."

"I know." He kissed her...began to move, deep inside her. And he whispered brokenly, "Teach me now."

"Teach you..." Gasping...breathless.

"To dance."

Warmth and laughter and purest joy rose inside her like a giant wave. "It's...simple. It's all about...rhythm...and movement."

"Ah," he said, smiling down at her. "Like this?"

She moaned. "I think...you've got it."

* * *

Abby fell asleep listening to Sage's heartbeat, in a state of happiness she could only have imagined...except better, more wonderful than she could ever have imagined. But then, sometime in the night, she dreamed of Pia, dreamed she heard her funny little chirp, always sounding as if she was asking a question. Dreamed she felt her sandpaper tongue, and the weight of her body sitting squarely in the middle of her chest. And she woke with a feeling of deep loss, and sadness.

She heard Sage's voice say softly, "Hey...'morning, Sunshine." She put her arm over her eyes to hide her tears, not wanting him to see her grief when she had so much to be happy about. She heard him laugh, and add, "I know, but I'm probably always going to call you that. I told you—it's not just a name, it's what you are to me."

She felt his weight on the mattress beside her. And then, incredibly, impossibly, she heard...that funny little chirp.

She sat bolt upright in bed, eyes wide open. Sage was sitting on the bed, and in his arms, was...*Pia.*

Pia. Looking wild-eyed and scary.

"How— What did you— How did you—" She dashed away tears and simply stared, first at the cat, then at him.

He shrugged and said gently, "You cried in your sleep, and called her name. So...I got to thinking. And...this morning, early, I took the dogs and went back to the crash site. It was Moonshine who found her—I mean, what's the point in having a bloodhound if not to find someone who's lost? Freckles is nursing a scratched nose, though. I'm not sure this *tuugakut* appreciated being rousted out of her hiding place by a couple of great big dogs."

"Oh, God, poor Freckles. I'm so sorry."

"He'll be okay. He just has to learn, she's part of the family, now."

Laughing, crying, Abby reached out to pet her cat, and got a sharp nasty bite for her trouble. She jerked her hand back, cursing the wicked beast, and said plaintively, "Why does she *do* that?"

"Cats learn from their mothers, their litter mates how to be part of a family. This one's never had that chance."

"Maybe that's why I like her," Abby said darkly. "She reminds me of me. That's the way I was, when I was a kid, in the system. Probably why nobody wanted to adopt me."

"It's not too late to learn," Sage said. "For both of you."

He leaned over to kiss her, and with a questioning chirp, Pia came pushing between them to lick their faces with her sandpaper tongue.

Epilogue

From the memoirs of Sierra Sam Malone:

I had sworn off love, after Barbara, though not off women. No...never off women. Of those there was always a plentiful supply, easily available and more than willing to please. Mine for the taking. And I took without conscience or regrets.

When Katherine came to me with a sensible business proposition, I thought it seemed like a good idea, at the time. Power and prestige, in exchange for the thing that mattered the least to me—money. The funny thing was, we were a good match, Kate and I, and we lasted longer than either of us expected.

But when tragedy struck, we lacked the one thing that might have seen us through the storm. And that was love.

* * * * *

SUSPENSE

Heartstopping stories of intrigue and mystery—
where true love always triumphs.

COMING NEXT MONTH
AVAILABLE FEBRUARY 28, 2012

#1695 OPERATION MIDNIGHT
Cutter's Code
Justine Davis

#1696 A DAUGHTER'S PERFECT SECRET
Perfect, Wyoming
Kimberly Van Meter

#1697 HIGH-STAKES AFFAIR
Stealth Knights
Gail Barrett

#1698 DEADLY RECKONING
Elle James

REQUEST YOUR FREE BOOKS!
2 FREE NOVELS PLUS 2 FREE GIFTS!

❧ Harlequin

ROMANTIC
SUSPENSE

Sparked by Danger, Fueled by Passion.

New York Times *and* USA TODAY *bestselling author*
Maya Banks presents book three in her miniseries
PREGNANCY & PASSION.

TEMPTED BY HER INNOCENT KISS

Available March 2012 from Harlequin Desire!

There came a time in a man's life when he knew he was well and truly caught. Devon Carter stared down at the diamond ring nestled in velvet and acknowledged that this was one such time. He snapped the lid closed and shoved the box into the breast pocket of his suit.

He had two choices. He could marry Ashley Copeland and fulfill his goal of merging his company with Copeland Hotels, thus creating the largest, most exclusive line of resorts in the world, or he could refuse and lose it all.

Put in that light, there wasn't much he could do except pop the question.

The doorman to his Manhattan high-rise apartment hurried to open the door as Devon strode toward the street. He took a deep breath before ducking into his car, and the driver pulled into traffic.

Tonight was the night. All of his careful wooing, the countless dinners, kisses that started brief and casual and became more breathless—all a lead-up to tonight. Tonight his seduction of Ashley Copeland would be complete, and then he'd ask her to marry him.

He shook his head as the absurdity of the situation hit him for the hundredth time. Personally, he thought William Copeland was crazy for forcing his daughter down Devon's throat.

Ashley was a sweet enough girl, but Devon had no desire

to marry anyone.

William had other plans. He'd told Devon that Ashley had no head for the family business. She was too softhearted, too naive. So he'd made Ashley part of the deal. The catch? Ashley wasn't to know of it. Which meant Devon was stuck playing stupid games.

Ashley was supposed to think this was a grand love match. She was a starry-eyed woman who preferred her animal-rescue foundation over board meetings, charts and financials for Copeland Hotels.

If she ever found out the truth, she wouldn't take it well.

And hell, he couldn't blame her.

But no matter the reason for his proposal, before the night was over, she'd have no doubts that she belonged to him.

What will happen when Devon marries Ashley?
Find out in Maya Banks's passionate new novel
TEMPTED BY HER INNOCENT KISS
Available March 2012 from Harlequin Desire!